The Rose of Jericho

by
Vanessa Davis Griggs

The Rose of Jericho
Copyright © 2000 by Vanessa Davis Griggs

Cover design by V. M. Griggs
Graphic sketches by Johnathan L. Griggs
Painting of 3 women (on back cover) by artist John Sims
"Ordinary Women With Extraordinary Talents" © 1997

For information write:

Free To Soar
P. O. Box 101328
Birmingham, Alabama 35210-6328
To call or email:
205-956-2889 Email: fts@FreeToSoar.com
Web site: http://www.FreeToSoar.com

If you're unable to order this book from your bookseller, you may order toll free directly from the publisher. Call 1-800-929-7889.

Library of Congress Catalog Card Number: **00-190134**

ISBN 0-9673003-1-2

First Printing **May 2000**
Printing Number 10 9 8 7 6 5 4 3 2 1
Printed on acid free paper in the United States of America

Special Sentiments To You

From

Also by Vanessa Davis Griggs

Destiny Unlimited

This book is dedicated to all who have come before me, and upon whose shoulders I now proudly stand.

To My Mother:	Josephine Lee Davis
My Father:	James Davis, Jr.
My Grandmothers:	Peggy Jane Lee Wiseman
	The late Lucile Davis
	The late Vashti Bell Davis
My Grandfathers:	The late Joseph Lee, Sr.
	The late James Davis, Sr.
In Memory of:	Countess Harris
	Maurice "fred" Plemmons

To: My ancestors and persons I have met, in most cases, through the spirit of those who have managed to keep their tales and stories alive by recanting those things no one else may have otherwise believed important enough to be heard.

Acknowledgments

First and always to God who is not only able, but has done exceedingly, abundantly above all I could ever think or ask.

Much love and appreciation to:

My mother Josephine Davis. You have been my greatest supporter for as long as I can remember. Thank you for giving me a great sense of who I truly am and what I can do in THIS LIFE, for believing in me, and for loving me unconditionally. You are the wind beneath my wings. My father James Davis (Jr.) for having taught me to be independent when I need to be and for demonstrating what it is to have a father who loves his family.

My husband, Jeffery Griggs for allowing me to be me and to do, what I needed to do. You are a very special man indeed, and I am blessed to have a jewel like you.

My children: Jeffery Marques for the wonderful words you have spoken regarding the gift you say I give to the world; Jeremy Dewayne for being such a caring son and for giving me the gift that put music back into my life...I needed it; Johnathan LeDavis Griggs for your love and artistic talent, especially with this book.

My sister, Danette Dial who not only reads the words I write, but tells me her true feelings about them. My brother, Rev. Terence Davis who always make me feel special and encourages me more than he'll ever know. My sister-in-law, Cameron Davis for taking the "in-law" out of the word. My sister, Arlinda Davis for being one who doesn't mind me reading words to her so I might see how they sound outside of my own head. My brother, Emmanuel Davis for being so supportive of his oldest sister and making me feel like "I am really somebody special."

My mother-in-law Florene Griggs; I have been blessed by
you, your love, and your support. My friend Rosetta Moore, you
have no idea how honored I am to call you "my" friend. You've
gone the extra mile with me—you, your love and support have
truly been a tremendous blessing in my life!

Bonita Chaney for your special love and words of encouragement. Ella Wells for the friendship you and I share as we laugh
and talk about so much. Pam Hardy, for never wavering in your
belief in my true dreams. Dr. Marilyn Elliott for caring about me
and my well-being. My friend Shirley Walker who proves that
distance is not an obstacle when it comes to true friendship.
Malinda Ramirez...I'll never forget that day when you came to
the hospital during a difficult time showing me so much love.

To Rev. James A. Frazier, Sr., who has always encouraged
me. First, when I was a young girl, then later, as a young woman
trying to be a blessing to others, and now as I continue in my life
full of unlimited dreams. Even in your own dark hour, you never
failed to ask, to ensure...that all was well with me and my family.

Destiny Unlimited introduced me to so many wonderful
people like Alice Gordon, the host of Alabama Now (lookout
world!) and Ophelia Cox of Ophelia's Art Gallery in Birmingham. What a blessing you two are...not just to me, but to all
whose lives you have and are touching! To my greatest internet
supporter better known as "BlaqMale" —Leland Johnson. Thank
you for helping to spread the word about me and my works.

Ms. Johnnie Hamby who has been so supportive of me with
Destiny Unlimited. Ms. Goneba Taylor, Ms. Georgia Frazier,
Mary Chavers, Russ McClinton of www.urbanham.com, Sheila
Allen of South Carolina, Beatryce Shaw, Ken Benion, Zelda
Oliver-Miles, Dr. Jesse J. Lewis, Laneta Evans, Crystal Cartier,
Johnnie Peoples, Evangelist John Young, Loretta Griffith, and
Ellie Conrad...thank you all!

My aunt, Naomi Session for taking the time that day to tell
me the wonderful stories of our ancestor from Africa. My aunt,
Mary Mack for showing me so much love over the years.

A special thanks to Phaon O'Reilly, Myron Owens, Jr., and
artist John Sims for being gracious to allow me use of your gifts.

Elizabeth DeRamus for your friendship and caring personality. A special blessing to Pamela Douglas for your professionalism and care with my hairstyles—I tell you, you do have a gift!

My publisher who truly believes in me and my mission as I strive to inspire, empower, encourage, entertain, and instruct others by way of words. Special thanks to the marvelous staff at Central Plains Book Manufacturing for your commitment to this book and your wonderful spirit of Excellence.

If I have missed calling you here by name, just know in my heart...you are not forgotten. Thank you.

To all who have been supportive of me, especially with *Destiny Unlimited,* thank you from the bottom of my heart! My prayer is that this book will bless many—by its truth and true to life situations. The only task it ever imposed, was in the balancing of its—and my—integrity. I am so proud to be the author of *The Rose of Jericho.*

May you truly receive in this life,
all the desires of your heart!
Remember, even the sky
truly knows no limits!

Vanessa Davis Griggs
Email: VanessaGriggs@FreeToSoar.com

It's been said a *fact* is something
with actual existence
and *fiction*, something
invented by the imagination.
Assuming a possibility
is indeed a *fact*
and that a *fact*
is actual *existence...*
and that *fiction*
is actually *fact* created by imagination
—first a *thought* then *manifestation*—
is there *then*
even a *thin* line
between the two?
And...whether *fact* or *fiction*
does it truthfully make any difference?

Factually speaking
is *"rose"*
a noun or a verb?
Or is its meaning
solely defined
by the context in which
it is being used
at the time?

The Rose of Jericho

April 18, 1863

Refusing to break her trance-like stare, a dark-skinned, tall, lanky young girl (no more than thirteen) rocked on her heels as she sang, "Green green the crab apple tree, where the green grass grows tall." She stopped the tune. "I free," she said.

"No," the young white man said as he stood towering over her with a toothless grin. "You're mine." He grinned more, showing he indeed had teeth. "Mine," he said gently pointing the whip toward himself. "My slave. This is America. You belong to me. And for what I paid, you certainly weren't free!"

"Free!" she said. "I free! Nam-o belong to Nam-o." She patted her chest. "Free! America...home of free and brave."

"No," he said again, narrowing his eyes. "You're mine. I own you. You," he jabbed her in her chest, "belong...to...me!"

"Nam-o belong to no one but Nam-o. Nam-o and God!"

"Your name is not Nam-o. Your name is Peggy. It's Peggy. Say it...*Peg-gy.*"

The young woman squinted, continuing to gaze up hard as though her staring would cause him to understand. "I Nam-o. I free. I born free, I die free. Nam-o gonna always know free."

He drew back and lashed her hard with his whip. "You're a troublemaker I see. That's what I done gone and bought my-self—" he hit her even harder, "a troublemaker! Well allow me to help you understand," he said, the whip cracking each time it made contact with her tiny body. "You're my slave. And if I say you're mine..." he struck her again, "...then that's what you are!" Again he hit her. "I'm the Master around here!" he said.

Nam-o yelled with pain as the whip cut open her flesh.

He continued to beat her mercilessly—smirking at her now torn bloody body. "I'll teach you to look a white in their eyes!" He struck her again and again until finally, his whip lay quiet.

She struggled to stand; tears now dry...white on her face. Her eyes held the ground as the young master spit tobacco juice past her lowered head. He flipped a silver dollar at her feet.

"Cost me 450 of them there—449 more than you're worth it looks like! I suppose you do get what you pay for. I knew I should have bought that one they had for six-hundred."

He turned to leave but stayed when he heard a laugh. And not just any laugh—but one later described as pure-dee-evil!

"You think you own some-body...some-thing?" Nam-o said clutching the coin and a shred of the green cloth torn from her body. "I tell you *what* then Master—*die* and *see*. *Die* and *see* just what you truly own! Nam-o show you a mystery. Nam-o know free. No whip gonna tell Nam-o no different. You sow, I sow. Soon both us gonna reap. Then all gonna see!"

It was two weeks to the day when the otherwise young and vigorous master fell dead. Ironically, in almost the exact same spot where he and Nam-o had stood that day.

The documented cause? *Unknown.*

It was the mild more spring than winter weather all across the South including Alabama that seduced quadrillions of dainty color blooms to burst forth early. The year two Friday the thirteenths did a tango back to back...

The year—I killed my own father...

June 9, 1998, at the grave site. I can recall so clear what Rev. Goodword read from the book of Psalm.

"*Into thine hand I commit my spirit; thou hast redeemed me, O Lord God of truth.* Amen?" he had said.

And with bowed heads and humbled hearts, we said in unison, "Amen."

From my journal—J. M. Taylor's. Mine. My thoughts, my words...the bearing of my soul. Still, no one has the right to it. No one unless I say so. No one—save me. Right? No one!

Truth? Yes truth.

Confession they say, is good for the soul. Well...maybe.

A novel— Is it solely fiction or riddled with facts? If you take the truth...change a name here, a place there; make what's short, tall; what's thin, plump. Who truly recognizes it? But if fact is *the* truth and fiction *a* truth, doesn't truth *still* manage somehow to be told? Does real life hold deeper truths—deeper meanings?

"Sometimes," my father once told me, "*it...*" (*life?...truth?*) "...it can be as simple as putting on or taking off an old coat."

Many accuse me of not allowing folks to get close to me. Making it hard to "sympathize" or "feel" for me. "They" say I and those around me build walls no one can seem to get past.

What do they know? What do they expect?

Who, in truth, can know all there is to know about another unless...until...time has been spent between them? And not all is known then. Even Jesus, had a Judas.

Time...trust...either...both bring to light who we—under the cloak of darkness—truly are. That's what *I* say anyway.

And just like the walls of Jericho, even the strongest structures do have their ways—in the end—to come tumbling down.

Oh. But I've gotten a little ahead of myself. I do that, from time to time. Sort of like a prologue before the story.

Yes...a *prologue.*

Still, I find it does help to begin at the beginning. Or at the very least—close enough to it.

"Begin At The Beginning"

One to Another

Lie not one to another, seeing that ye have put off the old man with his deeds: And have put on the new man, which is renewed in knowledge after the image of him that created him: Where there is neither Greek nor Jew, circumcision nor uncircumcision, Barbarian, Sycthian, bond nor free: but Christ is all and in all.

Colossians 3:9-11

 J. M. Taylor's Journal

They say I chose this life although I'm not so certain about all that. I can't imagine me, J. M. Taylor, choosing all the crap I've had to endure in this lifetime. However, if it is true—that I chose this life—then I am either a strong person indeed, or one in desperate need of some good doctor's psychiatric gifts. Personally, I favor the strong version myself. From where I stand, my mental state appears as much in tack as anyone else's I've observed of late.

So for now, I will continue to tell my deepest darkest secrets and thoughts to my oldest, truest, and most trusted friend—my journal. Just in the future, I'll attempt to do a much better job of protecting such a treasured and devout confidant.

May 15, 1998: I would recall that day even if I hadn't written one word in my journal...

I stepped outside the double French doors of my bedroom onto a sun-warmed deck while listening to a host of blue jays serenade nature with joy and contentment. Stretched on the lounge, I bathed my clean smooth face with lather from the May morning sun.

Once the chirping began to subside, I sat up and smiled—bowing my head to say, "Encore! Encore!"; however three from the group immediately took flight toward a clear Alabama sky—disappearing into the ocean blue like drops of spring water. Only then did I glance at my watch.

My doctor's appointment wasn't until eleven, but since I had decided to take off the whole day, I found time to be tame—allowing me refined moments of enjoyment for a change. Probably why I relished in the O'Jays mini concert on 98.7 KISS-FM as I cruised into town in my just-yesterday-hand-buffed, black inside—black out (with glittering gold trimmings), Lexus. Also why, I was able to draw the profound connection between the Blue Jays of earlier to *these* O'Jays singing their greatest hits now. Blue Jays...O'Jays—why of course!

The words to the song *Backstabbers...* *"They smiling in your face"* (an allusion to—as I would later learn—what was in store for me), replayed in my head as I strolled up to the sliding glass window of the doctor's office and signed in. Six names were crossed off; four remained...five now counting mine. I turned to take a seat and was happy to count only one person silently waiting.

"J. M. Taylor?" a pip-squeak voice that held the '*a*' in Taylor far longer than was necessary, called me back to the now opened window.

I stepped forward. "Yes?"

"You need to fill out these forms...your being new and all."

Was that a smirk? I looked from the top of her head to the half of her body as she appeared to be framed. "I'm not new," I said moving up even closer. "Where's Maxine?"

"Maxine? Oh you mean the girl who *used* to work here?" She allowed her lips to turn upward ever-so-slightly. "I believe they say she got herself another job. I'm her replacement." She held the clipboard back out to me again. "I've searched high and low but haven't found a file with your name on it anywhere," she said.

My lips barely moved. "Well that's odd. Because Maxine *never* had *any* problems locating my file. So I would suggest you go back," I pointed toward the open lateral filings behind her, "...and do a bit more checking." It was then—that I smiled.

The upturn of her mouth fell so much, the smile she first sported became more like a wounded frown. I turned and started again toward a lavender and red zigzag designed chair, when for some reason, an afterthought really, I decided to pick up a magazine from the table. Just something to pass the time.

The cool breeze from the pages fanned my face as I allowed them to tickle past my thumb; however, my upper thoughts continued to drift on life and what are truly individual choices. Yes, I must have been a strong one to have chosen *this* life all right. A life full of rejection every way I turn.

Rejection by blacks; rejection by whites—too dark for some, too light for others. Rejection by women (both black and white); rejection by men (again, both black and white). Straight folks, gay folks, rich folks, poor folks: there always seems to be someone somewhere waiting (seeking out even) for a reason to judge or reject me. Oh I chose *this* life all right. Now, what was it I came to this world to learn again?

Apparently I forgot everything once I arrived here, and from all I've been able to surmise of late, I'll be forgetting a good portion—selective portions likely—of what I have managed to discover before taking my leave. And as though it wasn't enough to have the old timers dilemma (once called senility), now there's the dreaded Alzheimer's disease. Yet, the downside to being only thirty-six is having nothing to honestly blame occasional short term memory losses on other than: "What did you say? I've got so much inside my head, I can't get to it all."

The nurse came to the door and called the last person left besides me. Little Miss *New-To-The-Office* slid open the glass window and glanced first at the register, then a practically deserted waiting area before making four quick strokes with her pen. She made eye contact with me and faked a quick smile.

"I *was* able to locate your file," she said. "It was under your *full* name."

I nodded my approval and half-smiled back. My *full* name. Well, at least she has lovely teeth. Rather large, but lovely. And she did look for my file without my even having to get ugly with her about it. I glanced down at my watch then back at the magazine resting in my lap.

My hand had started to bond to the shininess of the page. I looked closer and noted it was stuck on a short story. Fiction, not what I cared to read today, yet the title roused my attention. *Moroccan Rose*. Interesting...my favorite flower of late.

As I began reading, I was first impressed by the words—a mirror of many words I myself had expressed—but then my impressiveness turned into nausea. This was not just similar, they were my words exactly! Words I had written in my journal some time back. I hurried and finished the article as the drooping feeling continued to coat the insides of my stomach.

I then flipped back to the beginning to see who was this thief. J. T.? What kind of a name is J. T.? Not a name in my book! The blood in my body felt now like it was all surging to my head—my face, warmer and fuller with each clicking second.

My mind was taking far too much time to sort, retrieve, consider, evaluate, and decide all the information my eyes had graciously (and neatly) laid at its feet. I knew the nurse would be calling me soon, so I needed some answers—and quick! And my answers did come.

Yes! it had to have been someone close to me. Who else would have had access to my home...my room...my personal belongings. Yes! it was someone I trusted...probably still trusted. And yes! yes! yes!...this was sheer betrayal of the Judas kind. But who? Why? Who could possibly be close enough to me, yet not realize this was not their best move to make? Surely the two I considered my friends know me that well—don't they? And Solomon would *never* (not in a million years) do something like this—would he? Not willingly...not Solomon.

However one thing was for certain, someone had done it! I held the evidence—printed with skill—on this glossy yellow tint paper as it dared to glare back at me without so much as an embarrassing blink. Words—oh yes, *my words* that I never intended for another set of eyes to read (at least, not while there was still breath rattling inside my body).

Nevertheless, here in the June edition of a most widely read, tremendously circulated magazine, was proof. Proof! "A work of fiction," it said. I say, "Fiction my foot!" Oh yes, someone had smiled mightily in my face while thrusting into my back, sharp and quick, a rusty dagger—an undeniable violation of both me and my private possessions.

I jumped when I felt a hand touch me on my right shoulder.

"Excuse me, but you can come back now," the nurse said.

I folded the magazine—making the article now the cover.

"Are you feeling all right?" she said while directing me onto the scales. "You weren't looking so well back there a second ago."

All right enough to know the number on these scales can't possibly be right! She proceeded to search my face while jotting down that ridiculous wrong number where the metal block still rested. I nodded, stepped off the scales, then back on again and carefully balanced the lead myself.

"Fine," I said, barely above a whisper. Then boldly, "These scales are off."

She grinned, pointed me toward the bathroom, and ordered me—on demand—to pee in the clear plastic cup. Oh yes, I chose all *this* all right.

After I finished in there, she proceeded to prick my finger before directing me to Room 5 with her lukewarm smile. "Dr. Richardson is running just a little behind. She'll be in shortly."

"Carol must be on vacation," I said, mostly to fill dead air.

She wrote things inside my folder, then gestured for me to take off my jacket and roll up my left sleeve. "Carol no longer works here; I'm Peaches," she said, wrapping the wide blood pressure band securely around my upper arm.

"Peaches?" I did hope my voice didn't reveal my lingering distaste. "Is that your *real* name?" And like a large boa constrictor, the band squeezed me steadfast.

"If you mean my *given* name, then that's Desiree. But I go by Peaches." She pumped it even tighter.

"Well I think Desiree is a lovely name." A hissing sound began to slowly escape.

Desiree seemed more focused on my blood pressure than on what I was saying. "Hmmmm," she said with a serious look, then in one quick yank, tore the Velcro loose. "And so..." she said, "...is Peaches." She held a crisp folded white sheet up to my face. "Now, if you'll strip all the way please..."

Dr. Richardson strolled in about fifteen minutes later with my chart in hand—Desiree now her shadow.

"Why hello there!" Dr. Richardson a medium-sized, personable, though highly professional woman said while working magic with her signature sunshine greeting. "And to think, I expected to see you months ago." She skimmed my chart then made total eye contact with me. "So...how is everything?"

"Everything's...great. Work is fine. Home is fine. Life is good. Busy is all, but not complaining." I then sat more erect. "I see you've changed around a bit since last I was here." I cut my eyes over and smiled Desiree's way.

"Yes. You know how things are. People get bored, they want more...looking for something better. Life, I believe is what it's called. But I'm fortunate—Peaches is great! She's been with me about...seven months now?" She directed the question to Desiree. Desiree nodded and smiled.

I smiled as well but allowed a silent windy breath to flow, tickling past my lips. "I just wish this were over with and done already," I said.

Dr. Richardson was looking down at my chart. "Have you been under much stress lately?" she asked.

"You mean other than eating it for breakfast, lunch, and dinner. Okay, I confess, I've cheated and sneaked a little extra for my snacks."

She smiled. "Yes, I'm well aware of how you manage to live off stress that otherwise would break most folk's nervous systems completely down. Nothing like a good challenge to get your juices flowing, huh?" She quietly closed the folder. "No, it's just your blood pressure's never been this high before—"

"High?"

"Not high, high—it's still normal. Just never been *this* level, let me put it that way."

"Well you know how excited I get when I think of all the fun in store for me beyond your doors. Thoughts have ways of getting my blood to pumping."

"Uh huh...right. And now I suppose you want to pitch me a deal for a plot of land owned by a little old atheist who never used it except to walk to church on Sundays?"

She sat my chart down near the sink and began checking other things; then my heart and breathing with that straight-from-the-refrigerator little stethoscope of hers. "Fit as my girdle," she announced after a few breathing ins and breathing outs. "Now for the *really* fun part! You know the routine."

"I know I *really* hate this part. Really. When are you guys going to come up with a more dignified way of doing this and cut out the cheap thrills?"

Dr. Richardson laughed a soundless-like laugh. "I've told you before, if you can come up with something better, you and I will get together and make a fortune. Until then, all the way to the end please."

"Yeah," I said as I did as I was told. "But the only time I even think about it, is when I have to endure this god-awful process."

When she finished, she wrote feverishly. I struggled to sit comfortably as she strolled over and stood near me. "Looks like congratulations are in order."

"Oh?" I said with a smile knowing full well, like a script, what always comes next.

You're healthy and should live forever, if you don't die before then, she will say. Still, I played along as always. "Congratulations? Why is that, Doctor?"

"You're healthy and should live forever..." she began, "only it seems..." she looked grim, "well...it looks like you're going to have..." a grin began to cover her face, "...a baby!"

The smile on my face died—crashed right at her feet. "*Excuse* me? But what did you just say?"

"Johnnie Mae Taylor...seems you're with child. Pregnant!" Dr. Richardson was jubilant. "Expecting!"

"Expecting? What? Me?" I shook my head fast. "But how? What about my birth control pills? When could all this have happened?"

Dr. Richardson continued. "Now Johnnie Mae, the how shouldn't even be a question at this point. And there's no need for alarm...your pills are low dosage...obviously not foolproof as you can see. And if you can tell me the date of your last cycle, I can narrow down that due date...give or take two weeks."

I gazed into space...searching for words other than what Dr. Richardson had just uttered. She placed her hand gently on mine. "I'm a bit confused. I was under the impression this was what you suspected...had planned even."

"No I didn't suspect or plan...this! I only came for my yearly things. You know, the breast...the pap, and all that other crap. Your office...they send out those cute little postcards to remind us when it's time." I shook my head, but then tried to force a smile Dr. Richardson's way. She now seemed visibly concerned about my *not so normal* fluttering reaction.

"Johnnie Mae, why don't you get dressed. We'll talk more in my office."

Dr. Richardson had stopped years ago inviting patients into her office. The new way was more efficient: examine, talk, and dispense prescriptions all at one time, all from one place. It didn't bother me when she stopped, but according to Carol (the nurse "Peaches" replaced) many of Dr. Richardson's devout patients weren't so happy about the "cut back." Yet, it made good business sense—better than dramatically raising the price of visits. This way she could see more patients, thus increasing her revenue base.

"Sure. I'll hurry—" I wrapped myself better in the sheet.

She touched my hand...firm yet gentle. "No need to hurry J. M.; you're my last patient this morning. There's time before the afternoon rush." She smiled.

* * *

I knew she had called me J. M. to settle me. Few people are even allowed to call me Johnnie Mae; she happens to be one. A caring black woman—I've known Dr. Richardson since she began her practice in Birmingham fifteen years ago. I was among the first wave of anxious patients, and she has witnessed J. M. grow out of Johnnie Mae (J. M. being the more powerful and successful of the two).

Johnnie Mae usually snapped an instant image of some country bumpkin from the "good old South" whose folks really wanted a boy but instead ended up with yet another girl. Privately frustrated, they gave her the name they had planned anyway and stuck the Mae in the middle because...well, be-cause "that's what Mae is for!"...the middle!

Johnnie Mae, whose employer's address was most likely some white woman's house. Where—in addition to being paid miserably for scrubbing three-point-five pee stained toilets, who knows how many nasty floors, the cooking, the cleaning, and thousands of humble "Yes mam"s and "No mam"s a year—she could count on receiving all the hand-me-down clothing she could manage for her own use or sale. Johnnie Mae whose hair—most often than not—was not tied, fried, *or* laid to the side since she had to work six out of seven days in somebody else's home before dragging herself to her own home where she still had to answer to all that awaited her there!

J. M. on the other hand, set folks to expect some pros-perous well-to-do white gentleman who was either gracious or business minded enough to set aside a few minutes of his "precious" time to listen to what you might have to say. Someone you would be excited about having speak to your civic group or company employees. Someone who would *never* have even *one* strand of hair out of place nor would a speck of lint dare cling to his fine attire. Oh yes...J. M. commanded instant respect, sight unseen!

Maybe someday I'll find a more appropriate expression of the true me (a happy median between Johnnie Mae and J. M.). But until that day, J. M. will just have to suffice. And because Dr. Richardson understands both Johnnie Mae and J. M., either name this good doctor chooses to use, suits me just fine.

After I dressed, my eyes scanned the opened page of the article. Oh yes, my blood pressure was surely up Dr. Richard-son. And this J. T. person was most certainly the root of it. Just as soon as I am positive these words match up with the words in my journal, El Niño will not be the only storm wreaking mass destruction this year. Only they'll be tracing this devasta-ting origination all the way back to Coffee, Alabama. And should it become necessary for me to take out a few places in the Birmingham area in the process—then so be it! Thirty-eight miles between me and whomever...will not deter me.

Dr. Richardson stared at me from across her desk before leaning forward. "Johnnie Mae, forgive me, but am I missing something here? Are you telling me you *don't* want this baby?"

Yes I want a baby...just not now. But Dr. Richardson said "this baby." The question is, do I not want *this* baby? A fact already in existence...or at the very least, in the making. I'm just not ready though; I have too much left to be done.

She's determined I'm about six weeks. Six weeks! But what about my career? I'm too close...a baby now...in the next seven months... No, that would only topple all these years of effort.

I just can't be pregnant! Not now. I just can't be! I've worked too hard to get here. What would "this baby" do to all of that?

Yes, of course I want children...I've always wanted children. Every year has just always turned out to be the wrong year and the next year, always seemed better. Only now, I sit here at the age of thirty-six (thirty-seven by the time "this baby" is scheduled to be born)... "...a Christmas baby it looks like," Dr. Richardson says—and still, I say the timing's wrong?

What kind of a mother would I be? Here, as my doctor poses questions of my plans? For certain, no match juxtaposed with my own mother. She would never even be having such an interrogation about *her* baby. But then, she would have never planned a baby around every other thing in her life as I appear to have done...so far anyway.

Well, at least I'd be a heck of a lot better than my friend Rosalyn. Lord, now you *know* some people have no business with children. I do honestly believe that...some times, anyway.

I admit, there are days when I do feel sorry for Rosalyn and her four. Yet, one can certainly learn something from just about anyone. Rosalyn without a doubt, has taught me a lot of don'ts in life. One being: Don't have children before you're ready! And I do mean *really* ready. That might not have been her intention, but that is nevertheless, the conclusion I have come to. Watching her struggle most days, seeming to neglect those children at others. Then there's Pearl with one daughter attending Grad school, and her other two—

Just then, my right foot kicked my purse as my crossed leg swung up and out. Reaching down to move it, I picked up the magazine. "Dr. Richardson, would you mind if I got a copy of this article? Or I could just buy the magazine from you."

Dr. Richardson blinked several times before leaning back against her chair. "What?" she finally said.

"I'll bring it back...when I'm done. Or I can just pay you for the copies—"

"Johnnie Mae," she began, "just keep the magazine. I'm sure it won't be missed around here."

"Thanks," I said trying to muster more of a relaxed smile just as I stood up to leave.

"Johnnie Mae? Your plans? Have you decided...?"

Oh yeah, I've decided all right!—and someone's going to pay. Big time! Someone I trusted has betrayed me and now someone will have to deal with their own consequences.

"About the baby? Have you decided about your baby? What's going on in that head of yours? There are vitamins and iron, folic acid tablets, blood work...all kinds of tests and things necessary in the first trimester. That's if you care in the least about giving your baby a fighting healthy start." She looked at me hard, like she wanted more than anything to penetrate the deep recesses of my mind.

I managed a confidence of a smile. "I'll get back with you. And don't worry Dr. Richardson, everything's going to be fine. I just have a lot on my mind right now. That's all."

Dr. Richardson began to scribble fast. "Then here," she said. "While you sort things out, see about getting these filled."

I smiled as she handed me four small slips of paper—one with a familiar scripture scrawled on it. *Casting all your care upon him; for he careth for you: 1 Peter 5:7.*

"I'll call...soon," I said. *Yes, there are just three people who could have had opportunity and access to do a thing like this to me. But who...which one?* 1 Peter 5:7 is good Dr. Richardson, but had you included the eighth verse, we might have been in business. *Be sober, be vigilant; because your adversary the devil, as a roaring lion, walketh about, seeking whom he may devour.* J. T., whoever you are...you will assuredly be answering to J. M. Gates Taylor.

The ancient ones believed a certain power was possessed in one who had four names. Yet more than power, J. M. Gates Taylor can be ruthless—especially when dealing with one who would dare go so far as to betray her.

I can already hear my mother's mouth: "Lord—that's old Nam-o rearing her head up through you, God rest her soul." Nam-o was Mama's great-grandmother making her my great-great-grandmother. And based upon the mounds of stories I've heard so far about Great-Great-Grandma Nam-o, she was truly a great...great...and a *grand* mother— Well let's just say, Nam-o was truly a *force* to reckon with. Free in Africa, brought to America to be someone's slave, then pronounced an ex-slave as opposed to formerly-free. And I, well I, am her descendant.

My fate from Mama most likely would be slanted more toward a story about Great-Grandma Nam-o getting her eyes plucked out by the "*Doc-tor* Master" (or some tale equivalent to it) if Mama feels even the *tiniest* bit obliged to explain my "inherited behavior" of which I apparently have no control.

No, I don't believe I'll mention this to Mama. Yet anyway. The *last* thing I need is to hear another story about dearest and grand Great-Grandma Nam-o.

I took out the silver dollar I've kept lately tucked away in a pocket of my purse (green string and all) and squeezed it tight.

Oh yes, someone will have hell to pay for this! But who?
Think J. M., think!

I must not be thinking hard enough—back far enough. *Who could, and did, do something like this to me? Who?*

I didn't mean to be so longwinded today in my writing, but as you can see, I have much on my mind. Especially now that I know, beyond any doubt, the words of <u>Moroccan Rose</u>— this "work of fiction"—match the words in my journal...phrase for phrase...detail for detail. And to top all this off, today of all days, I learn I'm pregnant?

My mind drifted and I heard, *"Begin at the beginning."*

Rosalyn Benefield's Journal

THIS BOOK BELONGS TO: *Rosalyn Benefield*, GIVEN BY: *J. M. Taylor*, GRANTED THIS *4th* DAY of *August* , *1997*

That's what the inscription read. So I just lined through *Rosalyn* and scrawled in...*Honey*!

I don't know about that J. M. sometimes. In the first place, nooobody calls me Rosalyn. Nobody! Everybody calls me Honey. Rosalyn might be the name on my birth certificate, but I answer to "Honey." Yet, when I pick up the phone and hear, "Rosalyn—," I know right off, it's got to be J. M. I'm talking, even my bill collectors all call me Honey for Christ's sake!

"Honey...just when do you plan to pay this bill?" "Now Honey, I'm trying to work with you, but you've got to show *some* kind of effort." "Honey, well tell me...how much *can* you pay then?"

Sometimes, they even add a little something extra—"Honey Child, I'm gonna have to turn this over to someone else, and believe me, they're not gonna be *half* as nice *or* as patient with you as I've been."

So why I can't get Johnnie Mae—oops! that slipped. Heck!—this is my journal; I'll say Johnnie Mae if I want to! She ought not have given me something to write my "deepest thoughts and feelings" in. Just don't you go slip and say it around her. Heck you're liable to lose an ear, an eye, a finger or two if you do. The first time I did, she nearly bit my entire head off—in one gulp almost, it was gone! Couldn't see nothing but the inside of her mouth. Yeah, we laugh about that crap now, but it wasn't a bit funny back then.

I say, "J. M., do you remember the time you nearly bit my head off? That day I slipped and called you by the name your folks gave you."

J. M. said, "Girl, didn't nobody bite your head off—you ought to quit!"

I said, "Oh yes you did cause I was wiping spit off weeks later."

Then J. M., in that proper speaking voice of hers said, "I did not do any such thing." She was looking all serious, mean and junk. Then she said, "Your big old head won't even fit in my mouth. So there!" We both just burst out to laughing.

Yeah, we laugh about it now...make all kinds of jokes; but when you're either on the wrong side of friendship, or just happen to be a mere acquaintance of J. M. Taylor, you had best be careful. She doesn't allow many folks to get too close, but when you're in...you're in. I will say this much, she's all right once you get to know her. At least, to her true friends.

I just wish she would get off my case about how I should be raising my own children. She needs to get a few of her own—that's what she needs to do. Then she'll see just how hard it *really* is.

And stop—*stop* trying to tell me how to run my life! Just because she and I are friends and just because she has a wonderful relationship with Sugarman—oops!..."Solomon," that doesn't give her all rights to my life. Sure, I'll be the first to admit I've made a few mistakes...okay more than a few, but then, who hasn't? I told J. M. from the git-go, "I've got one mama—don't need a spare, Girlfriend."

She said, "Then *act* like it."

The nerve of her! But real friends can talk that way with one another I suppose. However, I *have* been *try-ing* to do better. If for no other reason than for the sake of those "darling" little brats of mine.

Hey this journal stuff is all right. I can say brats without hearing, "Don't call those dear children that." Yeah it's easy to call them "dears" and "darlings" when they belong to someone else, but take them home for a few days, hours, minutes even.

I wonder why J. M. bought me this book with these angels on it. Anybody, who knows anything, knows that angels aren't women *or* cute little chubby babies. She needs to consult that bible she's always telling me I need to "study and show thyself approved." Won't find a woman or baby angel in there nowhere...not by name anyway. There's Michael, Gabriel, Raphael, Uriel—all sound like men to me. Even Satan (called Lucifer) was the prettiest angel God ever created. Of course, that was before he got kicked out of Heaven.

Now I got nothing against women *or* babies for that matter being angels (I'm all for equal rights!—power to all beings!), and Lord knows, they make prettier ones than some giant-sized men— Maybe angels are men-like because of all the battles they seem to end up having to fight, (although I personally know plenty of women who can kick royal butts!—me, being one of them!). And there does appear to be quite a bit of butt kicking going on between Heaven and here.

There was Jacob wrestling with that one angel for a blessing, that angel that got delayed bringing a message to Daniel that time, the war between Michael and his crew against that old serpent called the Devil (Satan) and his crew when Satan and his gang "fell" so to speak (Revelation 12), and then my ex-husband Duke... No wait. I believe I took care of that devil myself. Tried to knock the holy sh— (oops, forgive me Lord) crap out of him. Changed him from a serpent to a worm with just one good knee to the groin, oh yes I did!

But this *is* a beautiful cover. Soft and serene. And I know J. M. well enough to know she didn't pick this out lightly. There's always something going on in her head for every action she takes. Sister (that's "Pearl") and I call it: The law of J. M. Physics. Simply stated: for every action, there is an equal and more powerful reaction!

* * *

I remember my first encounter with J. M. like it only just happened instead of ten years ago.

J. M. Taylor waltzing in that hot recreation center in her fancy tailor-made A-line suit. And if her body hadn't complimented that darn outfit so well, I would have at least had something to laugh about. But oh no—Miss Thang stepped off in there dressed to kill! And in that particular neighborhood, she had best be packing something more than just good looks and a lot of empty promises. She might have been a short little petite thing, but home-girl was obviously as powerful as a cute little pearl handled pistol.

Well Miss Thang didn't scare me one iota! If I hada had her kind of money I could have matched her tit for tat too. Don't get me wrong; I can wheel a mean sewing machine now when I need to. Get me a bolt of linen and some pretty lining material with some famous designer's name on it, and I could have had men stumbling over me just like her. Come stepping in there whipping her jet black hair from side to side. Yeah, I thought it was a weave at first. So now I know differently.

But as it were, I had spent most of my time, energy, and money trying to make our girls from the neighborhood look nice when they glided down that runway for that benefit fashion show. And oooh goodness! What about those g-i-r-l-s!

They were so excited, I'm telling you the truth. I taught them each how to walk without looking like they were weighted down in their drawers. I taught them how to talk to people without spitting their 'B's and 'P's in folk's faces. But I did have to get on a couple of them...you know—let them know who was running things.

"If *somebody* gonna spend *their* time trying to do *something* to help *you*, then *you* gonna learn how to show some respect!" I said. "And if you *don't* appreciate the fact that don't *nooobody* have to do *nothing* for your old black butts, but that they do it because they *choose* to, then you can strut right on out of here so there will be more air left for those who *do* appreciate it." Then I bore down long and hard...took my time to stare all serious at each of them...let them know I meant it.

One of the little smart mouths, a lanky looking old girl, grinned and started repeating over and over...just got louder and louder, "My mama have to!"

I smiled and got right up in Miss LaShonda's little skinny face. "Oh no, your mama *don't* have to either." Then I paused (mostly for effect). "Your mama does it because she wants to— she chooses to, *not* because she *has* to. All she *has* to do is stay black and die!" I started walking away but a thought smacked me right on the back of my last nerve so I came back.

"And you know...I hear there's a cream now that'll turn even licorice looking folks as light and as white as they want to be. But now me—I happen to be proud of my color. Don't want to change it. Wouldn't change it if I could. Don't wish to shame or disgrace it either by acting *pure-D-ignorant!*"

I declare if that child's hair didn't lose all its perm right then and there; rolled right nice into tight springy little strands.

But when I saw that child in the outfit I had sewn with my own two hands, make-up just right for a girl her age, that big old smile to die for as she came floating down that runway... Well, let's just say, it would have been hard even for her own mama to have been prouder than I was—had she come.

So when Miss Thang—J. M. Taylor that is—came around after making her grand entrance...turning heads in the process, I turned myself to find another *thing* to warrant my attention.

"Excuse me?" Her strong, power of a voice reverberated behind me.

I turned around with a just right smile—not too big, not too small; not too hot, not too cold. "Yes?" I said much too perfect.

"Hi, my name is J. M. Taylor." She held her hand out ever so slightly all sweet and polite and crap.

"Yes?" I said, tempted to ask her what she wanted *me* to do about it.

"J. M. Taylor," she said *again* (like I didn't hear her the first time).

I finally took that limp manicured hand of hers and gave it one good pump. "Honey," I said. "Honey Benefield."

"Hon-ey?" she said like something didn't smell quite right. "Is *that* your real name?"

I did try hard not to laugh, but it was difficult to hold it in short of biting my tongue (which I wasn't about to do, not even for *J. M. Taylor*). It sort of seeped out, you know like my car sputters when it's way past the E?

"My real name?" I asked. *Oh give me a freaking damn break!* Still I composed myself. "*Honey* is what everyone close to me calls me. But I'll tell *you* what. Why don't *you,* just call me Rosalyn."

She smiled. "Rosalyn? What a beautiful name." Then she sighed—deliberately if you ask me. "Well *Rosalyn*, you must be *awfully* excited."

I had the feeling she was thinking I should be excited about meeting her or something. Sure, I had heard all about her—her reputation did indeed proceed her.

"Excited?" I said after a pause (mostly for effect). "Now why would that be? Oh, I know!" I said. "...Because *you* get to meet *me!*" I laughed (so it was phony, so sue me).

She batted her eyes rapidly, smiled ever-so-slightly, then with her nose all high in the air, she sashayed away.

And *that*—I thought—was *that!*

J. M. Taylor.

Frankly, I could not understand why any woman, let alone a black woman, would choose to be called by some old initials. However, my path was destined to cross several more times with this J. M. entity.

To witness for myself the different reception Johnnie Mae Taylor received as opposed to the intelligent, powerful, and highly anticipated J. M. Taylor, I began to understand it better. And I must admit; the seed of respect hidden away deep in my heart on what was then our first encounter, burst forth a tree which grew to bend under the heaviness of its own weight.

Yet what I did not know—could not have known—was on that first day, I *too,* had made an impression. On J. M. Taylor.

Still she persists in calling me Rosalyn, no matter how much *I* insist she call me...Honey!

 J. M. Taylor's Journal

Rosalyn thinks I didn't see that funny look on her face when I gave her that journal. I know she's not crazy about religion and things, but those angels reminded me so much of her. She acted as if the cover was full of dead bats or something...turning her nose up at it and all. And it sure wasn't giving off an odor or anything—nothing that should have caused her to frown the way she did. But other than acting like those angels were foreign to her, I believe she liked it.

Everyone knows I've kept a journal most of my life. It was a diary as a teen. Mama started by buying me five-year diaries, but I had so much going on in my life, I used all five divisions for one day. Then she got smart and bought me a one-year diary—even larger than the five-year one. I used those kind until I outgrew diaries altogether and graduated to journals. Now and days I use plain notebooks...nothing fancy about them. I save my pretty journals for affirmations and cute sayings I don't wish to forget.

I gave Pearl a journal as well. All she said was, "Gee. Thanks," then promptly sat it on my coffee table. Almost forgot to carry it home with her...good thing I noticed it. I would think if anyone would appreciate a journal, it should be Pearl. Why, she's a writer for goodness sakes! Or at least, she's trying to be one.

Based upon some of what she's let me read, a journal might be just the thing to point her in the right direction. I know there's nothing that sparks the electrodes in my brain more than holding a pen in one hand and a blank canvas on which to bleed my soul in the other. I end up purging all kinds of junk out of my system before I find myself writing some simply beautiful things midway the process of my expression, even if I have to say so myself.

My journal has become like a best friend. The biggest difference being...that this friend will at least, allow me to finish what I'm saying without constant interruptions. There is no judgment...no guilt associated when I'm done. I don't have to worry about my words coming back to haunt me later either.

"It's over and done—now move on to the next day and let's begin anew," it wisely says.

My journal is always there when I need it, and I know whatever secrets I share, will remain safe and quiet within it. It doesn't ask anything of me or expect me to "be" a certain way.

"Just be honest and say what you feel," it whispers calmly.

It reminds me of my many strengths, helps me heal when I feel hurt, surprises me from time to time, assures me with loving support. It allows me tears when I feel I need to, encourages me to be free...to speak the truth—yes, the whole truth! I can admit when I'm bothered...or afraid. I can even tell it when I'm tired or just plain to the point where I want to quit—give up. But no, I won't...I can't; and deep down it knows this.

Mama called—said she had a surprise for me. I wonder what it will be *this* time. Some months back she ran across a box of my mementos from high school packed away. I had totally forgotten about them. There were my library club pins, Junior Achievement and many other awards...a few love letters from old goofy boyfriends—

Man! I had absolutely *no* taste back then! It's good my taste buds improved greatly with age or who knows what I might be waking up next to (or not) every single day. Some old sour ball I'm sure. Instead, I got me a taste of some sweet Solomon...my goodness, you talk about *sweet* dark chocolate—God he's sweet! That's probably why all of his old friends—and new ones—all call him Sugarman. Well I don't care how much like sugar he is, his name is still...Solomon.

Personally I don't care for nicknames. Let's see, there's Rosalyn who wants to be called Honey (at her age, her drip has to be pretty close to drying up). Then Pearl who prefers to be called Sister (well I have two sisters of my own, and I don't call either one of them "Sister").

I happen to like the name Pearl...believe me, real pearls are not cheap! And as far as Rosalyn goes, she can forget about ever hearing *me* call her Honey. I hate it when people call me that just in mere conversation. "Hey Honey" "Bye Honey" "Honey this, Honey that..." Pl-ease! Spare me!

I tell them quick— "I'm not your honey!" But it doesn't stop them.

I just figure if somebody went to the trouble of picking out a name for you (although some do take the job more seriously than others), then the least you can do is use it. A variation is okay. Take Solomon's brother for instance—Terence. But everybody calls him Terry. That's acceptable, although I prefer and *do* call him Terence. Terence just sounds so strong. Terence!

See?

"Solomon's name came from the bible," his mother has said on more than one occasion. "A wise son makes a glad father, but a foolish son is the grief of his mother. I named him, Solomon David and prayed that some of King Solomon's wisdom and wealth might come to his name sake some day. My desire for Solomon, all my children for that fact, is that they would never have to experience struggles like I've had to endure in my life."

Solomon's mother had ten children.

"Near 'bout raised all ten of 'em on my own," she said. "That no account husband of mine was good about depositing babies, but I never could pursuade him to take any interest!"

Her words, not mine.

Pearl Sue Hunter's Journal

As though I don't already have enough to be trying to write, J. M. Taylor's little "surprise" turns out to be this "cute" little book full of nothing but blank pages needing to be filled. So Sister, or should I say, "Pearl"; since this book is from the Right-Reverend-Politically-Correct J. M. Taylor, let's you and I take inventory of all we have right now and give thanks.

I've got a *blank* computer screen most days, with crisp white *blank* paper in my sleep-mode laser printer, a *blank* notebook that *should* be (but is not) full of story ideas, a *blank* when it comes to how I'm suppose to pay my *blank* bills, *blank* stretches of time to fill up *blank* days, and now I have this "cute" little *blank* journal to write all the wonderful *blank* happenings of my *blankety-blank* life!

"What's this for?" I had asked J. M. (not because I didn't know either).

She laughed with that sweet little business laugh of hers. "Why silly, it's a journal to write down all your daily thoughts and happenings or to just vent if you prefer."

"I know that much J. M.; I want to know what you think *I* have to write inside of it."

She blinked her eyes real fast like a calculator being fed too many numbers at one time. "For starters, why don't you write down all that you are grateful for. That's always a good place to begin...if you ask me." She smiled.

I smiled back. Yep! That shut me up all right! I sure didn't care to hear this lecture—not again. Not in this lifetime anyway.

"Gee. Thanks," I said and grinned a little more. Then I gently laid it on the coffee table where, frankly I had intended for it to stay. Un-for-tu-nate-ly, J. M. made sure I didn't forget it!

"Pearl, you almost forgot your journal. You do like it, don't you? They had one with little puppies on the front, but I know how much you love variety. Did you notice that big flower on the front as well as the back?"

"Girl, you know I'd forget my head if it wasn't made onto my body." I hugged her. "But I do love it! And you for always thinking about me." I kissed at her cheek and smacked the air. "I'm going right home and start filling this up tonight." I then hugged the book close to my bosom.

"Well, you do know what they say about writers?" she said.

I turned around, my hand on the front door handle at this point, and looked into that cheery face of hers. "What's that?" I said masking my frown with a slight grin of my own choosing.

"Why...a writer writes, of course!"

Now what would *she* know about writers? She has no idea what we go through or how hard this profession is. Constant unending rejections. I'll tell anybody, if you really want to feel good about yourself, don't choose writing as a career.

My self-esteem has seen more ups and down than all the roller coasters at Visionland Theme Park. I've been so high at times that I've done figure-eights on the three rings of Saturn. Then there are times I've been so low, I have walked—upright— under the belly of a snake and never even bumped my head or messed up my hairdo (and trust me, my hair at times has been stacked a foot high on top of my head...according to my style of the week).

But J. M. who had the nerve to start up her own company when she found she couldn't go any higher up within a com- pany mind you that paid her more money in one year than most people will ever make in three to four. A woman whose man—as sweet as he wants to be and as true as he is handsome and tall—this man who supports her unconditionally...a man who would give her the earth on a stick if she said she wanted to lick the world. J. M. Taylor, whose house's foundation is cemented in the secluded green country lands, under indigo skies encamped near the crystal clear waters of Coffee, Alabama. Coffee, a place of its own majestic wonders...rich with air designed to create heart's desires. A place where every house is incisively and openly planted and—like the people who reside inside them—no two are alike. This woman...*this* woman now wants to tell *me* about writing?

Well I'd love to see *her* get something published! Anything. A page or two from that sacred journal of hers maybe since she thinks her writings inside it are all that.

She is right about one thing though—I feel much better having dumped all this junk out of my system. Come to think of it....I even feel a story coming on.

Let me see now...*A rich young snob with everything already in the world one could ever hope for, suddenly finds herself...*

Solomon Taylor's Journal

This house used to be so warm when we first moved in here. Now the stiffened caulking falls easily away. Where things were once so tight, time has witnessed a loosening grip. There are other signs of strain and decay, cracks and chips...where none used to be. And a chill (which in past days never found its way inside), now strides in bold like a lion, and somehow manages to wrestle any true warmth into submission. The only means to staying warm these days, it seems, is by turning up the heat. But even that succeeds in draining necessary resources, from other places.

Johnnie Mae gave me this. A journal she calls it. She giggled, almost like a teenage girl, apologizing for its cover.

"Solomon Taylor, it was hard finding a journal expressly suited for a *real* man," she had said. "But I do hope you like and appreciate my ingenuity."

She had glued magazine pictures on the cover. Cut outs from my favorite copies of Sports Illustrated. My *favorite* copies. The ones I had put up. In plastic covers. She said I would be more inclined to write in *my* journal if it was covered with something *I* cared about.

If only I had known she had intentions of cutting up my *favorite* issues of Sports Illustrated (the ones I had in plastic); I would have assured her, promised her, made a vow to her even, that I would write in it just as it had originally come.

A *real* man wouldn't be bothered by flowers or cute little animals on the outside of *his* book. Plain would have pleased me tremendously. Black, brown, blue—pink even, if it had meant saving my *favorite* issues of Sports Illustrated from becoming sacrificial lambs. She could have used *any* of the Sports Illustrateds still slumped over like drunks in the magazine rack—any one of those would have been just as much, if not equally as deserving, to grace the outsides of *my* journal. My "*real man's*" journal.

As I towered over her, on occasion rubbing my clean shaven head...turning this "journal" over and over in my hand, my only thought was: How could she! What was she *thinking* when she decided to do this? I don't believe she cut up my Sports Illustrateds—not these anyway! Now how would she feel if I just rummaged through her forbidden things and took whatever, anything, without having asked her first? If I just decided to do whatever I felt with *her* stuff? No, she wouldn't like that the least little bit!

So *what* in the name of Peter was *she* thinking when she did this to mine? God!

But deep down, Johnnie Mae has a good heart. And she does believe this journal kick she's on is the most wonderful thing; that it will "save the world" from all *her* inner problems.

"If everyone could just go deep enough inside themselves..." she says, "we would all be the better for it."

Now me—I just figure if this will make her happy and keep peace in the house, I can write a few words in here from time to time.

She was so proud when she handed it to me. "Now let me know before you fill this one up completely so I can get you another one in time."

Another one? Honest to God, I don't see myself *ever* needing *another one*. Not for *many* years to come. Oh—did I say years? Then let me say h-e-r-e, a while. A good *long* while!

"All right, Baby," I said licking both my lips, "but will you just do me *one* tiny favor the next time?"

She stepped up close to me like a cat rubbing against a post. "What's that?" she said with a slight growl behind that sweet little purr she sometimes makes.

I cleared my throat and considered just the right words. "Please, *please*, don't cut up any more of my favorite issues of Sports Illustrated. Please Baby. It's going to cost me a fortune just to replace these you've already mutilated."

The look in her eyes kind of made me think, *maybe* that wasn't the best choice of words I could have used during this "special" moment.

Well, she just has to understand...these were my *favorite* copies of Sports Illustrated. They were minding their own business on a shelf in their own *individual* plastic covers, put up way out of the way—hidden practically. Weren't bothering a soul! And still, my darling little wife managed to find them and then proceeded to mangle each and every one—one issue at a time. I'm talking about my *favorite* issues here!

And whether she knows it or not, I happen to do more than just look at the pictures, too. There were some really great articles inside those issues...some you can't get anywhere else!

Damn! And tell me—why can't women learn to push the toilet seat back up when they're done?!

Oh—and...I'd like to retract what I wrote earlier...about a pink book. Not pink. But now any other color...would have been just fine.

Countess W. Gates' Journal

A mother would know that a birthmark, now up past the wrist, was once near the middle knuckle on the back of her own child's hand. A mother would know because she was there...in the beginning. She would know where it was, and where it is now. A mother would know what had—and had not—moved.

Johnnie Mae's cute little tattooed strawberry birthmark, I do remember so well. Strawberries were the only things that calmed my digestive system enough not to return half-digested food back once downed. How I craved those plumps of sweetness. Maybe that's why Johnnie Mae gave me this book—a journal she calls it—covered with pictures of huge strawberries. It said: *To Mama—Countess W. Gates.*

I'm not quite sure where she got it in her head that I would be interested in keeping records of my days, but I'm doing my best. I missed a few days some time back...

"That's to be expected," Johnnie Mae had said. "Just keep at it though. It takes twenty-one days to form a habit."

I'm only doing this because she asked me to. And Lord knows, I try not to deny my children their simple requests. With five grown ones, sometimes I find myself going from ABC to CBS to NBC to FOX to whatever that station is that causes us to spread the antenna flat like a tight rope just to see it. There was a time when all my children sought *my* advice, but I suppose they want to show me how grown up they are here of late. Rachel, my oldest, teases me every chance she gets.

"Mama, how on earth did you get to be so smart?"

"The University of Mother Wit," I always say, then I laugh because they all know I never went to a real college and almost didn't finish high school. Not because I wasn't smart enough (I have plenty of Mother Wit), but because I fell so in love with Mr. Gates and wanted too much to still be a virgin on my wedding night. Nine months later, Mr. Gates was calling me "Mama" as he gazed into Rachel's sweet little face.

Mr. Gates has been kinda puny of late—black Lung is what the doctors attribute it to. But he declares he's as fit as he ever was. Nevertheless, after forty-one years of marriage, the man *still* knows how to make my toes curl...Lord have mercy!

Oh my—maybe I should be careful what I write in here; who knows who'll find this later. God knows my children giggle today if me and Mr. Gates go to steal a kiss in their presence. But Mr. Gates is just hopeless...forever my Romeo. He swept me off my feet when first I met him...and vacuums me off them today (though I'll be the first to admit, there's more of me now to whisk than ever was before).

But to let our kids tell it, we couldn't possibly know a thing about sex. I just laugh and wonder how any one of them think *they* got here. However, I also know, the thought of "it" is much too great for any of them to accept when it comes to us. What? Me and Mr. Gates getting it on...doing the wild thing...knocking boots...making whoopee...having S-E-X? Yes, I have lots of grandchildren, and as they put it, "Grandma is *down* with it!" Or is it up now?

* * *

Mr. Gates has felt much better the past few weeks. We were able to visit some of the children and grands around Labor Day. Johnnie Mae is the only one of our offspring without offsprings of her own. I admit I'm concerned about her being able to conceive, but she assures me everything is in working order (as far as *she* knows).

Of all my children, I really expected Johnnie Mae to have had a house full by now. Granted, that would be more than all thirteen of my grands put together (because Johnnie Mae has some kinda house!). Six bedrooms upstairs, two down, and then there are two bedrooms in that guest house of theirs out back. If she were to put two children in every bedroom and only filled up seven of them, that'd make fourteen right off.

She keeps telling me the guest house is mine if I ever want to move to Coffee. I'm sure she means me and her daddy, but she says, "Mama, I'll always have a place for you." I don't know, maybe she feels her father don't have long with us. I'm certain that must be it.

The last time I visited her, I could only stay three days. She hates it whenever company pops in on her unannounced, but I think she hates it even more when it's time for me to say my good-byes. Or—so it seems of late.

I can't wait to show Johnnie Mae the surprise I have for her. But I guess I'll just have to. I suppose if it's kept this long; it will hold a while longer. I can hardly wait to see the look on her face when those pretty big brown eyes of hers behold *this!* I'm sure she won't know *what* to say.

But then again...who would know their own child, better than their own mama?

 J. M. Taylor's Journal

February 5, 1998

I called Maxine today to make a doctor's appointment for May 15th...my annual exam. Maybe I'll talk with Dr. Richardson about starting a family, though she probably won't believe me this time either. I've only been saying this same thing every year for, at least, the past ten years.

And every year, I mean it. It's just something always seems to come up. Going to college at night to get my degree, getting four promotions in a ten year span where I worked almost seventeen years...those weren't good times to start. Not when you want to make a good impression...prove to them that they didn't make a mistake by trusting you to handle even greater responsibilities.

A nine month ordeal with possible morning sickness in the beginning, slow downs during, gaining some twenty-five (if I'm lucky which for me would probably be closer to fifty) extra pounds, the actual birth (which is rarely ever scheduled unless you're having a repeat C-section...it's hard to repeat when it's your first time), and finally a three-to-six weeks recuperation time *after* the blessed event. No, right after a promotion is *not* the best time to start a family.

Then the following year I would work my butt off to get everything running like a well greased axle and boom!...another promotion, and the cycle begins yet again.

Two years ago, I hit the glass ceiling everybody eluded to and realized it wasn't some made-up tale to intimidate the faint of heart. Oh yes, it's there all right! And heels taller than one inch and with any kind of a point, need not apply. I guess they're afraid we might put our foot down with those spiked heels, thereby cracking and breaking away that cheap glass.

So I just figured since I was practically running a small company without the pay that should have accompanied it anyway, I might as well run one of my own design. What did I stand to lose? Really?

When I mentioned my ramblings to Solomon, his eyes lit up like a two-hundred watt bulb (a glow that was to be short-lived). Believe me, two-hundred watts screwed into a sixty watt maximum socket...oh well, something had to give.

"Johnnie Mae, I think you *should* leave that company," Solomon said as he nestled up close to me. "Then you...and I..." he started to smile, "can get started on that family we've been putting off for so long. Take as much time as you like—"

"Whoa! Hold up there cowboy." My laugh was one and short. "Before you saddle up and get ready to ride me off into the sunset, hear me out first..."

And it was right there, I saw his brightness begin to dim. Seconds later, sharp pieces shattered all over. Leaving cutting edges to be wary of. Have you ever tried to unscrew a broken light bulb from a live socket? Trust me, you'd better be certain the switch is turned off completely. And even then, it's not always a safe thing to do.

Solomon wasn't even trying to understand why I felt it necessary to delay having a baby a few more years...the time I felt it would take me to cement this new venture.

"It's a major undertaking, starting a consultant company from scratch."

"You know what Johnnie Mae? I'm starting to wonder if you *ever* intend to get pregnant. What is it? You don't want children?" The pain filled up his soft brown eyes.

"Yes, of course I do Solomon. You know I do. I merely want everything to be *just right* when we do begin—that's all." I inched closer to him, pressing my silkiness up against him, and kissed him lightly on his chest.

"Yeah...?" he said calm, "that's what you said when *you* decided we *had* to build this house. 'This house will be *just right* to raise our family in,' you said."

I pulled back. "What do you mean by, *I* decided? I thought this was what we both wanted...we both wanted this house."

"A house is a house to me. A place to come to, a place to leave from. So tell me, Johnnie Mae...why have fifty-million rooms for only two people to romp around in?"

"*Romp?* Romp?!"

"Oh you're right Johnnie Mae! Johnnie Mae's right again," he said shaking both hands at the ceiling. "*Romp* is not *even* the word I was looking for! You and I don't *romp* anymore. Not the past few years anyway. You're either too busy too tired or in too big of a hurry to get it over and done with to—"

"Solomon! You're not being fair! This is only for a couple more years. Tops! If I can just get everything going, then—"

"Save it Johnnie Mae!" He was gentle. "Don't even bother; I've heard this speech so many times I can recite it backward, forward, and up the middle."

"But I'll be able to spend more time with a child if I can only get things ironed out first. Don't you see? Solomon what's a couple years when we plan to give a child a lifetime? Children are a minimum eighteen to twenty-three year commitment— some even longer than that."

I tried to laugh it off as I rubbed his long, smooth, dark chocolate body. A rich deep dark smooth chocolate. The deep rich pretty cocoa chocolate you simply can't resist. The kind you crave, melt in your mouth, chocolate bunny kind of deep dark chocolate—

"I'll be thirty-eight this year," he said looking down at me, "...and you're...almost thirty-five? Will we be taking care of our children *or* will our children end up having to care for us?" He pulled his hand from mine leaving me with a chilling ache.

Shattered—Solomon left the room. And I was left to change the bulb as I prayed, neither of us would end up hurt.

But now my business is almost there! Almost where I want—need it to be—to grow. In another year (year-and-a-half at the most), it will be running just the way I envision it. Six more months, and I can at least start to working on a baby. Hopefully, it'll be another six months before anything takes hold, and that, would frankly be just *too* perfect! But this means I'll need to work extra hard for the next six (to ten) months if I even plan on *considering* beginning our family.

Come to think of it, that would actually shell one pod of peas with one quick swoop. Solomon...Mama—

Mama—she's convinced I simply *can't* get pregnant. I told her I could if I wanted to, but that Solomon...and I...had made the decision to plan our family so everything would be...perfect.

"Perfect?!" Mama had said, jerking back with the force of the word. "Who ever heard of *perfect* when it comes to babies and families? Lord, if I hada waited on perfect to have y'all, you'd *still* be waiting somewhere for your number! I'm gonna tell you the truth Johnnie Mae, I love you and all, but I'm entirely too old for anybody to be trying to come here by way of me. You'd better thank God I didn't wait on perfect with you!"

"Oh Mama, things are different now—"

"Different?! Do you love Solomon?"

"Mama, now you know I do."

"Well I know that Solomon—every inch of his six feet frame, 185 pounds—loves you," she said. "So unless that much has changed—" She began to giggle a little. "They do still use sex to create babies don't they? With all this new technology—"

"Mama!" I frowned; I hate it when she talks like that.

"What? You can do it but you can't talk about it? Sex is *not* a dirty word, and I know I never taught you it was. What I said was, 'Wait until *after* you're married.' And that was the only *wait* instruction I gave you regarding sex and babies. Johnnie Mae, how long have you and Solomon been married now?"

"Seventeen years."

"Then that's *wait* plenty! Give that man some children before folks be mistaking you two for the kids' grandparents."

I arose from the kitchen table. "You and Solomon have been talking, haven't you?"

She smiled and came over to give me a quick hug. "I talked; he listened. I'm satisfied the problem's not coming from his end, so now...I'm talking to you Johnnie Mae Gates Taylor."

I sighed long and hard; I hate it when she calls me by all my names...my full names at that.

She grabbed my chin and lifted my face toward her eyes, her lovely long-lashed eyes.

"What..." she said, "my dear child, does it profit a man... or a woman...?"

I pulled my face gently from her grasp. "Mama, it's not about profit."

"That much I do understand Baby. But let it go, okay. Just let it go. 'Living without living, ain't really living at all.' At least, that's what Great-Grandma Nam-o used to say."

When she smiled, I noticed the silver on the right side of her teeth that held in place her new partial.

"Go on and have that family you always pretended you would have back when you were a little girl—*my* little girl. My precious little girl." She laughed. "Time moves on Johnnie Mae. Too fast for some, yet too slow for others."

All right! So this is 1998. In another year...year-and-a-half maybe, I should be able to make everybody happy! I just need to put things in order. And there will be no baby, making any grand entrance, one day before that.

That's my decision, and it's mine to make. Whether anybody believes it...likes it...or not!

Countess W. Gates' Journal

A purple and pink sky—I've not seen many things more lovely. I wonder what is the scientific reason for such an unusual beauty. I already know what my explanation is...and I hear you Lord! I hear you.

Mr. Gates at times forgets what year it is. Sometimes he seems to go back in time. His travels aren't long though—and he usually snaps back to the present pretty quick...much like a rubber band come to think of it.

I'm almost embarrassed to say this, but he was trying to *feel* on my legs today!—like he used to when we were first dating. I wouldn't have paid it much attention probably had it not been for that twinkle in his eyes when he said, "I can't wait till we can be together Coun-tess."

That's just how he said it... "Coun-tess"...like he was singing a song or something. Hasn't called me Countess since... well, since Rachel drew her first breath actually.

It's always, "How you doing today, Mama?" "Mama, you 'bout ready for bed?" When I heard Countess, I nearbout dropped that glass bowl I was drying at the time.

Still Lord, you've given me some grand years with this man...and I sure do thank you for that. I just pray the elasticity holds when he stretches back in time like that. Please Lord, don't let it break, or worse, lose its fancy to at least spring back.

When I think about Johnnie Mae and Solomon, I can't help but see me and Mr. Gates all over. I thought as much about Rachel and her husband, Trouble, now living in Chicago. That was until Rachel caught him stepping out on her.

Except for her five kids, why she took him back three times I'll never really know—but then, I'm not one to get in my children's business. Not *too* much, anyway.

Marie has her four, and she has no plans to ever put up with such foolishness from poor old Phillip. Told him from the get-go, he didn't have but one time to cheat on her and the watch began ticking the day he said, "I do."

Skipping past Johnnie Mae (in birth order...she's more like a middle child) and there's Donald. He has one child by that first wife, but has been married almost six years to old prissy Jessica now (good thing it was *he* that married her and not me). But to each his own.

Lastly my baby boy, Christian with Justin and two of the sweetest little girls. He married that girl down the street—Denise—right after she found out she was pregnant with Justin. And L-o-r-d, it wasn't a whole year good after the first one came before she come up pregnant again. Then a year later—again!

Now Lord, if Johnnie Mae could just have favor. She's a good child. Of course, I know this is your business—but if you might see your way to granting her a sweet little one—

I don't care what she says; I know she would have had a baby by now if she *could.* Not even Great-Grandma Nam-o, as headstrong as she was, would have been so set on a course she would have risked losing such a fine a husband as Solomon. And Sol *is* a good man...been good to my Johnnie Mae. But, of course...you know that too already, don't you?

Mr. Gates keeps asking about Johnnie Mae. I'm sure he would love nothing more than to sing and bounce one of her little ones on his old bony knee. "La-dies trot..."

Oh who am I kidding? I'm the one! He only wants our children to be happy. He has a special way of looking way past their eyes, no matter what their mouths say, and telling for sure whether they're truly okay. Johnnie Mae refuses to let him look in her eyes anymore. I don't know.

Yet, who amongst us can be sure how long we get to see orange suns play hide-and-seek behind blue waters? Purple and pink clouds scroll across a sky? To taste sweetness from the juice of berries or the creamy flesh of succulent peaches? To be charmed by the rising effects of yeast in fresh baked bread in and out the oven—that feel of its light texture melting in a cool mouth? The scent...the aroma of roses as they breathe from their own pores—the red, yellow, pink, white, orange and now that new kind Johnnie Mae likes so well. Moroccan Rose—a beautiful brown. I think she just admires the way that brown subtly makes its presence known...and then...acknowledged.

"Minority or not," Johnnie Mae said, "...you always know it's there."

Lord! She and that man gonna surely make some beautiful children together when they *do* commence to having them. And I'm not just saying that because she's my child either.

A purple and pink sky, huh? Purple for royalty, pink for a little girl, and the thickness of the colors stacked says it'll be a few more months before any of this takes place. Which one of my children this time though, Lord? Which one?

Word or Deed

And whatsoever ye do in word or deed, do all in the name of the Lord Jesus, giving thanks to God and the Father by him. Wives, submit yourselves unto your own husbands, as it is fit in the Lord. Husbands, love your wives, and be not bitter against them. Children, obey your parents in all things: for this is well-pleasing unto the Lord. Fathers, provoke not your children to anger, lest they be discouraged.   Colossians 3:17-21

Pearl Sue Hunter's Journal

I've got so many papers that need attention. I believe some of them multiply overnight...like rabbits. Sign this, pay that, file this, read that, throw this in the trash. No, on second thought, better shred that stuff...it's got too much information for a would-be gold dumpster diver. I hate paperwork! Some of these things need to be notarized...some only need a witness.

I'll get J. M. to witness the ones I need signed when she comes tomorrow with her comments on that last story I asked her to look over.

I'm really kind of excited about it...the story that is. I've got a real good feeling about it too. Not deceiving myself...it's not the best I'll ever do, but everybody's got to start from somewhere. And I desperately need to get paid for something soon. My funds are starting to get mighty low! About down to drugs now.

Not *that* kind of drugs; the bottom of the barrel kind. Yet, I feel I'm destined for a breakthrough any day now. I only need a little something to encourage me...keep me going. A small *yes* to add some heat to the oven.

Flick's been terrific about my decision to take that early buyout over eighteen months ago, but I need a *yes* on my writing soon or I'm going to have to go find me another job. A *yes* may help Flick to see I really am working, and maybe he'll stop expecting the house to be clean with a full course meal waiting on the table by the time he gets home.

"You didn't clean up today?" he said. "Haven't cooked yet either? Damn woman, what the hell do you do all day? Sit on your fat butt eating up all the food, watch soap operas or that that—what's his name? Jerry Springer? Yeah, that Jerry Springer Show."

"I don't watch Jerry Springer, Flick. I was working on my story—"

"What story? What the hell story you talking 'bout woman? Anybody paid you yet?" He stood in front of the opened refrigerator, gazed from me to it, then shook his head. "What's that you say? Speak up, I can't hear you."

I turned away. "Well no, but—"

"But...hell! Then I don't call what you do, work. Look...I personally don't care how you choose to waste your own time, but the least you can do is keep this house clean and have my food ready when I get home. Is that too much for a man to ask? I mean, at least one of us is working and deserves to eat."

"Flick—"

He closed the refrigerator door and walked over next to me. "Hey baby, look..." he grinned and smoothed down the sides of his mustache with his forefinger and thumb, "I need a couple of Benjamins. Why don't you spot me two or three crispy one hundred dollar bills 'til next month? You know I'm good for it."

"Good for it? You still owe me from the last three times—" I whispered.

"Yeah? Well okay. And I haven't charged you a dime for all the electricity and heat you've been wasting either! But look a here, I have this hunch you see I want to play at the track. A sure-fire, can't lose Superfecta! I'm telling you these dogs can't lose! When it pays off, I'll have all your money and then some. I can have it all back to you like that!" He snapped his fingers.

"And just where do you think I might get my hands on an extra couple hundred dollars? Flick...you know I still have all my bills to pay, and the house note—"

He smiled and pecked me on my lips. "You know baby, you still got some money left from when you left the company."

"Flick, I can't keep dipping into that money like that—"

"Yeah, right. You decide to leave work to pursue some stupid dream like writing and I get stuck taking up the slack. So you're going to be like that, huh? If you could figure out how to do that much, then you can spot me a measly five hundred. Yeah, I hear what you're saying...I can work my tail off trying to rub two sticks together for a fire, but you can't manage five hundred dollars every now and again when I need you to help me keep the home fire burning. You heard the preacher on Sunday...you gotta give to get. And you know, it wouldn't be so hard on the black man if you black sistas would just work with us!" He began to stammer, "Rather than against us."

"All right!" I said, "I'll get you the money, okay?"

He kissed me and smiled. "Mmmmm, now that's *my* girl." He began to dance...walking the floor with me in his arms, singing all up in my ear as we slid across the linoleum with an occasional dip. "All right now...who's the man?"

"What?" I said trying not to smile. It was hard to stay upset with him when he acted like this.

"I said...who...is...the...man?"

I let him draw me even closer. "You?"

He laughed. "Again—but this time, try and be a little more convincing."

"You!" I said louder, then laughed.

"You damn skippy! And don't you forget it either."

Yeah, I'll get J. M. to sign these papers for me. She's so use to signing things, I don't even believe she reads them anymore. I just hand her a piece of paper, point where she needs to sign, wait for her to scrawl that fancy signature of hers on the straight or dotted line, and she keeps right on with what she is saying.

How I *do* appreciate our friendship!

Solomon Taylor's Journal

The refrigerator's acting up—making this weird humming sound—and the water seems to be freezing up right before it flows into the ice-maker tray. The washing machine is leaking to the point now that the floor gets mopped every time clothes get washed. Everything seems to be either breaking down or falling apart. The washing machine, I can wait on; but we're having company up this weekend and it's not the best time to be worried about not having ice.

I asked Johnnie Mae if she'd called a repairman (and after she finished making her point, I promptly revised my question to repair*person*). After which, I received a lecture on the functionality of my fingers for punching in numbers just like hers are able to do. I don't disagree that she is just as busy as I am, but she has always been the one who has taken care of all these matters. Frankly, I had "assumed" it was something she enjoyed; yet here she was going on and on. *Beam me up somebody!*

"Just because I'm the woman, you've somehow mistakenly *assumed* I should be the one to take responsibility for getting everything done that seems to get done around this place," she said almost too smooth (okay, first gear).

But then, Lord-have-mercy if she didn't just skip right past second and third and shoved that baby straight into fourth!

"And tell me!" she said, "Exactly what kind of relationship is it when one-half does ninety-five percent of the work but receives only forty-percent of the return?"

Forty? And the longer she spoke, the faster she went. Louder...meaner...accelerating in the curves! Phrases seemed to bump into each other. She'd ask me a question then turn right around and answer it before I could fix my mouth to answer her last question. Then she had something to say about how slow I was about answering her. The pedal was to the metal, and she wasn't braking for anything or anybody! Finally, I threw up my white flag and surrendered.

"I'm sorry I even brought it up," I said. "I'll call somebody tomorrow—"

"Don't bother!" she said, "I've called somebody already, and they will be here some time tomorrow."

*Some time tomorrow...*set up again! So I did the only thing now left to do; volunteered to be home when the repair*person* arrives "some time between the hours of two and four." *There goes my evening appointments.*

"It's no problem," I said as I walked back to her office cradling a load of papers. "Really. And while we're taking care of business, here are some papers you need to sign."

"I really don't have the time to read a bunch of papers tonight Solomon. I have this deadline I'm trying to meet for Phoenix Electronics—"

"Johnnie Mae, they're just standard proxies. We get them all the time because of our various stock holdings. We signed as Joint Tenants, so we both have to sign in order for our vote to count. You've put this off for so long now, either you sign it or they vote our shares the way they want."

"Fine!" she said taking the bulk from my hand. "Show me where, and I'll sign the things."

"Don't you want to know what you're signing for?"

"Solomon...frankly, I really don't care! These are your babies. Whatever you think is best, I agree." And she began signing all six papers, not once bothering to read one thing.

"I'm glad we're having this get together," I said trying to dispel the dense fog lingering in the air. "We both need time to relax...to unwind for a change. Johnnie Mae..."

I began massaging her neck, back, and shoulders—definitely tight. "You know I'm really looking forward to the sounds and laughter, the maxing and relaxing..." I began kissing her on her shoulders.

She jumped up and pressed the papers into my side. "Here!" she said, "all done!" She then hurried toward the opened doorway.

Turning with a jerk, she said, "I'd love to stay and play a while, but bees don't make honey by simply flying and buzzing around. I've got *too* much to do to be buzzing and flitting with you right now Solomon Taylor."

I don't know...maybe she noticed the look on my face, or maybe it was the sound of what she had just said reaching her own ears. Maybe she thought a little more about what she had just done. Whatever the reason, she walked back over to me and pecked a kiss on my closed lips—just the way a hen snags a worm out of the ground.

"*You* might be all excited about this party," she said, "but *I* have a lot to do *besides* it," she pecked me again, "and *with it*," another peck, "*if it*," two pecks, "is to be..." peck, "worth," peck, "all the effort," peck...peck.

She smiled, tapped me on my nose and was gone—again.

I just wonder. Why *does* everything manage to break down right about the same time? Or maybe it just seems that way.

Hold up...did I just write hen and pecked in the same place? Well what I really *meant* was...she kissed me lightly on my lips—several times.

Countess W. Gates' Journal

I got Johnnie Mae to look over a few papers me and Mr. Gates got in the mail three days after the new year came in. I could have asked Donald or Marie, but Johnnie Mae does have such an eye for business. Lord, I don't know where she gets it—probably from her daddy. I've got Mother Wit, but she has a different kind of smart about her. But then, so did Great-Grandma Nam-o if I recall correctly. She was quite a little wheeler dealer herself...no matter if she was a slave. Lord only knows what she might have accomplished had she not been so oppressed.

I suppose Johnnie Mae got a lot of good *Xs* and *Ys* from both sides of the family. She and Solomon's children would probably end up little geniuses, I've no doubt about that either. There I go again; after I vowed I wasn't going to start stirring a pot this year for Johnnie Mae and a baby. But I can't seem to help myself! I desire so for her to have a little leaven in the dough. I can almost smell the loaf!

Yes, I could have asked either Donald or Marie to look over those papers since they both live much closer than Johnnie Mae. She's way on the other side of Birmingham... way out there...they call it the suburbs. Ain't nothing but a fancy word for *the country* I don't care how folks try to dress it up and pass it off as something more.

I've not dared allow a word to slip past my lips to Donald or Marie about how Johnnie Mae's been looking over our important stuff here of late (every since me and Mr. Gates got burned so bad those few times—). Nope! Said I wasn't going to think on that again either, so I won't go there.

"Didn't you read this before you signed it?" Johnnie Mae had said as she studied hard the "intent" of the words printed as though her gaze might change things.

"Well...yes," I said. Suddenly, I felt like I was standing trial for conspiracy or something. "I even had Donald to check it out, and he said everything looked all right to him—"

"*This*, looked *all right* to Donald?" she said waving the papers in the air. "You're telling me Donald looked at *these* papers and he didn't see all these red flags? There are so many things that should have been questioned about this before you and Daddy signed one blessed thing!"

I tried to play it off...take full responsibility for this quite costly blunder.

"Blunder? Blunder?! Mama, this is more than just some blunder believe me—"

"Well Johnnie Mae, you can't un-bake a cake Baby. Everything's gonna be all right. See—it hasn't killed us," I said. "We'll pay the extra and just consider this an expensive lesson for the future. We'll just have to be more careful the *next* time, that's all."

Johnnie Mae couldn't do one thing but stand there and shake her head. The way she does when she's in total disbelief.

"Mama, please don't take this the wrong way, but Donald— I know he's my brother and all but...," Johnnie Mae stabbed at the words, "...the next time...will you get someone to look at it who...," again she started and stopped, "...let somebody look at it who...," she chewed it like it was leather in her mouth, "Just get somebody else other than Donald to look at it, okay?"

So the next time I asked Marie. And when the dust flew back in the house after we'd swept that ordeal out the front door, Johnnie Mae sighed hard, shook her head over another piece of certified mail while drenching her soul trying to make it right.

"Mama...the next time you have something that needs a closer look, let me know. Okay?"

"All right Baby, but I know how busy you are. It may take me a while to get it to you—you living so far away and all. That's almost a two hour drive even if I speed and do fifty."

"The speed limit is seventy now, Mama. Coming to my house, you can drive seventy."

"Well all the signs say forty."

"Forty is the minimum, Mama. It's the *minimum* you should be driving." She smiled. "But if you'll just let me know, I'll arrange something. If I need to, I can give you my Fed Ex account number and you can send it to me that way. It could all be taken care of in a matter of days. We'll see when things come up."

I smiled. "Well, thankfully we don't get all that many important papers that need scrutinizing so close. And I really don't feel good about bothering you Johnnie Mae...you're always so busy—"

"Mama...it's no bother. I promise. Besides, look at all the time we can save by not having to undo what ends up getting done wrong."

After Johnnie Mae started getting bogged down in every little minute matter, she started relying upon my summaries of what the papers were about to determine whether she needed to take a closer look or not. Most of the things we have really aren't major.

"Johnnie Mae," I finally said one day when I knew she was too weighted with her own matters (she was deep into getting that company of hers on its feet at the time). "Johnnie Mae, we really don't need advice with every little matter. Take this one... all it needs is a witness to my signature. So you can just sign it since I'm here, and give it back. I signed it, you saw me—now attest to that."

She opened her mouth to say something, but I flashed her my world famous *I'm still your mama, Child!* look. Apparently she hasn't forgotten that look because she smiled, shook her head as she bit down on her thumbnail, and signed it in that graceful handwriting of hers...without so much as one word.

Yes...I'm *still* the mama now!

Pearl Sue Hunter's Journal

I asked J. M. to explain to me how Caller ID works. She laughed at first. I told her I understood it from the billing side because that's what I did for the last five years before I took that early buyout. I figured she could shed some light on the network side. She said things were changing at the phone company, even as we speak, so she didn't want to tell me something that was out of date already.

That's the problem with J. M.—she never loses her manners. Not even quiet-like...in her own presence. No burping. No passing gas—she just holds everything inside like it's just going to go away eventually or something. If something doesn't sound right, smell right, look right, taste right, or feel right, J. M.'s not going to come near it.

"Call the phone company and ask one of the reps there if you want to know," she had said.

"I'm not interested in getting it," I said. "We already have it—Flick had it put in."

"Flick?"

"Yeah."

"You mean your *husband* Flick?"

I wanted to laugh, but I was just as baffled as she. We both knew Flick won't get up and go to the kitchen to fix his own plate after I've slaved over a hot stove all day long cooking it. Heck, he only half wipes his butt (and I should know, I do all the laundry). So the thought of him getting up from anywhere, looking up a number and calling to get something done, was beyond belief.

"Yes, J. M. My husband, Flick."

"So now what's he up to?"

"I don't know. That's what I'm trying to figure out."

"Well I do know Caller ID let's you know who's calling most of the time anyway." She paused. "Do you think he's trying to see who all's calling your house?"

"I erase all the calls I answer. I have no idea what that man is doing."

"Do you think he has some kind of way to retrieve the calls you're erasing?"

I sighed louder than I meant to. "That's what I was wondering. I don't think he can, but I can't say for sure."

"I still have contact with someone in Network. I'll ask, see what I can find out and get back to you."

"Thanks."

"Pearl?"

"Yeah?"

"Why do you put up with him? I mean...really?"

I bit down on my chapped bottom lip. "I love him I suppose."

That was the only answer I could come up with.

"But Pearl...love is *not*.." She stopped. Probably tired of repeating the same words to me; I know I've grown tired of hearing them.

Is it, love is not a verb or love is not a noun? All I know is, I really don't care to hear it anymore.

"Hey!" she said, her voice more upbeat, "you're still planning to come to our place this Saturday, right?"

"February fourteenth? You know I'll be there. Of course, Saturday *is* my birthday as well. I mean..."

"Sure, but it's also Valentine's Day. Solomon and I figured it was a good time to have a get together with a few friends."

"A few friends? As in, other than the faithful few?"

"Yes, but not a whole lot. Possibly even some you might know. Come on, you're not thinking about chickening out on me, are you? You know I won't have anybody to be myself around if you and Rosalyn don't show up."

"Oh I'll be there, don't you worry about that! One thing I'm not...is shy. And it sure beats sitting here counting the number of walls in each room of my house."

J. M. was silent for a minute. "Pearl, are you sure Flick's not planning something for your birthday? He might be preparing to surprise you—"

"Surprise me? And break a twenty-seven year tradition? Girl ple-ease. Stop dreaming...I certainly have."

"Well now if you're sure, I might even spring for a cake or something...possibly Rosalyn and I can sing happy birthday to you."

"Oh no! No torturing me on that day, please I beg you," I said laughing.

"Okay. It's like *that*, huh?" Then she laughed too.

"Now on the other hand, Sugarman can sing to me all day long and it would be just fine with me. Your man know he has a voice on *him!* So deep and—"

"You mean *Solomon?*" she said—just *had* to correct me.

Oh but I know Sugarman better than most folks (even dearest J. M. doesn't know everything). I happen to know how he *got* the name "Sugarman," and I could tell her...if I chose to. So having J. M. practically demand I call him Solomon just because *she's* decided that's what he should be called, really ticks me off at times (although this is not one of those times).

"Look..." I said to J. M., "I call *you* what you want; leave a sistah something okay?"

She laughed. I can hardly believe it, but she actually laughed after I said that.

"Well Rosalyn and I *might* see...oh all right, we'll *allow* Solomon to sing with us—"

"With? You don't take hints very well I see." But then, I became a little more serious. "You know, what I'm really thinking is—Saturday *will* be Valentine's Day. Don't you and Sug... you and Solomon...the two of you, wouldn't you like to do something more romantic that day?"

"What? And let your birthday slip by? Let you sit home, possibly alone, and pass quietly *over the hill* into that great and wonderful beyond—that *big five...O?*" She laughed. "Pearl, there are 365 days in a year. Solomon and I can surely give up one of those days for someone we both care about. And we'll *still* be left with 364 days in which to celebrate Valentine's Day. Alone if we so choose."

I smiled, though she couldn't see it. "Thanks," I said.

I really don't care to spend that day alone—not my birthday. Everybody wants to believe somebody cares that they were born, at least enough to pause and acknowledge it did happen. It doesn't matter how long ago it might have been.

J. M., Sugarman, and Honey are all being so wonderful to take a few minutes out of their schedules for mine, so I'd say that's something to be grateful for. Something to be written...in a journal maybe?

However, I don't care what J. M. says or thinks. I really do love Flick, and I believe...know, he really loves me—just in his own way.

Solomon Taylor's Journal

Johnnie Mae is so tired lately. I told her when you work every waking hour as hard as she does...pushing herself beyond tired (I know for the past twenty years we've been together, counting the year we met), even when her body says, *"No, I will not move another inch. No. Give me time to catch my breath. Not until we rest"* yet she continues to make it, force it, press it even further... "Johnnie Mae, what do you expect?"

Not the answer she desired or cared to hear, so she did what she has done more lately, than in the history of our marriage. Stared first, then rolled her big brown eyes at me.

"Solomon, why do you work against me? You know how hard it is already out there," she said pointing past the walls of the kitchen. "I don't need this from you too! Why are you men so afraid of us women? My God! y'all even set us up to take the fall for what happened in the garden of Eden.

" *'It was that woman thou gavest me Lord. She gave me of the tree. And me being the man you created me to be...I ate it.'*

"What kind of crap was that? Wasn't it Adam who God told not to eat of the tree? I haven't found one place where it says Eve tied Adam up and forced that fruit down his throat. And do note...I did say *fruit!"*

I knew that to mean it never said an apple anywhere in the scriptures. I eased over and sat on a bar stool...hypnotized by the pendulum that now swung fast and hard before me. *Okay, so she's reverted to y'all; she'll be awhile from this point.*

"But everybody wants to say it was an apple," she said. "Nowhere in the Bible does it say an apple! It could have been a peach, a pear, a plum...anything. Yet *everybody* spouts 'an apple.' I guess because it makes it easier to explain why men have an Adam's apple and women don't.

"Oh you know...when Eve *shoved* that *apple* down poor old Adam's throat...it got stuck, thereby being the plight of every man who was to come after him." Johnnie Mae went back and forth, pacing like a tigress determined to protect her young, stopping only to pounce firm a point.

"And *why*—Solomon Taylor, do all you *BLACK* men..."

Oh God, there she goes. She said BLACK men—officially appointing me the spokesperson for every black man past, present, and yet to come.

"...why do all you *BLACK* men have to find some white woman to marry—especially, you *BLACK* men who finally get a little piece of money? Everybody knows those women weren't studying y'all's old broke butts when you didn't have a pot to piss in!"

My shoulders began to sag, so I hunched them back...holding them on top as best I could under the circumstances.

"I'm talking about the *b-lack* woman who put up with all y'all's crap when you didn't own or have one thing...most of you not even owning your own name. Who stood by you?

"No matter that, when they brought our people over here on some crowded, stanking ships, the smell alone killing many, who stepped forward?...who stood up for us?...who fought for us?...the black woman?

"No matter that when the master came and defiled us—even after having allowed their slaves to 'jump the broom,'—if the *Mas'sah* desired himself a taste of some sweet brown sugar or dark sweet molasses, he just *came* and *went* as he pleased. But you know what...we still made it."

"Johnnie Mae...Baby, what does this—any of this—have to do with me and you? Look, you're tired. Maybe you should—"

"What does this have to do with me and you? See, that's precisely my point; it *did* affect us!" She rubbed her forehead.

"No matter we had *your* babies...*their* babies...*our* babies— some times only to have them ripped away from our breast, tearing out chunks of our hearts as they were sold or willed away like we were not human. Who was for us? Who fought for *our* family? Now, even after being free, some of y'all *still* have that slave mentality. Thinking it your *god-given* duty to impregnate the strong black woman and to keep right on to the next one." She stopped and tried to look into my eyes.

"When you didn't have two nickels to rub together to make a dime...who was it that stood by you?" she said. "When you couldn't get anybody to hire you for a job, who was it that worked night and day...doing whatever she could to keep the family together while at the same time trying to convince—undo no less—what damage had been heaped upon *their* men? Reminding you of how great you are, in spite of what '*they*' said.

"Working till we heard our own backs crack, only to come home and have some fool waiting with a clenched fist and a chip on his shoulders—a chip we did not put there."

She flopped down in a chair in the kitchen nook and gazed out the window...no sound...just a certain look that could be heard in the silence.

"No, we weren't the ones who did wrong by you. But y'all have the *nerve* to look at our various tones of hues...our natural tans...our blackness and say to us, *We are not good enough, pretty enough, smart enough, for you?* Now that you are free to choose, you don't—will not—choose us?

"The water. The rock. The one who always and has always wanted, cared for, and loved you when nobody else thought you worthy—deserving of such a love..." She looked into my eyes and this time, I looked back. That's when I saw the flame now almost spent to a flicker.

"When *nobody* else," she whispered, "*did* or *would*...now that you have something to give, you'd rather give it to *any one*, any one, other than the one who gave to you?"

She stood and walked over next to me. "My words are not racist; I don't deny some truly do love those they are with...who can rightly say? I just want you *black* men to know, that we your *black* women, do—at times—take it personal. And Solomon, I am J. M. Why is it so hard for you to call me that?"

I stood there realizing this was not at all about color or men or women. I pulled her together by her shoulders—every shred that had come undone.

"Johnnie Mae," I said, "I can't speak for all my fellow black brothers of the world. Nor can I speak for my white brothers. But I can tell you this—black or white—I am one blessed man. I love you, and I am sorry you carry the pain of all our mothers, sisters, and daughters so deeply within you.

"What I must say is...had you been white, red, yellow, or green; I would have married you and *cursed* what any one of any race thought—or felt about it. I married *you*...Johnnie Mae Gates Taylor," just hearing her name settled a smile over my face. "And it's true, a rose—Johnnie Mae—by any other name—"

Her whole self suddenly turned to water and fell upon my body as she washed me all over. I felt the cool wet seep through my silk shirt, then warm as it reached and touched all the way down to my bones. Bone of my bone, flesh of my flesh.

And I rocked her. The way her mother rocked her in times past. The way my mother rocked me.

"Johnnie Mae...woman...do you have any idea how much I love you? Too much, some say; never enough—say I. But I want you to know, to always know, how much I love everything about you—I declare I do. Inside and out, my spirit bears witness with your spirit. And spirit—crystal clear—is without color and not limited to a set form."

Right then and there, while locked inside my embrace, her tired caught up with her. And she surrendered to it—body *and* soul. And all that was left standing was the rock...the water... and the spirit.

Later, I called my mother, Johnnie Mae's mother, all my sisters, and special friends who are mothers and simply said, "Thank you."

 J. M. Taylor's Journal

Okay—so fat is bad for you, fat is necessary. Salt is bad, salt is not. Wine will make you drunk, a little wine is good for the stomach. Oh! just found out, it's also good for the heart but then, so is grape juice. Now coffee will make you black, no coffee won't...but it's still bad for you, right? No, that was last month, this month, it's not.

Man was created by God, man evolved from apes, but not all apes evolved because apes still roam the earth (those who haven't been killed or poached). Hey did you hear?...they found fish fingers? Man was once a fish! Yes, fish grew fingers and already had lungs, so they crawled right out of the ocean to live on land as a man...was that before or after that meteor struck the earth and took out those mean old dinosaurs? Are they sure that wasn't just Jonah crawling out of the belly of that whale?

"Evolvers and adapters," that's what *man* says *man* is. "We always find a use for old genes."

Kind of validates my theory about black folks and all that we've endured in this land of the free. It's like this: when you have a disease you want to overcome, you create a vaccine to combat it.

The concept is: a thing that could destroy you is introduced into the body (a milder strain of course) so that the body's immune system can examine the foreign matter and begin immediately creating its defense. Then when the actual *thing* (whatever that happens to be) attempts to invade and attack the body, it comes up against a more intensified protector.

There's one flaw to all this...some of these attackers are re-creating themselves...a stronger version...stronger than its past self. So strong, there is nothing that eventually will be able to stop it. One day anyway.

I watch the Tiger Woods, the Toni Morrisons, the Michael Jordans, the George Washington Carvers, the Oprah Winfreys, the Ben Carsons, and so many others (too many to name in one sitting), and I can't help but smile.

Fish fingers, huh? Well, I suppose it's possible. For nine months before a baby crawls out of the mother's womb (the ocean), it has swam, flipped, sloshed, kicked, and transformed in the warmth and safety of its own reservoir. So why should this fish theory be such a marvel?

But Pennsylvania? That's where they say the fossils were discovered.

Pearl Sue Hunter's Journal

I do love Toni Morrison's work! Oprah picked her latest book for her book club. I'm going out today and buy the book so I can get my letter in. I'm pretty smart; I bet I get picked for this one.

If I could go to this—at Princeton University too... Shoot! I could possibly get Oprah to choose my book (whenever I finish it), and maybe Toni and I could become friends and...okay, so I need to slow down a little. Getting a little ahead of myself. First thing—buy the book. Read it. Send in my letter. Get picked. *Then* I can go from there.

Honey wants a ride to J. M.'s house. I wish she would hurry up and buy a car that runs! I don't care if it's the ugliest piece of junk welded together riding on the road. If it will just run—that would be great!

And to think she wastes good money buying a tag for it too. If I were her, I would ask the people at the Courthouse to prorate my fee for the time it's parked in one spot (generally about nine months of the year). And the one month it travels back and forth to that jack-legged mechanic she calls Doctor K. Prorated, that would be about two months she'd owe. I'm starting to favor assisted suicide; somebody should put that pile of junk out of its misery! That's my vote, but who asked me.

I sure hope Honey gets somebody to keep those bad children of hers. Make one of those two older children stay home with them instead of out prancing in the streets showing their behinds. My children are all grown. One daughter is in college, and none of them ever acted like Honey's kids. Honey just lets them run wild.

J. M. will put up with it, although I don't understand exactly why. It's evident she doesn't want to be bothered with children otherwise she'd have some of her own by now.

Nope, J. M. has her eyes set on a larger prize. She intends to make her mark, and nothing's going to get in her way. I can't help but wonder what drives a person to that point?

Who could have known when I met her in the copy room that first year she started working for the phone company—so shy and timid—that things would turn out like they did.

She started moving up so fast, it made all our heads—black and white alike—swim. And did she ever move fast! Everybody had something to say about it too. Some claimed she had to be sleeping with *somebody* to be rising like that.

"A woman and a black woman at that?" People said. "It's because of her skin tone, I tell you. You know how they prefer *her* shade of black whenever it comes time to have to pick one of us."

"It's the quotas."

"What you talking about skin tone...she's darker than me. Where's my promotion then?"

"Well she's *way* lighter than me, and I'm not dark by any stretch of the imagination."

"Now what are you talking about? You're darker than you *think!*"

"Rose too fast for her *not* to be doing something not entirely upstanding," a manager—a black woman no less—said. "I'm black. Been here longer than her too! How could she pass me? Explain that much, then tell me she's not doing something immoral somewhere?"

So the code word to speak ill of Johnnie Mae Taylor without saying her name was "Rose."

"The sun *rose* mighty early today."

"Mr. Flinch's *rose* doesn't *ever* appear to fade any."

"Child, I wonder how *that rose* can still be blooming after all of *that?* I've never heard of a *rose* that didn't lose a *few* of its petals at some point in time."

"Don't know exactly why, but I hear the higher ups have their eyes set on a certain *rose* again."

Ironic now. Seems there's an actual rose that describes J. M. perfectly—the Moroccan Rose...a magnificent brown.

I knew the answer for her rise just as they all did but were refusing to admit. Before she started calling herself J. M., she would stay late and come early. She took work home by the grocery bag full, literally (she didn't even own a briefcase back then). She sacked the extra work in a bag just like I used years ago when I'd tear brown strips, twist them and roll up my hair.

J. M. willingly did the work three people wouldn't do receiving only one paycheck for it. So when she got promoted the first time, everybody figured she would now slow down and quit making everybody else look bad.

"Did you know she's going to college *too?*" my friend said.

But she didn't slow down. If nothing more, she got worse. Around this time, she and I were speaking more often and longer whenever she ate lunch in the break room (she wouldn't take but fifteen minutes of the hour she was otherwise entitled).

"Got to run," she would say.

I thought she was being paid overtime for it, but those who worked alongside her said that was not the case. She was "the kind that made it hard" for others because now "white folks are looking for every person of color to step it up like her."

"Shoot!" people said, "she's even making the white folks look bad. But they're white...so you know how all that goes."

Most folks thought she was snooty because she started moving up. But the truth is, they were the ones who changed toward her. And I should know; I watched them do it. Here was, in actuality, this child younger than most of us, only doing what she needed to do to protect herself from being torn apart by unmerciful wolves on the prowl. God gives every thing on this earth a way of protecting itself and J.M. was no exception.

I figured out, all by myself, she just didn't like to feel at all rejected. She'll never let anyone know that for sure because when people know your weakness, they'll use it against you. So she'd just act like it didn't bother her.

She said once, "I don't get paid to make friends; I get paid to do a job." *Reject before rejected.*

As J. M. Taylor, she was featured many times in publication. Sometimes they placed her picture alongside the article, sometimes it was just the words standing alone. Words on recycled paper—who had any idea what color she was.

There were many whites who talked like J. M. was a member of their family. Some, I happen to know for a fact would "just *die*" if a black were to show up at their neighborhood meeting.

Still, they'd read about her accomplishments and ideas and brag about the wonder of this fine person...this J. M. Taylor who is/was/will be...if only he/she keeps focused on what he's/she's doing. "J. M. Taylor—this power player of a lifetime."

J. M.'s private life was just that—private. People known not to have any use for her in the past or had declared they'd never offer her the time of day were her watch to stop, began trying to hang out with her. "Just being friendly," they said.

They speculated about the house they heard she was building. Three people in my own office spent an hour discussing it.

"I hear she's building a mansion way out in what, Coffee Alabama," one began.

"Pray tell! You'd think they would have red-lined that area already."

"I suppose they didn't expect they'd have to...being that I hear just the land alone starts upward of $95,000."

"*That* wouldn't be called red-line. Red-line is when whites move *out* of a community and Realtors conspire, '*unofficially,*' to zone it as a black neighborhood—*only show those to blacks.*"

"You do know why they call that place Coffee don't you?"

"No, why?"

"On account of if you've got *that* kind of money, it's okay for a cup of blacks to *stir* in a white neighborhood."

"Did you say a *cup of* or a *couple?*"

"Same difference."

"You need to quit!" The three laughed.

So when J. M. invited me to her house (a year after they moved in five years ago), I was just as shocked as those who had wanted to go but had not—and would not—ever be invited.

There were plenty of invisible walls erected in her home... both in what she allowed herself to say and where a visitor was allowed to roam alone.

You can go this far and no farther, is what was whispered clearly, yet not said.

I respected those boundaries. So, the first time I was introduced to her husband, no one was more surprised when we locked gazes...than he and I.

Well no one except maybe, J. M.

Oh well, if I'm to finish this short story tonight and mail it off tomorrow, I'd best get back to it.

Application fee is ten dollars. Money, money, money. I'm still waiting on my change though Lord. Just working and waiting on my change! And I don't mean the kind that jingles either!

Rosalyn Benefield's Journal

Sister said she would come pick me up around six; it was closer to six-thirty by the time she pulled up. I do like her car. She bought it brand new off the showroom floor. Cash. Used much of the money she got when she took early retirement from her company of almost twenty-nine years. Should have been quite a nest egg; she got a buyout.

So now the only retirement money she'll have until Social Security kicks in (if Social Security is still around by then), will be what's left after she finishes nibbling away at it instead of leaving it invested. Sister's the oldest between me, her, and J. M.—today was her birthday. The big five-zero! I turned thirty-four in January; J. M. will be thirty-seven August the 4th.

Sister thought I asked her to come pick me up because my car was acting up again (it is, but that wasn't the reason). J. M. was throwing her a for "real" surprise birthday party, and we figured we could better control Sister's arrival if we had a plan.

The last thing we wanted was for her to change her mind at the end and not show up at all. "Surprise!" "Oh! where is the birthday girl?" No, that wouldn't work. So I told J. M. (like she didn't already know) that my car breaks down a lot and Sister would think nothing was odd about me thumbing a ride.

The plan was for Sister to come pick me up around six but I would be running late, so we wouldn't leave until around six-twenty. Sister would be upset since she despises folks who operate life on "CPT" (Colored People Time).

As it turned out, Sister was the one running late, so we were speeding down the highway to get to Coffee (a good forty minutes from my place), by seven. That LeSabre sure can fly! It's so pretty too—four matching doors...steel gray. I mean she drove that baby right off the showroom floor the same day she paid for it. It had never belonged to another before her...she was its first. Even if it ends up with another person later, she would always know...it belonged to her before anyone else.

"Nice...outfit," Sister said alternating long glances between my fake leopard skin top, black wrapped skirt bottom, and a busier than usual freeway.

"Oh you like? Thanks, Sistah. You know I made it, right?"

She smiled. "Of course."

J. M. keeps telling me I have talent just wasting away. She thinks I could be some famous designer if I were to set my mind to it.

"What do you have to lose by trying?" she had said. I don't know; I've seen too many unsuspecting people get sucked in by human shredders...ripping to pieces whatever got thrown in their paths.

Sister is already running low of funds out there trying to follow her dreams of becoming a famous author.

"My aim is for the New York Times Bestseller's List some day," she says.

It's all she talks about. "Honey, that's my confession...my daily affirmation. I'm going to be on somebody's list, mark my words, you just wait and see!"

Over and over—like if she says that enough, it will be so.

J. M. explained to me that repeating something is not the thing that makes it so.

"It's really about getting it down in your spirit. Then your spirit convinces your mind to do what it needs to do," she said.

Then she went on talking something about the mind creating pictures, then action and action moving you in the direction you need to go in. J. M. can be deep some times.

"But it's action with imagination that makes a thing so. Words are like the spark plugs in a car," she continued, "...it gives off the sparks that lights the gas that eventually causes things to get moving."

"I've got brand new spark plugs now...and gas, but Doctor K says it must be my carburetor that still needs to be adjusted," I said teasingly, although J. M. didn't crack a smile.

So that's what I believe Sister may be in need of...a tune up with minor adjustments. She lets that fool husband of hers talk her into dipping into money that should be left to grow, and now she's in a panic to succeed. Except it's harder to concentrate when your mind is stuck on 'E'.

Nothing's worse than a desperate woman than a desperate black woman. And the only thing worse than her, is a desperate *broke* black woman. Now desperate broke white women are a different matter altogether although most, at least, have family or friends who can lend a helping hand.

Desperate broke *white* men...well, the last recorded time when a lot of them went broke was 1929. I hear a bunch of them believed they had grown wings and decided to test them out by leaping off tall buildings—all they got was a single bound. And you know they were all white—a brotha jumping off some building because he's broke? Shoot! They'd have to pass out tickets just to accommodate the crowd.

Even then, ninety-nine point nine percent of them would have reasoned that things were surely starting to look up. "Hey check this out! I was just standing in line there, and some funny looking guy came and handed me this ticket. Looks like my luck is about to change! Think I'll hang around to see if I win."

J. M. is about the only person I know with any real amount of money to speak of. And anyone who knows her, knows: *Every pot must sit on its own bottom.* Family, friends, the man begging on the street, makes no difference to her. Sit!

Now me, I don't have a problem with that philosophy myself. I believe in paying my own way or stay my butt at home (unless it's a date, of course but that's a different matter).

J. M. will listen, but you're going to have to take responsibility for your own decisions...good or bad.

She says, "Everyone has the power of choice. You may not think so, but that doesn't change the truth."

Sister looked so surprised when she pulled up and saw me outside waiting.

"Where are your children?" she said.

I wondered at first why she would think I would be so tacky as to bring them. It's no secret she's not crazy about my children...especially when they start to get on her nerves. I see the way she rolls her eyes at them. They do too—they're *just* children. She acts like she doesn't have but one child and that *sweet* little Christine is *so* perfect.

"You know Christine's in her last year of grad school. Made the dean's list," she said. "Christine was never one to run after those mannish boys when she was in high school."

I know that was a throw-off on my daughter. But ask her about her other two—the two older ones. The ones she don't talk about much...the ones she practiced on *before* Christine.

Her boy (well, not a boy anymore...he's twenty-eight), is in jail for killing his best friend (shot him in the back, self-defense was what the papers said). And her oldest daughter is so strung out on drugs, the state came and took her children away for their own protection.

Who ever heard of repossessing children to protect them from their own mother? How bad of a parent do you have to be for this? I've had many things taken from me, but never my children. Never.

Ask Sister about her four grandchildren being placed in four separate foster homes. Ask her why she won't take them in—her own flesh and blood—and raise them so they can grow up with family. Ask her. Ask her why Flick wasn't at the party? Why she was spending her birthday with us instead of him?

So we arrived on time to Sister's surprise birthday party in a car that still smelled new. J. M. had erected the invisible walls by the time we made it inside. Perhaps Flick could have come after all. No one was allowed past certain points; J. M. made certain of that...watching like a hawk, swooping down...steering those back on track who did—at times—wander "off-course."

Yet never a more gracious hostess than she. Everyone marveled at her attentiveness not fully knowing why. Sister and I knew as we exchanged smiles and glances a few times in between the "shaking of our booties."

J. M. didn't get where she is being vulnerable or stupid... that's for sure. God, I do admire that woman!

"Honey got a big old butt!" "Oh yeah?" the crowd sang.

"Hey! The bigger the onion, the harder I'll make you cry," I said.

Man! what a party!

 J. M. Taylor's Journal

They always need someone to blame...it's always somebody else's fault. God forbid what might happen if they ever owned up to the truth. Just once. The only real way to heal...true therapy...the road to being well, is to own up to it. Stand, state your name, tell the problem in one short sentence. Then deal with it. No added sugar. No honey or artificial sweeteners. Hold the ice...at least for now. Take it straight. Make it quick...and to the point. Because time can work for, or against you.

Somehow, they all manage to gaze into the crack in the mirror of their own lives and see only the distortion reflecting back. "See?" they say, "See!"

But for some reason, they never really do. Not things. Not themselves. Not even others...not as they truly are anyway.

All they see is what the crack allows them to see. If only they would take the time to confront—face to face—they would find that even past reflections viewed through a faultless mirror...a perfect unbroken mirror...was, is, and always will be...a reversal of the truth. What's right...is really left. And what's left ...will be right.

"What?" they ask. "What do you mean? Why can't you talk so people understand? I hate when you speak in riddles!"

So I try again. "That which is right is always left; therefore, what is left will always be right."

But still, they seek someone to blame. Yet, in the end it's true: *Every pot must sit on its own bottom.* The only questions left to be answered are: When? Where? and How?

Solomon Taylor's Journal

Man, that was some party! It was just like the house parties of years gone by. And I was a dancing fool back in the day.

"Get down Sugarman!" "Stomp that Roach!" "Gone and get with it then." "Ah sooky sooky now! You cut that rug, Boy!" "Oooh, can't touch you with a sugarcane, can they Sugarman?"

Sister was really surprised. One because she discovered the party was mainly for her. And two, because some of the people there, she hadn't seen in decades. Must have been about fifty folks, all total—counting the four from my job that came, the three from Johnnie Mae's company, a few people Sister knew from the phone company back when she and Johnnie Mae worked there, and a slew of people from the old neighborhood.

People I grew up with—pretty much have known since before they got their permanent teeth (many of which have lost a good bit of theirs now). There was Jawbone, Doc, Hotshot, Knock-Knock, Didi-bo, Brenda (aka Crawl-the-Bottom), Blue, Dosha, Baby Doll, and Dog (only I didn't invite Dog and don't have a clue who even told him about it).

Neither Rosalyn or Sister had an escort there, but that didn't stop either one of them from buffing the shine on the dance floor. Stocking bare feet, them just twisting and shaking like two teenagers. Yeah, counting couples, it was about fifty.

Johnnie Mae barely broke a sweat. I had to drag her out on the dance floor just to get a slow dance. Then a fast one came on, and I wouldn't let her walk away without finishing that one out too. I really can't understand why she doesn't like to dance; she's great! Now Rosalyn, shoot!—that girl, a couple of times, looked like a fish trying to flop its way back into the ocean.

It's hard to say for sure but I believe Jawbone had his "good" eye on Rosalyn (his glass eye looks straight ahead all the time anyway so it's hard to tell for sure by that one). And if it hadn't been for those two front teeth missing she might have let him finish his tired old rap with too many 'L's and 'F's.

I believe Rosalyn had her sights set on Doc. (Doc is the one who had the brother called Preacher and when Preacher died—drowned he did—then Doc became a preacher.)

Right now Doc has questions he's waiting on God to answer so he's sort of on a sabbatical until his answers *do* come. Then he plans to step back in the pulpit without having to think himself a hypocrite, which is why it was okay for him to be at the party in the first place and not worry about sneaking his Canadian Mist on the side (being that he *is*—technically speaking...officially anyway—not on duty).

Knock-Knock almost got into it with Didi-bo because Didi-bo was still (in private anyway) referring to Knock-Knock's wife by her *old* name of Crawl-the-Bottom.

Of course, all the fellows knew "Brenda" (because of her loose reputation) by the name of Crawl-the-Bottom which is what they dubbed her (though she never knew it because no one would ever say it to her face—one never knew when or if he might have a dry spell in between women and end up desperate enough to have to *"Crawl the Bottom"*).

Knock-Knock said he wasn't about to tolerate anybody referring to "Brenda" that way any longer, so Didi-bo decided to knock it off (even if Brenda *was* the one flirting with him).

And Blue just sat there staring at Dosha. We all noticed how he didn't look away and wondered whether he was planning to make a move before the night was over.

They both are about the color of midnight; Dosha more like a Tootsie Roll—a chocolate taste without all the fat, and Blue more like a giant Hershey's Kiss—a rich gooey chocolate (especially when he gets too hot), small on the top, big around the middle, and simply loaded with fat!

Now Hotshot, having noticed Blue's gaze locked tight on Dosha, and then Dosha—every now and then—seeming to be sizing up Blue as well, whispered in my ear, "Man, I'm gonna tell you...if *those* two get together, I pray to *God* they practice some form of birth control. Lord-have-mercy help us Jesus!"

Blue finally struggled his way up...seeming to have gotten the nerve to stagger Dosha's way.

I can still hear the words...the way they flowed like a song from his mouth. How he hit the high notes just right...holding long the low ones in that baritone voice of his as he said to Dosha (and we all heard it), "You's one ugly sap-sucker!"

Dosha stood up. It got quiet fast. You could hear our *neighbor's* roaches scampering a mile down the road.

Everyone who recalled—and believed—Dosha's reputation, knew Blue was about to turn a bright shade of red. And those who didn't know, must have sensed she might possibly miss when she cut, shot, or slapped the mess out of him.

Dosha stood and walked up just beneath Blue—cataloguing his body parts from his head to his toes. She smiled, then spewed in a cigarette coated voice, "Kind of like looking in a mirror at the fun house, ain't that right you big-fat-no-account-skillet faced-elephant-jack ass-hunk-of-coal!"

Blue took one more step up to her...it was like watching a live rendition of a miniature King Kong getting ready to devour a king-sized Tootsie Roll.

"So?" he said, cocking his head over to one side...a smirk spreading over his face. "You wanna dance, or not?"

Dosha walked away, then turned around. "Well, are you coming?" she said. "Or are you waiting for that lard butt of yours to just *r-o-l-l* over here? Cause if you coming, you'd best come on." She began swooning and swaying, singing loud (and off key) to the point she just plain old drowned *out* poor Marvin Gaye. "*Let's get it on*!" she sang, "*Awww Baby!*"

I hated having to tell Hotshot, "Blue and Dosha...they left, Man. Together. Sucking all over each other's face." When Hotshot heard it, he promptly fell to his knees...and prayed.

Baby Doll was there. We all recalled how she killed that man. Well, *she* didn't really kill him, but you might as well say she did it. She was about nineteen or twenty at the time. And old Mr. Charlie was close to ninety. He lived in a pretty nice size house and had just bought a brand spanking new, fully loaded, completely paid for, red El Dorado Cadillac that he couldn't even drive all that well.

Consequently, Baby Doll married Mr. Charlie, and just two weeks later...he was pretty much gone. There was even a jackpot started: The How Long Before Mr. Charlie Croaks pot.

"How long do *you* think?" my sister asked our mother.

"Disgraceful!" Mudear said. "Just a crying shame! Folk's betting on a man's life like that."

So naturally I was just as surprised as everyone else when I won that ninety dollar pot, God rest his soul. It did buy our school supplies that year, paid a month on the power bill; and I was able to buy Mudear a dress from Newberry's downtown.

Someone (I still don't know who) invited Dog to the party; I just know it wasn't me. But I dared not to tell Johnnie Mae that. I have nothing against Dog, but he and Sister once had a thing for each other. Dog had his chance and he crashed like a computer system with a major virus.

So when I caught him teasing Sister, naturally I stepped in, although the frown on her face hissed at *some* hidden feelings.

Johnnie Mae whispered in my ear later, "Hmmm, Pearl seems to have a way of attracting all the *mangy* mutts. You mean to tell me she could have ended up with *this* Dog instead of the *dog* she married?

"Looks to me she just might have lucked out after all. Now that's sad when I have to admit that." Johnnie Mae's stare seemed locked on his waist as his pants rested a quarter inch below the wide band of his—now exposed—BVDs. "Oh well," she said, "at least *Flick* has the decency to wear clean drawers. Or at least he doesn't go around advertising his dirty ones."

Johnnie Mae can always manage to find something wrong with any and everybody I grew up with. If she'd just give them a chance...like she did with Sister. Only, she had no idea I even knew Sister back when she introduced us to each other.

Yes, that was a great party! Everybody appeared to have enjoyed themselves, and that was the goal. Most weren't too drunk to drive home or at least, they had sense enough to have a designated driver. Those who didn't...we called them a cab.

Sister, in particular, seemed to have had a great time. All of us laughed as she tried blowing out fifty candles at once. Dog stood there waiting breathlessly, hoping it seemed, that she would need mouth-to-mouth (and I'm sure he would have fought off ten men, happily for that privilege).

"Man! You gonna have to do this again! Soon. Real soon!" Dog said as he staggered away—half-drunk now. He was one of three who was still there after one o'clock.

I looked over at my dear wife whose face seemed to scream, without apology, "I'll be *so* glad when these fools leave my house and take their butts on home!" and I knew this might well be the last time *this* crowd would ever assemble again in *our* home.

Johnnie Mae did say she enjoyed it, after the last person was gone. Then she went about the task of unlocking all the locked doors inside our house. Why she locked them, I do not know. But after a while, you grow used to certain things.

Showering and quickly sliding between the satin covers, she shivered and said, "I'm cold! I'm putting the T-shirt sheets back on the bed first thing tomorrow."

I reached my hand underneath her fluffed pillow and pulled out a velvet box.

"Be my valentine?" I said. The light from the moon that flooded through our bedroom window, somehow caught and seemed to add a special touch to the diamond tennis bracelet just as she dangled it in the air.

She smiled, and I gave her a passionate kiss before laying her ever-so-gently down. She nestled closer to me. We didn't discuss the good or bad of the night; the only words uttered, were words of passion and love. I think she said, "Yes!" several times.

Yes, she'd be my Valentine. And if I'm not mistaken, I do believe I actually yelled, "Ah...sooky sooky now!"

Oh yes, it was definitely a *good* night!

Pearl Sue Hunter's Journal

Flick wanted to know why I was so happy today. I told him about my surprise birthday party J. M. gave (I didn't dare say *Sugarman* too, although he was as much responsible for it as J. M.). To keep peace, I told him it was a Valentine's party as well, not *just* a party for me. I thought he would care that somebody cared enough about his wife to remember—let alone celebrate—her birthday (even if he seemed to go out of his way *not* to).

"Yesterday was your birthday?" Flick said, with a look of bewilderment.

"All day long. It's been the same day since I was born, as a matter-of-fact."

"So how old are you now?"

"Fifty."

"Fifty?! That's all?! Why'd I think you were closer to..." he started to grin, "...wait a minute...didn't you turn fifty last year or was it the year before?"

"No. It's this year, and you still haven't wished me happy birthday yet, either."

He kissed my cheek. "Well happy birthday, baby." But it was what happened afterward that upset me so. "You do know why your little short friend had that party for you, don't you?"

"Because she's a friend who really cares."

"Oh yeah, she *really* cares all right. Got her sweet eyes on *you,* I do believe."

"*Ex-cuse* me?"

He held his hands up and stepped back like I had pulled a double barrel shotgun on him. "Your *girl*-friend is into women."

"Flick, take that back!"

"Why? We men know these things; I'm just trying to school your old naive butt. J. M. wants you Sister. Why else do you think she would go to so much trouble on your birthday? You see I didn't." He laughed. "Why do you think she would let someone like *you*—and Honey too for that matter, hang around somebody like her? You know that woman has too much class to be desperate for friends."

"Flick—"

He laughed more. "The two of *you* really think you're good enough to be friends with a piece of class like her? Come on woman, get a life. Grow up, why don't you!"

"She's not like you say. I don't appreciate what you're implying either. And frankly, I could care less what you think."

"Yeah, probably one of those closet kind. I'm telling you... I can spot one a mile coming. Sister alert! Don't you see?"

I shook my head. This was low, even for Flick. I know he doesn't want me having any friends but to attack J. M., Honey, me for that matter...like this? Uh uh!

Flick grabbed me hard by my shoulders and made me look in his face. "All right then, why do *you* suppose she insists on being called J. M.? How many women do you know who introduce themselves by initials?" He grinned. "The girl likes to play with live dolls, I tell you—play with *soft* things."

I pulled from his clutches, snapped back the tears that threatened to flow, and stomped away—leaving Flick standing there in the middle of the kitchen laughing like he'd lost his ever-loving mind. Obviously, he had.

"Don't be upset with me," he yelled as he stepped up behind me laughing that horrible laugh. He then grabbed my upper arm...squeezing tight my muscle.

I struggled to free myself. "Flick. Stop! You're hurting me!"

He tightened his grip and pulled me up to his now sober face. "Just be sure you let Ms. J. M. know—you're only in-

terested in the real deal. Tell her, maybe she should try what
you got some time. Because once they've had Flick, who wants
to go back to...anything else." He kissed me hard. "Tell her,
money back guarantee. Tell your friend *that* why don't you, the
next time she calls here."

Then he walked over to the Caller ID box and smiled.
"Nice little gadget there, don't you think?" I glanced at the
innocent box and felt somewhat intimidated. "Real nice little
gadget," he said. "Be surprised at all the things one can learn
from these new electronic devices. You do know I took electronics in school right? Of course you do. You're not like me
and forget important and—sometimes—*not* so important
things." He sucked wind hard and loud through his teeth.
"Yes, yes...and people are left wondering how on earth you
know what you know." He grinned. "I'm going to step out for
a while. You be good now, you hear." Then he left and went
who knows...or even cares...where.

I just don't understand Flick these days. The sun must be
frying what little brain cells he has left. Talking about he took
electronics in school...high school, almost thirty-five years ago!
An old radio, he *might* be able to fix. But the things they have
now—shoot! he can forget about them.

It was really good seeing so many I knew at the party...even
Dog—my first. I sure am glad I didn't marry him! He's on his
fourth marriage now and says it's on its last leg. And to think, I
used to wonder where he got his name. Only no dog I've been
around has breath that smells like his—that babe was *kick-ing!*
The kind of stank you can taste (even when you try hard not
to)...the kind booze can't even mask. And then, he had the
nerve to be all up in folk's faces...exchanging his breath for
theirs. Thank God! Sugarman rescued me when he did!

Old Dog...suppose he's due for a name upgrade. How
about...Atomic Dog? Oooh...better!

The phone rang. I saw from the Caller ID who it was.
Imagine my delight when I heard, "Hello there...Sister."

I'd recognize that smooth silky voice anywhere.

"Hello...Sugarman," I said.

Countess W. Gates' Journal

I dreamed of fishes last night. I know lots of folks don't believe in that, but every time I have one of my fish dreams... somebody in the family comes up expecting a baby. So I made my rounds as always—calling all those who hadn't had themselves fixed already, that is.

"Now Mama, you *know* I got my tubes tied three years ago," Rachel said. "Don't even start with me!"

"Yeah? Well Pauline's daughter down the street had hers tied also. Seems those things, at times, do come loose. Yes... had herself a fine little boy too," I said. "Just as cute as he wants to be."

The rest of my children who didn't laugh me off the phone, begged me not to bring it nigh them. I started not to even bother Johnnie Mae—her acting like she's *planning* when hers will come and all. When I *have* called in the past, she always pretends to be thrilled when it turns out to be one of the others instead of her. Her way of coping, I'd say.

That daughter of mine...she's a strong one all right. I came right out and told her one day, "If any of my children *do* decide to adopt, I wouldn't treat that child any different than my own flesh and blood." After all, aren't we *all* descendants of Adam and Eve anyway? If we traced our roots all the way back to the beginning, wouldn't we *all* arrive at the same place?

Adam or Eve...neither one had a belly button. Were they not created by God? We're all connected, whether we want to accept it or not. Who is my mother, my father, sisters, and brothers? Do children truly belong to any of us, or are we all merely caretakers for the Almighty?

Anyhow, Johnnie Mae cut me quick and to the bone—with respect though, mind you. I *still* don't allow back talk, don't care how grown they think they are.

"Mama, why would I adopt when I'm not ready for *any* children?" Johnnie Mae said. "If I were going to adopt, I might as well go on and have my own."

Yes, that Johnnie Mae *is* a strong one. Keeps things to herself too much though if you ask me. From what I can tell, she has a few close friends. I've met the one she calls Pearl (who whispered to me it was all right to call her Sister), and that kinda tall, big-boned one...with the short hair...calls herself "Honey." That *Honey* is a mess! She keeps me doubled over whenever she stops by and I happen to be visiting.

But those kids of hers—Lord-have-mercy-help-them-Jesus—a couple of them need their butts *whipped.* Hear me?! One good time, that's all it would take! Like that old mischievous baby boy of hers. I told her she'd better get a handle on him before he ends up getting a handle on her. Young parents today trying out all this new parenting junk—listening to Oprah. I'm sure even Oprah's been introduced to the scripture about not sparing the rod—probably why *she* turned out so well.

Shoot, she'd likely pop some of these old bad butt children herself if she had to be the one raising 'em. Children now will threaten to dial 9-1-1 if you look at them too long. Well I told that grandchild of mine, "You can call 9-1-1 if you want to. I'll beat your butt and *then* send you on back with 'em when they get here!" I'm not having that mess! I mean it! Not me!

Mr. Gates is suppose to be getting one final check from that Black Lung settlement. The coal mines were good in providing folks—especially "Coloreds" and poor whites—with regular work, a means to get food, clothing, and a home back then. Paid more than most jobs blacks could get (though not nearly as much as they should have). But those who did make it out from its death traps, discovered their lungs were just full of coal dust. Many of them are just now finally getting some real compensation, though for most, it's too little too late.

I think my husband's deepest sorrow these days, is Johnnie Mae. She can't seem to find many words to exchange with him. I admit, I'm in the dark when it comes to what happened—though I'm positive it wasn't of a sexual nature (they've both confirmed that, and I saw it was the truth they spoke as I looked in their eyes when they said it wasn't). But whatever it was, it rent the veil from the top...and that tear has continued to split down to where it appears to be held now only by a thread. Johnnie Mae attributes it to growing up.

"Mama, I can't be Daddy's little girl all my life," she said. "All goo-goo and ga-ga eyes."

And Mr. Gates keeps spouting off things from the bible. About seeing through a glass darkly—then face to face...about scales falling from the eyes...about in a moment in a twinkling of an eye we shall all be changed—I declare if I don't believe that man has no idea *what* he means sometimes!

Well, at least Johnnie Mae seems to have calmed down about her name.

"How come I couldn't have had a pretty name? Like Rachel's...or Marie's? Why did y'all have to name me after a boy?" Johnnie Mae said when she was about thirteen. "Even Christian's name is better than mine."

"Child," I said, "your name could have been Suzy Q, Charlie Mae—"

"What's the difference?! Johnnie, Charlie...they're still boy names."

"Oh Johnnie Mae's *not* a boy's name; it's your name. And you're not a boy. Are you? Besides, it's not the name that defines the person, it's the person that defines the name. And power belongs to the person who learns how to possess his or her *own* identity. Have you ever heard of Sojourner Truth?"

"Yeah, I guess so," she said with wind poking out of her jaws.

"Well how many folks you know by that name? Probably none. Not one. But Miss Truth picked that name for herself straight from the bible...sojourn and truth, and she made something out of it. If you're strong enough and can go deep enough...to know the true you, it shouldn't matter *what* your name is. Then and only then, will people know and respect you. That's if you do something respectable with what you're given."

It sounded good when I said it back then anyway. But somewhere in her search she discovered someone named J. M.

Well, she might be able to make the others call her by some initials, but her name is *still* Johnnie Mae—still *my* baby! And had we *named* her J. M.—she would be having a fit about *that* instead I suppose.

Lest I forget, she is descendant of Great-Grandma Nam-o. Johnnie Mae wears a pendant around her neck...jade, she calls it...surrounded by 18 karat gold. It has Chinese symbols that translate to good luck and longevity.

Great-Grandma Nam-o wore a silver dollar hung from an old green cloth (green for life and growth she had said), and whenever she was worried or wanted an answer to a thing; she would sit, hold that silver dollar up to her squinting empty eye sockets—just batting away...and would talk to it. Then after she found peace, she would tuck it back in her bosom and go right on. You would have thought it had some special powers or something. I've seen Johnnie Mae, many times, swing her green and gold pendant close to the same way. Johnnie Mae and Nam-o...different worlds, yet so much in common.

So when I *did* call Johnnie Mae and told her about the fish, she sighed so hard I think I felt the breeze rush through my one ear and come out the other.

"Mama, I don't know who's worse—you or the psychic net-work people," Johnnie Mae said. "And you probably need to ask God to forgive you—"

"Forgive me? For what? I can't help it if I got the gift to dream dreams. Did Joseph the Dreamer need to ask for forgive-ness? Was not his gift from the Lord? This is God's work—"

"Mama, I *really* don't think your fish are God's work—"

"Oh no? Well if you'll read that bible for more than just ways to condemn folks, you'll find plenty of fish doing God's work. There were the two fishes that fed the five thousand...

then the fish that had money in its mouth—enough to pay taxes mind you, and even Jesus said he'd make us fishermen of men. There's something to these fishes, I'm telling you, you'd better hear me."

"Okay Mama. Okay."

"Okay my foot! And don't be trying to patronize me either. Somebody's about to become a mother in this family. I've not dreamed a fish *yet* that hasn't produced."

Johnnie Mae laughed. One of her *It just won't be me* kind of laughs. That's just fine with me too. I know how to bide *my* time. Somebody's gonna come up wobbling...sooner, rather than later. I'm marking it down on my calendar right now...I spoke it on the nineteenth day of February, 1998. They'll see. I've got nothing but time.

 J. M. Taylor's Journal

Mama dreamed about fishes—again. She thinks every time she dreams about fish, somebody's pregnant. I want to tell her so bad, "Somebody's pregnant somewhere every minute of the day," but I just laugh and let her go on. She maintains every time she dreams about fish it's always followed by one of her children learning they've conceived. Well, I remember a *few* times when she's had her famous fish dream and nobody in our family ended up expecting.

"What about those times, Mama?" I asked.

"Miscarriages," she said. "I know none of my children would ever abort, so they must have been miscarriages. And if they miscarried, they probably either *didn't* know it or just wouldn't tell me to spare me the grief."

"Well Mama, I can assure you, your fish do not belong to me."

"How can you be so sure?"

I wanted to say, *Because I'm too busy to even have sex these days*, but *that* wouldn't have gone over too well.

Solomon declares already we only do it every two months, but he also exaggerates—just like a man. But truthfully, I'm still a ward of the pill. I had to change to a different brand though. Dr. Richardson said sometimes one brand stops agreeing with your body. I guess that's what happened with me.

"Johnnie Mae? Tell me. *How* can you be sure it's *not* you? You never know." Mama's voice was laced with a grin.

"I just *am*, Mama. Okay?" As soon as the words left my mouth, I knew she had gotten it wrong again. Now she's most likely thinking...*my poor baby.*

"Johnnie Mae, I'm still praying for you. You know there's nothing too hard for God."

"Okay Mama. You keep praying for me," I said. "I need all the help I can get." I hoped that had put this fish tale to bed. "Well I hate to run but Pearl's coming to drop off a copy of her latest revision to her story."

"All right, Baby. Tell Sister I said, hello. Has she gotten published yet?"

"No Mama. Sometimes it takes awhile. I'll tell her you asked about her though."

I just don't understand why Mama can call Pearl, Sister... and Rosalyn, Honey. But with me...I have to be Johnnie Mae, whether I want to be called that or not.

I noticed a few 45s and LPs were still stacked in the corner from the party we had last week. Everybody appeared to have enjoyed themselves. Solomon had such fun pulling out all our old records...he had even talked about wearing a pair of old bell bottom jeans. I'm glad I talked him out of *that* notion. He has too many nice things to be embarrassing me like that. However, as soon as I saw most of his friends from his old neighborhood step in the house, I realized he must have only wanted to make them feel comfortable. Vintage clothes galore!

The repair*persons* did come fix both the washer and the refrigerator. Turns out they sent "two men"...Solomon ensuring I caught *that* point. Charged us forty-nine dollars just to step foot inside our house. Each! Both came from Sears, but they had sent out two different people since one only worked on refrigerators while the other only on washers. Yet, what we paid to get a new pump for that ten-year-old washer ($144), we could have bought a brand new one. But of course, Solomon let him fix it. Had it been me— Oh well...like Solomon said, I wasn't here to do it myself... "So what's done, is done!"

Miss Ruby catered the party for me. She is such a sweet woman and can plain throw-down when it comes to cooking. Her cooking is so good, most folks end up slapping their own selves. She know she can put her foot in some barbecue sauce!

I probably *should* have forced myself and invited Flick to
Pearl's birthday party, but I just know him *too* well. Number
one, he wouldn't have come. That would have been fine, but
he would have told her about it just to ruin the surprise. I can
name the times he's done something like that before.

"If he were *my* man...G-u-r-l," Rosalyn told Pearl once as
she bobbed and weaved her head, "I would have *been* kicked
his royal behind into next week!"

But Rosalyn's choices in men *ain't* all *that* either! Married
twice—the first time for seven years...as she puts it, "Six years,
eleven months and thirty days longer than I should have stayed." And the second time didn't last long enough for her to get
her name changed. She'd probably be on number three now,
had I not shaken her baby doll eyes open before she bit into
that *last* apple full of worms.

But Flick, as he has made it clear *he will be called*, knows I
won't stand for any of his crap. And when I *do* visit Pearl at
her house, he conveniently finds a reason to vacate the pre-
mises. He told Pearl he would never again step foot in my
house if I believed *he* was going to go outside just to smoke.

"Who the hell does she think she is?" he had said making
certain I heard him. "Somebody needs to tell her this is a free
damn country; I'm free to smoke where I damn well please!"

The last time Pearl and Flick were here together for dinner, he made the comment to Pearl as he smiled and smacked
his fat lips at me, "The rich booze-wah type tends to upset my
stomach, Baby." He then smoothed down his mustache on
both sides, licked his fingers like I was a piece of fried chicken
he had just sunk his teeth into and said, "Still, it *is* finger licking good." He's such a *jerk!*

Nope. Not even for Pearl's birthday would I stoop low
enough to call him. I *was* hoping he would have made some
plans to cause this *one* birthday to be special—this year at least.
So when I learned, not even for her fiftieth birthday, was he
intending to do one thing—I agreed to have her a party.

Although I admit, this is an extremely busy time for me.
But hey!...we're only fifty once. Right?

Flick has already shown me who he really is, and I, unlike Pearl, believe him. He's a low down dirty dog, and I just don't like him! Period! I have no problem accepting what and who he is. And it's true...he is free to do whatever he likes. Just not in *my* house.

Mama's dreaming about fish and people are talking about fish having grown fingers and crawling out of oceans. I wonder ...how *do* they know how old a fossil is? Is it engraved somewhere? Is there some kind of chart?

Mama had asked if I wanted to speak to Daddy. I said I would, considering he was sitting right next to her listening when she said it.

"Hello Baby Girl," he said in his still...deep...strong voice.

"Hi Daddy."

"How's everything?"

"Fine. How about you?"

"Good. Good. If I could just get Mama to quit so much fussing over me. She acts like I'm helpless or something." He laughed. "But you know your mama."

"Yes...I know Mama."

Then silence.

"Well, let me let you holler back at your mother," he said.

"Okay."

"Johnnie Mae?"

"Yes?"

"You planning to come see us anytime soon? It's been awhile, and of course, you know I'm not able to get out like I once did. Maybe we could talk—like we used to...when you were my little Jay. You remember don't you—"

"We'll see, Daddy. I'm just so busy—"

"Yeah," he said sounding a little disappointed, "I understand that. Well, here's your mama back."

I wanted to say more, but I don't know. I know he and I really need to talk. I just *can't* right now. And I don't have a clue what to say. Is there even anything *to be* said? We're from two different worlds; I know that. So what is left to say? Still, he is my father. And even though I didn't tell him—and I should have—I do love him. There will I know, forever be a tie that binds. It's just unfortunate now, there is that one thread which seems to have pulled me straight down my middle to the point where it continues—in its own way—to still tear me apart.

Reward of the Inheritance

Servants, obey in all things your masters according to the flesh; not with eye-service, as menpleasers; but in singleness of heart, fearing God: And whatsoever ye do, do it heartily, as to the Lord, and not unto men; Knowing that of the Lord ye shall receive the reward of the inheritance: for ye serve the Lord Christ.

Colossians 3:22-24

Rosalyn Benefield's Journal

I told both J. M. and Sister about my call from the Oprah Winfrey Show when we met up at Ryan's for a late supper.

"Rosalyn, that is so great!" J. M. said. "But what did they call *you* for?"

"The book club. Toni Morrison's new book. I read it, sent in a letter, and one of her producers liked what I wrote and called me for a little more information," I said.

"*They*...called...*you?*" Sister said, looking down her fork at me.

"Yes...on February the sixteenth as a matter-of-fact." I was still bubbling.

"I sent in a letter and nobody's called *me* yet," Sister said.

I stopped and looked over at her munching on her salad like a white bunny rabbit. *Is she trying to say I'm lying about getting a call?* "What is it, Sister? You don't think I'm smart enough to have gotten a call? Just because I don't work for some fancy company like you did...once-upon-a-time."

Sister laid her fork down and looked hard at me. "You know...Toni Morrison's books are no easy reads," she said.

Ohhhh...so she is *saying I'm not smart enough!* "Well Sister, personally I appreciate the effort Toni puts into each and every word she writes. I just sit, focus, and begin reading...one word at a time. I've learned to trust her; I've found her to be a master at what she does. And she plays *me* like a violin."

"So you're telling *us*," Sister shoved shreds of lettuce into her mouth, "you *understood* this latest book, *Paradise*, then wrote a letter, and someone from the *Oprah* Show has already contacted you?"

"They say they received thousands of letters but haven't chosen anyone just yet. She also said, if I didn't hear from them later, that would mean I didn't get picked."

Sister forced a smile (not a very good one at that). "Oh. So what did *you* say?"

"I said, 'Well, it's been a pleasure talking with you, and I do appreciate the enlivening conversation'."

Sister speared a cherry tomato and rammed it in her mouth. "Cute," she said. "I hope they *do* call you back."

I'm not going to profess to read minds here, but I got the distinct impression Sister was wondering about where her call was then...while also thinking, *Yeah sure, Honey got a call all right.*

J. M. only sat and watched the two of us; she didn't have much to say either way.

"I'll be right back," J. M. finally said, "I need to visit the ladies room."

Sister hurried to dab the corners of her mouth. "I'll go with you," she said.

I sat smiling, stirring my broccoli and cheese soup.

"Then I suppose I get to stay and watch the purses," I said while grinning even more.

It was at this point, that I heard my Hallelujah Chorus begin to sing in my head: "I got a call from the Oprah Show. Na-nan-ne-nan-na!"

Countess W. Gates' Journal

Mr. Gates has been working in the garden...tending to the cabbage, the turnips and collard greens today.

"Just getting soil ready for spring planting," he said.

It's cold out—and this kind of weather is so hard on his arthritis and gout in his knees. But I can most times, find him outside somewhere working every day.

Johnnie Mae always plants an herb garden in the spring. Not a big one, but one that might make that Martha woman green with envy. She's most successful with rosemary. Great-Grandma Nam-o had a way with plants, too. Had all kinds of "fixes" for all kinds of ailments— Cherries! That's it...or cherry juice, pure cherry juice. That's what Great-Grandma used for gout. The purer the form, the better. I knew I'd remember it sooner or later. I'll just have to run get some tomorrow—see if that might help Mr. Gates' gout.

Now rosemary—

Great-Grandma Nam-o would make tea or a "bag" for the bath water with *her* rosemary. She claimed it relieved all kinds of aches and pains.

She'd say, "Where rosemary thrives...the mistress is master." Well, Johnnie Mae's garden is always full of it...with that strong aroma that tends to ride on a strong breeze.

"Mama, all it means to me (talking about the rosemary when I pointed out what Great-Grandma Nam-o had said), is a richer flavor for chicken breast, other meats, veggies maybe...a different smell coating my kitchen," Johnnie Mae had said.

Yeah, old Nam-o. Great-Grandma was subject to strike up at any time with something that just *had* to be said. And oh! how her tales mesmerized me...it's practically impossible to forget most of anything she shared with you either.

Like how back when they were coming up, they believed in Hoo-Doo. How people would ward the spirits away by keeping a bag of things…"mojo," is what she called it…"greegrees." Who even knows what all was in it.

Even though Great-Grandma Nam-o had long ago lost her eyesight (back when the Doctor Master had both her eyes plucked out), there were many days when she seemed to just sit and stare at us. Then she'd ask if we didn't see those standing behind or beside us.

"What y'all doing here?" she would say. We would look around, then from one to the other—me, my two sisters, and four brothers—and although we looked, we long ago understood it was none of *us* she was addressing.

"Great-Grandma…there's nobody else here other than us," we would always say.

"Oh yes there is! I see 'em. Don't tell me y'all don't see 'em too!" Then she would squint and concentrate that much harder just above our heads (since we were children, I guess we were shorter than they were). "Why don't y'all show yourselves to them? These children ain't gonna bother y'all none."

But they never did—thank goodness!—show themselves to *me*. Although one brother, the knee baby who himself later became susceptible to *spirits* (of the bottled-kind that is), does claim to have seen them on certain occasions—especially in his later drinking age.

Great-Grandma Nam-o was a tall dark mountain of a woman with long bony fingers that grew more animated whenever she spoke. By the time I knew her (of course she was long past her youth by then), she didn't have any hair—unless you count that small patch of white laying flat on the top.

Yet I was amazed, even then, at her resourcefulness. She would take what we called a "roll" and make a "rat"; then she'd drag her long wrinkled fingers through the soot of the wood burning stove, and paint the whiteness of her hair black. After which, she would take a black hair net, put that "rat" at the back and the bottom of the net. It looked just like she had a head full of jet black hair when she finished!

It was Great-Grandma Nam-o who taught me how to use that same soot from the stove to thicken my eyebrows. "Child, just take that little stick next to your feet, and drag that thing through the soot," she would say as though she actually saw the twig from the branch that had fallen next to my run-over shoes.

"Thicker?" my then grown children said in unison when I repeated the story. "Who would even *want* thicker eyebrows?"

"It's all I do just to thin mine. Have to pluck, wax, arch—" Marie said.

"I don't pluck mine," Rachel said. "Love me like I am or not. I don't care. There's already enough pain in the world without conjuring up extra unnecessary things to have to go through."

"Yeah, well...I see you shave that mustache of yours," Christian teased.

Rachel threw a green pea at him. "Shut up boy!"

"Well I hope you do at least shave from under your arms," Donald said as he shivered. "Gives me the heebie-jeebies just thinking about hair sprouting all out from under a woman's arm. This is America not France."

"We could say the same thing about you old hairy *boys*," Marie said. "I'm talking about be *long* enough to plait too!"

"Yeah, but a real man—" Christian stood and started pumping muscles...posing like Mr. Olympia (with his little self), "is *clustered* with vitality. I'm Samson—"

"You don't know what you're talking about. Why don't you sit down boy!" Marie said.

"Why do you always have to call men boys?" Johnnie Mae said. Her voice was so cold it put a chill in the air.

Marie turned and looked at her. "What?"

"I said why do...you...always...have...to...call...men...boys?" Johnnie Mae was so intense as she glared. "He's not a boy; he's a man now. A man! Do you hear? A man! So *why* do you feel you must call him a *boy?*"

"Dog Johnnie Mae, lighten up! Didn't nobody mean nothing by it."

"In that case then, it shouldn't be so hard to call a man, a man. It shouldn't be a big deal to treat a *black* man with the courtesy of respect. They are *men* first then...black. Men."

The silence in the room was deafening. I decided I'd best do something quick, so I broke out with an old spiritual. *"Way down yonder all by myself,"* I sang.

Rachel turned and looked at me, then she started to laugh and sang, *"I couldn't hear nobody pray."*

Marie and Donald belted out with voices that could quicken the souls of the dead—just like Great-Grandma Nam-o used to do. *"O Lord!"* they sang.

"I was way down yonder all by my-self," I wailed.

And everybody—with the exception of Johnnie Mae—joined in and sang, *"I couldn't hear nobody pray!"*

Great-Grandma Nam-o would sing that song just as loud while she banged on that old out-of-whack piano that sounded more like a clanking box than a musical instrument. She'd take out her harmonica, slide it in, up and down her lips, and twang that *old* spiritual...right on out through her bony fingers.

I remember the corn pipe she held tight on the side of her mouth just smoking away...her sprinkling of salt in and around the bed to "ward off evil spirits."

I know about the salt for a fact; I was the one who ended up having to sleep in the bed with her many nights. Thankful—if truth be told—to have some place to lay my head. I can't say for sure whether the evil spirits were chased out, but those grains of salt sure did take *out* my hair! Probably what caused her to go bald too. The salt, I guess, just never reached the top of her head. Which explains why hair still sprouted there. And me? I have *yet* to get my hair to come back right. Old thin stuff!

Every spring...Great-Grandma Nam-o would have us catch "May" rain water. Then she would add about a teaspoon of sulfur to glassfuls of that old water and make all of us drink it. That was how we got ready for summer. All I can say about that is: we were *never* bothered by mosquitoes. That's a fact!

People often ask how did I come to speak as well as I do. If they had spent any time around Great-Grandma Nam-o, they would have learned to speak well too. She didn't hesitate to whack you with her walking stick either. Eyes or no eyes—she *never* missed. Never!

"Don't chew up them words, Child!" she would say. Then whack! "You best learn how to speak plain." Whack! "Talk right!" "Say that again." Whack...whack...whack!!!

So that much, I suppose, I did get and pass along to my own children. That, and so many of the wise sayings of my Great-Grandma Nam-o.

"When somebody offers you something," she said, drawing long on that corn pipe she held tight between her teeth, "...you take it! Because you never know when you'll need it."

Take it...because you never know.

Rosalyn Benefield's Journal

It's been over a week now...and I haven't heard a word from the Oprah Show. They said if they didn't call back, it meant I didn't get picked. I really want to go. I believe I'm gonna go. Everything is pointing that I'm gonna go.

This little horoscope scroll I buy every month said: *Many of you will be linking up with an important power figure this month. Creatively, you may have been using only a fraction of your charisma, possibly because you've been reluctant to put your talents on the line.* Now that is true...J. M. tells me that all the time. *You might feel apprehensive but this influential person's assurance and assistance could inspire you to apply your concept to a risky or artistic venture and make it a success.*

See!

Now I know these horoscope things aren't always fool-proof, but a few months ago when I had this bleeding problem, I was afraid to go to the doctor because I just knew he was going to say I had colon cancer or something deadly like that (I never knew hemorrhoids bled and that *it* was even a possibi-lity). So I decided I wasn't going to any doctor.

But this scroll said: *A minor health concern—your own or someone close to you, even a pet—that may arise near the 20th can be easily remedied if a health professional is consulted promptly.*

Well, I still wasn't convinced my problem was minor, but when it got really bad, I decided to bite the bullet and go see my old prune of a doctor.

"Hemorrhoids," the doctor said. And he prescribed a $65 dollar medication (which there's no way I could *ever* afford). I got the generic brand instead, and it was only fifteen. Now what's up with that big of a difference?

Besides my horoscope scroll, I just happened to be reading this book on intuition, and the exercises I had to do all confirmed I would be picked for the Oprah Book Club™ and get to go to Princeton to be in the study group with Toni Morrison and the rest of the gang. No...it didn't say it right out like that, but the answers to all the questions turned out to be a *Yes*.

But just to be on the safe side, I took out my tarot cards—and this one card turned up called *The Magician*. Now this card points to potential skills and creative abilities which have not yet manifested...an intuition of exciting new opportunities. It presages insight and an awareness of unexplored possibilities. *It is clear that the journey is possible and that one has capacities yet to be developed*, is what the book said.

I *almost*...(almost I said) called the *Psychic Network,* but then I remembered where CNN reported they were filing for bankruptcy. I figure if they didn't see *that* coming, then what could they *possibly* see for me!

So I just wait and pray now. "O God, please let them call me from the Oprah Show again. I really do want to go. Really!"

Now...I've meditated, visualized the phone ringing and me hearing the words, "Honey, this is so-and-so from the Oprah Winfrey Show. You've been chosen." So please dear God...let them call me. Please let them call.

Rosalyn Benefield's Journal

I am so depressed. The Oprah Show hasn't called back *yet!* What else can I do? I've done everything I can think of. I've chanted, prayed, spoken in tongues... "Sha-sha-bo-ba-co-see Bu-shun-da," but *nothing* seems to be working. What Lord? What?!!! I'm a pretty good person. I don't bother anybody. I try to treat everybody right. I work on the usher board at church... the usher board Lord. The *usher board!*

You said you'd give me the desires of my heart. I desire this Lord. I don't curse like I used to—that should count for something. I know J. M. was the one who encouraged me to cut back, but Lord, I was the one who worked on it. Come on, give a sistah a break! And you know how long it's been since I had sex last. Oh yeah, of course you do. Strike that last one, but the usher board now...Lord. *I'd rather be a doorkeeper in the house of my God* usher board.

According to my calculations, Oprah should be airing the book club dinner on March the sixth. That means they *have* to tape it next weekend. Next weekend Lord...February 28th. Today is Friday. I know Oprah can fly us there fast, but don't you think she's cutting this a little close?

You know she's got a lot on her mind...what with the trial, and being in Texas and all. She just might need a little reminding. Oh ple-eze God, just grant me this one thing. You know I'm not asking for ill-got-or-gain reasons. I don't want a thing from Oprah *or* Toni Morrison. I just want to be a part of the discussion for the book.

I read that book Lord—you know I did. And I *know* that book better than anybody they could ever possibly pick! The answer to the mystery of those women who got shot?...it's in First Corinthians 15th chapter (mainly the second through the fourth verse) and Second Corinthians 12th chapter too. I'm not coming to you empty handed this time Lord. This time, I did my part. I read the book. Twice! I'm not asking you to cheat for me, just *help a sistah out.*

Will you just see what you can do? You can even send one of the lesser-known angels. You know...Uriel, Raphael, either one of them will do just fine for this small of a job.

Sister called chomping at the bit. "Well, have you heard anything yet?!"

"No," I said.

"Oh."

I'm not sure she really even believes they called me. Still, she's being quite supportive about it. Maybe I shouldn't be so surprised.

"I'm sure you'll hear something soon. I just *know* you're going to get to go!" Sister said.

I sure do hope so! I only want to be a part, Lord. Can you imagine...me, old no accomplishment, Honey. Honey...a single parent with four children from the good old South, getting picked for something as grand as *this?*

Honey, who can read a book by the great Pulitzer Prize, Nobel Prize writer Toni Morrison, and Honey...who actually understands it all the way down to her bones.

My bones Lord. Honey Benefield. Oh, but you may have me listed under Rosalyn in the big book or computer system...I just know you guys are hooked up and on-line now. But either name you have me listed under, I just want you to know, it's fine with me. Just as long as I'm there.

Oh please God—just this time! *P-l-e-e-e-e-e-e-a-z-e!* Let them pick me!

Rosalyn Benefield's Journal

I can't believe it! The Oprah Show was just about to come on when my phone rang. I thought she was a saleswoman, but she said she was calling from the Oprah Winfrey Show! She said they were narrowing it down...were almost there...almost there. I figured they would have to be, since this is Monday and the taping should be this weekend.

Oprah sure does cut things close. It's a good thing I don't have any plans. The woman who phoned said she just had a few more questions to ask. I really wanted to watch the show Oprah had on today...she was speaking with that guy who talks to heaven. But between *watching* the show and being picked for the book club...well all I can say is—Mama didn't raise no fool!

So I pressed the mute button on the TV and tried to talk with as much intelligence as I could muster on such short notice.

I know this was it. They've got to pick either tonight or tomorrow. I think we had a nice chat, but it's torture not knowing for sure. All I need is one more call and I know I'll be going. Just one more call! Let the phone ring just one more time. Please Lord.

Oh...and Lord, have I said, "Thank you?" Then thank you, thank you, thank you. I knew you wouldn't let me down.

Rosalyn Benefield's Journal

I told Sister about my last call from the Oprah Show since she's called me every day just to see if I'd heard anything. I told a few other people as well; J. M.'s out of town on business so I haven't told her yet.

Sister just babbled...like a running brook. "Great! Honey, you're going...I just know you're going! I can feel it in my bones." She laughed. "I'm so proud of *you*. Look, I'm going to give you a fresh copy of the novel I'm working on so you can take it when you go—"

"Excuse me?" I said, stopping her before she got too wound up.

"My book. I know you're going to help out a friend. You know what a hard time I'm having trying to get an agent to even *look* at my manuscript. But if you'll take what I've written already...show it to Oprah...and she likes it...she might pick it as one of her book club selections. Honey, we'll *all* be on easy street then! Taking baths in liquid gold when we want."

"We? What *we?*" *How did I get in this?*

"Me and you. Now you know I'm going to share with my friend; that goes without even saying. And Flick...Flick's gonna flip when he learns he has messed around and married a famous author."

"Sister...I am *not* going up there peddling yours, or anyone else's, book."

"Peddling?" She stammered. "What do you mean by *peddling?* Look, all I'm asking you to do is take it—and *if* you get an opportunity, to *give* or *show* it to Oprah or Toni. Now how much trouble could *that* be?"

I could not believe her! And I didn't even see it at first, as her trying to use me...Oprah...or Toni Morrison. To think I would even consider taking her manuscript when my greatest desire was just to be part of a wonderful book discussion, was beyond me. "Sistah, I don't use people," I said.

"*What?* Use? Who's using? All I'm asking is a small favor. Minute. If I had gotten picked, I could do it myself. But I didn't—and you seem pretty close to going. And who's going to take you to the airport when they do call? Me, of course. Hey...I thought we were friends?"

"We *are* friends."

"Then this shouldn't be a problem. When I'm famous, whom do you think I'm going to remember for having helped *me?*"

"But I couldn't dare disrespect either Oprah *or* Toni Morrison that way. I want to go to be part of something special. I just know it's going to be a *phenomenal* (I do like that word... phenomenal) a *phenomenal* discussion."

"What does showing my book—"

"At best, I'd just like to thank them for what they've been in my life. It was one of Oprah's shows about spousal abuse that moved me to get out of my first marriage to old hateful Duke and not to stay so long with old backward Dex."

"But—"

"My only true desire. And I'm *not* going up there peddling some manuscript!"

"Well then...what about your own sketches?"

I shook my head. "I'm not peddling my fashion designs either. It's just something I play around with. No, I wouldn't—wait, couldn't dare dishonor this grand opportunity *should* I get chosen, which...by the way, hasn't happened yet."

"Look, Honey...all...I'm...asking of you...is—"

"I'm not trying to see what I can get out of this, Sister. Not this, anyway."

"Sure. Okay. But still, let me know when you do hear back from them. Call me the *minute* you hear," Sister said.

After I hung up the phone with her, I caught Oprah's Tuesday Show where she announced they had picked the twenty for the book club. They *would* be taping this weekend. Only...nobody's call *me* yet. Okay, phone—ring. Ring!

* * *

I called all my kids together and made them line up on the couch.

"I want y'all to tell all your little friends you can't talk to them on the phone for the rest of this week," I said.

"But how come, Ma?" Sonequa asked.

"Because I'm expecting a very important call and I don't want y'all tying up my line, that's how come. And if the phone *should* ring when I'm here, I don't want anybody to touch it. Understand? Nobody but me. And if I'm *not* here, and you happen to answer it, you had *better* write down the message. Write it down! Understand?" I looked at the three older children...individually, smack dead in their eyes. "Now...have I made myself perfectly clear?"

"Yes ma'am," they all said slowly nodding.

"And I'm not playing with y'all about your little friends calling here this week either. You tell them don't even pick up the phone to dial *this* number, you hear?"

Every head nodded again—including the youngest one who acted like he could care less *what* I was saying.

I walked over to the telephone and concentrated real hard. Ring phone. Ring. Come on now...ring why don't you!

Rosalyn Benefield's Journal

Oh please ring. Ring and let it not be a salesperson this time. Or a bill collector. Or somebody begging for a donation. Then finally, it did ring. It was a different ring. Different from a salesperson. An upscale ring. Don't ask how a phone can ring differently for some people...all I know is, it does. I took a deep breath and composed myself.

"Hel-lo," I said in my best voice.

"Hi...Rosalyn—"

My heart sank. Here it was already Thursday, and on the other end of the line was J. M. Even the Oprah people who called those two times, both said "Honey."

"J. M.," I said. "Hi."

I told her about all that had happened with the Oprah people, and she went up and down with each of my happy and sad recollections.

"Well, there's still tomorrow you know. Oprah has enough clout and power, she can call on Friday, fly *you* out there Saturday, tape the show, and jet set you right back here to Alabama all in a day's work."

"Hel-l-l-heck, I'd go if she called Saturday morning and said to be at the airport in an hour," I said.

"I saw where she won that lawsuit in Texas."

"Yes. Wasn't that something. She went down to Texas and won."

"So are you certain she's still having the club meeting this weekend? I mean, she may have changed her plans since she can leave Texas now. You know...that may be why you haven't

heard anything...maybe they're changing it because she's finished with the trial—"

"No, I don't think that's the case. Oprah's a woman who's
going to do what she says. If she says she's taping this weekend, it's this weekend."

J. M. laughed. "Yes, Oprah is both powerful and a woman
of her word from what I can tell."

"Yep. And home girl did go to Texas and win with the
prayers of the righteous."

"Prayers and money. Money helps when it comes to afford-
ing a good lawyer," J. M. said.

"Then don't forget truth...she did have truth on her side."

J. M. was quiet for a minute.

"J. M., you all right?"

"Uh huh. Sure." Then she seemed to snap out of her
funk. "Yes," she said cheerier, "prayer...money...and truth."

"Do you really believe there's a chance they still might call
me and say I've been picked?" It was hard to be optimistic.

"Sure...there's a *chance*. But Rosalyn—"

"Yeah?"

"If you don't hear anything by tomorrow, I'd let it go."

So after I hung up, I decided if I didn't hear anything by
Friday, I *would* let it go. But faith is the substance of things
hoped for; the evidence of things not seen.

Ring phone! Come on now...r-*i-i-i-i-n-n-n-g-g-g!*

 J. M. Taylor's Journal

I taped the Oprah Show on Friday...because of the book club discussion with Toni Morrison. I wasn't sure whether Rosalyn would or had taped it, so I figured better safe than sorry.

I was aware both Rosalyn and Pearl had read the book and both sent letters hoping to be selected. What neither of them knew was, I had also read the book and mailed in a letter.

So when I learned Rosalyn had heard back from the show from her letter, I was so excited for her! Although I got the feeling right off, Pearl's sentiments weren't the same as mine.

"J. M., what do you think? Do you really believe the Oprah Winfrey Show called Honey?" Pearl had said.

I gave her a funny look as I handed back the third marked up version of her latest short story.

"I mean, I am the writer here. I never heard back *even* once."

I tried to answer the question as one, though really it was three questions braided together. Did I really believe Rosalyn got a call from the Oprah Winfrey Show? Did I believe that Pearl never heard one word back from them? And the third question (which was a tricky one)...do I believe she is a writer?

My answer to each would truthfully be Yes, Yes, *And if you keep working hard enough at perfecting your craft.*

So I said, "Pearl, what reason would Rosalyn have to lie about a thing like that?" Effectively taking care of *that.*

"If she did get *two* calls, then why didn't they pick her?"

I started to say, *She got farther than either you or I*—or I could have said, *She got farther than you*—but either of those would have been tacky.

Instead I smiled to myself and said, "Well Pearl, I'm sure she feels bad enough about not being selected. The last thing she needs, after beating up on *herself* about it, is for you or I to do the same." I smiled as I thought how much like my mother I was beginning to sound then added, "And as Great-Great-Grandma Nam-o would have said," I mimicked Mama, "...No matter how much you kick a dead horse, you *still* not gonna get a ride! Not from that one anyway."

Pearl's mind seemed to switch gears. "J. M.? Did you ever get a chance to check on that Caller ID thing for me?"

I had meant to call and tell her, but there was the party, then that trip...and everything else running into each other.

"Yes I did. This guy in Network says after the information is deleted from your box, it cannot be retrieved. But as you already know, any calls that come in, will accumulate until erased."

"I just don't understand what Flick is up to. He already *knows* everybody who calls me. So why is he doing this?"

"Just playing with your mind, knowing him."

"I don't know...I just don't know."

I didn't know how to ask—it wasn't like I really wanted to know—so I just asked. "Pearl, do you think, he thinks...you're fooling around or something?"

"You mean with another man?" She pulled back. "Oh no. He knows better than that...I would never...no, J. M., that's *not* what's on his mind at all. Uh-uh. I just wish things would go back like they were when he and I were first married. He used to take me places...used to hang around the house...he even would help me out with a few things believe it or not. But now...oh well, now he's almost a totally different person."

It felt like Pearl wanted to tell me something though I can't imagine what it might have been. I know the kind of man Flick is. I know he has, a few times anyway, hit Pearl. That much, I do know.

She would like to pretend it was a long time ago; that he doesn't do it *now*. But I don't believe that. I'll never understand how a woman—any woman—can let a man beat on her and she stay there continuing to take it. Talking about, "But I love him, and I know he loves me." "He's under a lot of *pressure* right now." "If he just wasn't so frustrated..."

Everybody gets frustrated at one time or another—just don't take your frustration out on me! Do *not ever* put your hands on me in a way that will hurt me!

Pearl does seem to stand up for herself a lot more than when I first knew her. But I would have "gotten my pocket-book, children, and hat and been gone." That's what Mama told Daddy once when I was a little girl. "I'll get my pocket-book, children and hat...and be gone!"

Nothing is better than what some folks already have inside themselves. When will women look in the mirror and see what great beings they are? To see what they truly have going on for themselves—and quit letting jerks take it, knock it, or "love" it... from them?

Greater is *he/she* that is within *me*...than *he/she* who is in the world. GREATER is HE/SHE that is WITHIN ME...than he/she who is in the world. GREATER is ME (inside me) than THEY (those outside me) that are in the world.

When will we *truly* get this?

Pearl Sue Hunter's Journal

Honey got her little putt-putt of a car to run long enough to make it to my house.

"Sistah! Look at what I got from the Oprah Winfrey Show!" She held up a T-shirt with the words *Found in Paradise* on the front and *Lost in Paradise* on the back with an official Oprah Book Club™ emblem on its left sleeve. "And, look at my letter..." she shook a bright white piece of paper in my face, "Go on...hold it up to the light! See...it's got *Oprah*...embossed in the paper...like a secret code!"

Sure enough, the letter was addressed to Honey...on Oprah's official stationery (Oprah didn't sign it though).

"This is nice, Honey," I said after reading and handing it back to her. "I'm so happy for you." I tried to sound as excited about it as I could muster.

Well, it still wasn't a ticket to the book club. I may even be able to write and get them to send *me* a shirt like that. Oh I'm not saying she *didn't* get those calls, if that's what she thinks (her letter proves she did); all I'm saying is—*so what!* She got a T-shirt...what's so special about that?

I'm still waiting to hear something back from one short story—the one I sent to that magazine company in New York. It's been over three months now, but that's a good sign. Usually I get a form rejection letter back in four to six weeks.

If I could just get *something* published. The publishing business is too much like the loan business in my opinion. If you have money, you can get a loan. But if you need to borrow money because you don't have any, then they don't want to loan it to you. It's the same way with publishing. If you have something published, they'll consider publishing you. If you don't...most times—they won't until you *do* get something published.

And don't become a best-selling author, because when you do...then everybody wants you! Those same folks you couldn't *pay* to read your query letters, now want to call and take you out to lunch. Come to think of it, it's just like when I tried getting my first job.

"Miss Martin (that was my maiden name), do you have any experience?"

"No sir, but I'm a fast learner and a hard worker." I tugged at my white gloves (you had to wear gloves back then).

"We're sorry...we'd really *like* to hire you, but we *were* hoping for someone with some experience."

"I understand sir, but how am I ever suppose to *get* any experience if no one will hire me?"

He laughed. "Like the chicken or the egg, huh?"

"Pardon me?"

"What came first...the chicken or the egg?"

And now that I *have* experience whenever I apply for a job to tie me over (until I get money coming in from my writing), they tell me, "We'd love to hire you Mrs. Hunter, but I must be frank—you're a bit *over*-qualified for this position."

Now tell me, how can you be *over-qualified* for a job you need? *Some* money is better than *no* money. Why should they care if I'm over-qualified or not? That's so stupid!

I knew Honey wouldn't get picked for the book club—God don't like ugly! All I asked her to do was take a copy of my manuscript, just in case she got an opportunity to show it to either Oprah or Toni. That was all I asked.

But she said, 'No.' Trying to be all that! But when she needs to catch a ride, who does she call? Me! Now look what happened; she didn't even get to go. She sat home and watched the show on TV. I really rather enjoyed it myself (the show not the fact that she didn't get to go).

J. M. said she was taping it—afraid Honey might have been too down to watch it (after all she went through waiting for them to call). J. M. was thinking later on Honey might wished she had seen it, so she'd have it...just in case.

I would have told them to just shoot me and put me out of my misery! I wouldn't ever want to go through what Honey did for those weeks. Don't make a person die a slow and painful death—then ask them to sit and watch you eat the supper too.

Nope—just shoot me quick. I suppose that is what they did, come to think of it. Shot me down from the beginning. Well, at least I didn't have to go through all Honey did, thank God!

Flick asked me how J. M. was doing. I asked why he wanted to know. He grinned, looking like a fox just casually strolling past a leaning hen house.

"She's your friend," he said licking his lips. "I care about who *you* care about, baby. In fact, I'm going to make more of an effort to be nice to her when I see her next time. You just watch your man dazzle and be amazed."

I wish I could believe him—but I'm not a *complete* fool.

I'm going to this ball at the end of March...a place called Zamirs (pronounced Zi-mirs) is hosting it. I asked Flick if he would go with me, but he said he has this job he's lining up for some woman named Carol.

"I gave her an estimate on fixing her roof, but she said she couldn't let me start until the end of March. Said she was helping out a friend who had just left her job working for some doctor downtown—until she gets straight. Her friend's name is Maxine. Now those are two *you* should meet and get to know better. They seem like *real* down to earth women. I overheard them talking about this doctor named Richardson. Sounds like the good Dr. Richardson is a lesbian or something. I caught only bits and pieces of the conversation. I was trying to list—"

Dr. Richardson...? That's J. M.'s doctor. I sighed. "Flick, what does fixing a roof have to do with your going to a ball with me—held at night at that?"

He smiled and kissed me quick on the lips. "Nothing. You just never know what might come up. What if I'm just getting started and it starts to rain? I can't just leave the roof because

you and I are due for a ball. I may even end up having to work
late into the night...to do all that needs to be done around
there." He hunched up his shoulders and pulled his shirt tight
and straight by the collar. "I'm a very important man, in case
you haven't noticed."

I asked J. M. if I could borrow that charming little Y-
shaped necklace of hers. The one with the cute little diamond.
I promised I'd take good care of it.

"Pearl, I'll go you one better—it's yours. My gift to you,"
she said.

"Oh no J. M.! I couldn't let you do that. That's *too* much
now. I just ne—"

"What do you mean *'let'?"* She laughed. "A gift is never a
let, it's a gift. When someone offers you something...you take
it. So when's your fancy to-do?"

"March 28th."

"Good, I'll get it to you before then."

"Well if you're being nice enough to give it to me, the least
I can do is come get it."

"I'm sure I'll be out your way soon. If you happen to be by
before then, fine. But I'm going to be busy the next few weeks,
and frankly don't know when we might have a chance to hook
up. I've a meeting scheduled with Phoenix Electronics on the
twenty-fifth of March; I can run it by after I'm finished there."

Every time I think I've figured J. M. out, she jumps up and
does something to shock me. Still, I have seen many sides of
her—and not all are those I care to know better.

When Sugarman called that day after my surprise birthday
party, we ended up talking longer than I believe even he
intended.

"Yes, Sugarman. I *really* enjoyed it! It was great seeing all
those folks without someone being rolled and stretched across
the front of a church," I said.

"Well, I'm glad you liked it. I just wanted to tell you...you
still got it going on," Sugarman said.

"At fifty...oh stop."

"No. I'm serious. I was watching you out there on that dance floor, and—"

"All right now...you're going to get yourself in trouble if you don't stop."

"*What?*" he said sounding innocent. "You know how I feel about you—"

"Yeah, right. I know."

He laughed. "Sister...are you making fun of me?"

"So what did J. M. say?"

"Say?"

"About the bracelet?"

"She said..." he paused, then continued, "...she loved it."

"Told you she would."

"Yeah. You told me." There was silence. "Dog asked me for your phone number," Sugarman said. "Is there something going on between the two of you you'd like to share with me?"

"No."

"No, you don't want to share?"

"No," I said, "there's nothing going on between us. Tell me, did you *not* get a good look at him...did you even get *close* to him?" I turned up my nose.

"I thought you two were hitting it off pretty well from what I could tell."

"Sugarman..." I tried to find a way to say it nicely, "his breath was stank! I could hardly keep my face from literally withering away." We both laughed.

"Sister...you're something else. You know that?" Sugarman said.

Oh well, I do hope Flick changes his mind about the ball. I'm tired of sitting around here doing nothing but wait on him. Doesn't he realize I'm bored out of my skull?! At least Dog acted interested.

Lord! I'd rather be by myself!

Rosalyn Benefield's Journal

I don't know how much longer I can take all this. Nothing seems to be going right. What is it?

"Shawndrika Laquita, Sonequa Moné, Duke Junior, and Darryl LeDale...if y'all don't get your butts in here and pick up all this stuff out of my den—I'm gonna beat y'all till you rote like okra! I'm tired of telling y'all to clean up what you mess up. You ought not take it out if you're too sorry to put it back!

"If you opened it, you can close it. If you threw it down, you can pick it up! Taking clothes off and too lazy to stick them on a hanger—I'm tired of this mess!"

I don't know sometimes, why I even bother. Working at that two bit job all damn day—from six in the morning to two-thirty...three in the afternoon. My feet losing all feelings on the bottom—and for what? So I can come home and have to yell at a bunch of lazy kids who have no idea what I have to do just so they can have a roof over their heads, food on the table, a warm house in the winter...cool in the summer—at least *somewhat* cool anyway.

Sonequa...holding the refrigerator door opened while she stands there gaping. Fifteen years old, and I've had to say the same thing every day since she first learned how to operate it.

"Sonequa, will you close that refrigerator! What are you doing—trying to cool off the whole house?"

Duke Junior, thirteen, ain't no better. He opens the door to go outside or come in and just leaves it standing wide open.

"Hey old nappy-headed boy! Close that door! You weren't born in a barn! What do you call yourself doing...cooling off the whole neighborhood?!!!" (Or heating it, depending on the season.)

Shawndrika is the oldest...seventeen and graduating this year. She lays around yakking on the phone all day and all night, has on every light in a two room radius, the stereo thumping, every radio on that still works, while watching television. Then she has the *nerve* to have school books sprawled everywhere.

"Do you have homework?" I said when I walked up close enough for her to realize I was standing above her.

"I'm doing it Ma. Can't you see?"

"How can you concentrate with all this noise blasting around you?"

She twisted the phone cord around her index finger and untwisted it just as fast. "*Hold* on a minute will you Keisha," she said as she pressed the mute button. "Ma, can't you see I'm talking here? Dag—"

"Talking? Talking—oh excuse me. Excuz *M*-oi! How dare I—your *mama*—be so rude as to come up in here in *my* house and interrupt *you*...on *my* phone while *you* obviously have important business with *who?* Keisha? Yeah, Keisha, the girl who managed somehow to stay back a few grades just long enough for *you*...my child whom I carried nine months and struggle every day to house, feed and clothe to catch up with her? *My* child—who—if she doesn't hang up the phone won't even have to worry about whether or not *she'll* be marching with the class of '98 because *that* will be the least of *her* worries. The least! Which is just where she's going to find herself in about two hot seconds if *she* doesn't get off the—"

Shawndrika released the mute. "Keisha, I'll talk with you later girl. Ma's tripping—*again.*"

"Tripping? *Tripping?* Oh you haven't s-e-e-n tripping yet if some of these lights don't get turned off and all the rest of these earsplitting distractions. You gonna see tripping! How do you expect to do your work when you can't even concentrate? I can't concentrate and all I'm trying to do now is talk to you!"

"But Ma...I can't study if it's *too* quiet. I can't hear my brain think!"

I looked at her and wanted to slap that stupid look off her face right then and there. Here I am barely making it to work every day in that sorry excuse for an automobile...trying to live off that measly salary I get every week. I know where she's gonna end up if she doesn't take school work more seriously. The girl is smart; she could go to college and be somebody if she'd just apply herself.

"You can't think when it's quiet? Is that what *you* say? Well try it," I sang, "you'll like it!" Then I clicked off the TV and stereo and stomped out of the room.

Darryl LeDale, ten going on eleven, is definitely his father's child. And that's all I'm gonna say on him. He loves to play but when it comes down to real work...uh uh.

"I want *you* to do it for me," he says. "My arm hurt." "My legs hurt." "My feet hurt." "My finger-head-throat hurts."

"Funny, it wasn't hurting when you were pulling *out* all this *stuff!* It wasn't hurting when you were having so much fun playing a little while ago. But now that it's time to pay, you act like you're gonna die any second." I waved my hand over the area. "Get it up! And I mean now, Darryl LeDale or your *butt's* gonna be hurting!"

Darryl mumbled as he picked up three miniature cars. "Ma be tripping too much," he said. "Making speeches to Daddy when Daddy ain't nowhere around to even hear them."

"What did you say boy?!"

He looked up at me with his mouth stuck out. "I said—I ain't gonna be nothing like Daddy woman. So I wish you'd cut me some slack!"

"Oh I know *that's* right! 'Cause I'm not gonna let you lay around here on your butt messing up and thinking *I'm* gonna clean up behind you! No—you're not gonna grow up and be some no account, no showing up, sorry, good-for-nothing man for somebody's daughter to have to be bothered with..."

"Who says I'm gonna *get* married to somebody's daughter? Maybe I'll grow up and be gay?"

"What?"

He shrunk down a little...like he knew he had gone too far with me this time. "Maybe I'll turn out to be gay," he said barely above a whisper...head hanging, eyes stretching upward. "That's what Junior says about me." He held his head up higher. "Junior says I'm just a little sissy and probably will grow up to be gay! And folks on TV say it's not a choice but the way God made them—"

"That's it! No more television for you till you're grown! Or at least, until you're old enough not to be influenced by what folks say on television. Now pick up this mess before you cause me to lose my religion! Lord, help me Jesus, please don't let me hurt this child!"

I stood there with both hands on my hip. "Duke Junior!" I yelled.

"Ma'am!"

"Bring your butt in here boy!"

"Ma'am?"

"Right now Junior. Bring your *butt* to *me!* I mean now!"

So I wonder...why *did* I sell my self into slavery which is what this feels like most days. You get a little lean-to to live in, a ration of food, a few pieces of clothing for you and yours...all in exchange for every ounce of your soul they can manage to squeeze out of you. And if you miss one day—or two...or if you're late to the old job; you might end up without even *that* much.

Lord, could you please send Moses back down. Except to Alabama this time. And could you tell him to tell *these* Pharaohs we got now...to please sir...let your people go. Please!

Countess W. Gates' Journal

She didn't lose that baby. I'm not stupid now. I don't care what she says. That was no accident. Talking about she fell down some steps. She didn't *fall* any such thing! Just never wanted a baby. So why can't she just be woman about it and tell the truth?

"What happened?" I had asked as soon as I arrived at the hospital.

"She fell down a flight of stairs at work. Said she got dizzy and the next thing she knew, she was in the hospital in an awful pain," Donald said trying to fight back the tears.

"What about the baby? What did the doctors say about the baby?"

"She lost the baby, Mama. She's real upset about it too. I don't know how I'm going to help her get over this. You know...I just found out she was even pregnant on Friday. She was planning to surprise me, but I came home and overheard her on the phone. Then I called you because you saw it before *we* knew it. You know...your fish dream. And now, this had to happen today."

"She was at work when this happened?" I asked.

"Yeah. Mama, what am I going to do?"

"Donald, why did she take the stairs? Why didn't she use the elevator? She hates walking up and down any kind of stairs, we all know that—"

"I don't know, Mama. I know she's probably asking herself these same questions. Why did this have to happen? You think God is trying to tell me something?"

I patted his hands, clasped and locked as though he were in prayer. "No child. God ain't trying to tell you nothing. If God wants to tell you something, he ain't got to bring you trouble like this for you to hear Him."

"Then why? Am I being punished? Why did God bring this on us?"

"You stop it! God didn't bring this. What the scriptures say...God wants us to have and have more abundantly. God doesn't take—Satan does. That's why you lost that precious little one...it was a devil what done *that.*"

I don't know who Jessica thinks she's fooling. Upset! She ain't bit more upset than nothing. I heard her with my own ears that day, right in their house.

"I'll *never* disfigure my body letting some baby grow inside me," she said. "Stretch marks and junk...no, not me. If I even accidentally get pregnant, I'll abort it." She was talking on the phone a few months ago to one of her friends.

She must have forgotten I was in the house; when I stopped by to visit that one day. I'd gone into the kitchen...to check on my roast. She must have thought I was still in the den watching TV, because she was talking so loud, so freely to this particular friend.

"I'll drink a cup of cotton seed tea...I hear that'll make a baby turn loose." She giggled. "And if that doesn't work, then I'll...I'll...I'll just throw myself down a flight of stairs!" The words ring in my ears even now. "That's what I'll do!"

The person on the other end must have commented on how she doesn't use stairs because she said, "Well I'll use them *that* day. And I will *fling* my whole body...hard down the steps...hard enough to jar loose a baby."

Maybe she thought I was somewhere taking a nap, but I heard her with my own ears speak those words. I shouldn't have heard it, but it was too late for me to let her know I was in the kitchen. Maybe I *should* have let her know I did. Maybe if she had known I heard her, she would have decided against hurling herself...and that baby...that poor precious angel...my grandchild— There she was telling all this to her friend—a girl friend—or so I thought. Then I heard something a husband's mother has no business ever hearing. This friend was not a woman at all! And from all I gathered from what she had to say to him, *he* even wanted her to have a baby—his baby! The two of them...together. So this baby she just lost...was it even my grandchild?

Donald came out of her room heartbroken. "Mama, you can go on in and talk to Jessica now. Maybe you can help make her feel better...you always have a way of doing that."

I stood up and smiled...or at least I thought I had smiled. But the look on his face, made me know I apparently had not succeeded in a smile at all.

"Mama? What's wrong? What's the matter? Are you all right?"

I told him I was having one of my dizzy spells and I sat back hard against the chair.

The poor baby. And she didn't lose that baby *nothing!*

 J. M. Taylor's Journal

Donald called today...quietly sizzling.

"So Johnnie Mae—what exactly did you tell Mama?" he said.

"Excuse me?" I said, tapping a stack of papers on my desk to even them.

"What did you tell Mama about the papers...about Jessica ...about me? I know you've been looking over their important matters here lately."

"Donald, I don't know *what* you're talking about —"

"Their papers...that settlement from the lawyers...Daddy's Black Lung money. I know she asked you to look them over. So what did you tell Mama? I can sense, she knows something she's not saying. Have you said something...about me or—"

"Look Donald. I've got more important things to worry about than you and your little problems and situations you manage to get yourself into. So if she knows *anything,* it didn't come from me telling it."

I heard a sigh of relief. "Thanks Sis. I owe you—"

"But since you brought it up, I *am* going to tell you this much...you had better not *ever* try and play Mama or Daddy with some crap like that again! Just because you got crap falling all around you and your little household—"

"Hey Johnnie Mae—you're really upset with me, aren't you? I don't think I've ever heard you go off like this before. Not with *me* anyway."

"It's because of you they got messed up so bad those other times. Look—I don't care how much junk you all have going on...you...Jessica...your first wife; you leave *our* folks out of it! Do you hear me? Because if you do anything even close to any crap like that again, I will not hesitate to tell Mama...flat out—"

"O.K., Sis! O.K.! It's cool. I get the message. I was wrong. But I appreciate you for having my back."

"It's not *your* back I have; it just would break Mama's heart if she knew all that's going on. But I mean it Donald...if you ever try some crap like that again, heart or no heart, I'm going to tell Mama and Daddy everything they need to know in order to protect themselves from you—"

"You won't have to. I promise. I'm straight." He was suddenly quiet. "You know Jessica lost our baby yesterday, don't you?"

"Yeah," I said much more solemn. "I'm sorry to hear it. I know how much you've been wanting a little sister or brother for Ashley."

He was silent. "Man, I did. This would have been Jessica's first. And she really wanted this baby I believe. Just told me about it Friday, and yesterday...this had to happen. I told her we'd try again later, but she insists she can't go through this twice. She wanted to get her tubes tied—"

"She *what?*"

"Oh," he laughed, "I wouldn't sign for it. I told her she was just in shock—didn't know what she was saying or doing at this stage. Then she started crying and screaming how it was her body and she should be able to do what she wants to with her own body without having to have some man's consent. I don't know Sis."

"Well...I'm really sorry you're having so much trouble lately."

"Kind of brought some of it on myself though, huh? Sowing and reaping."

"As long as you understand...I do mean what I say."

"Don't worry...the next time Mama or Daddy asks, I'll keep *their* interests ahead of my own. I promise. But you and I...we're straight, right?"

"Straight—as long as we understand one another. You mess up your affairs and life all you choose, but leave our folks out of it. They've already sacrificed more than enough for us...Donald you of all people should know *that*. Every time you've gotten in trouble, they've bailed you out. They deserve something for themselves for a change. And Donald...nobody owes y'all one red cent. That money...ain't due to none of us—"

He started laughing.

"*Now* what's so funny?" I asked.

His laughter came under control to where it was more a hiccup-like giggle. "Well...it's just— Here we were thinking you had grown so seddity you didn't say *ain't* and *y'all* anymore, and you're rattling them off like an old pro."

"Well...apparently I *ain't* as seddity as *y'all* think!" I said. I tried to hold in my giggle, but it began trickling out, then just flowed freely like a dam had burst inside me.

That delusional brother of mine! Still...I love him dearly.

Solomon Taylor's Journal

Women have strange conversations. Some of the things they find to talk about...

I was in the den watching the basketball game (they're saying this might be Michael Jordan's last year since the Bull's management can't seem to come to terms to bring back Phil Jackson next year as the head coach). Why they're messing with this team at this point (especially with them heading back to the NBA Finals for sure)...causing a ruckus that could distract Michael so close to play off time, I'll never understand. But Michael's a pro. Besides...not everyone can sport the bald-look and still look good (lots of players have definitely proven that!). Yet Michael and I seem to do it quite well—if I do say so myself.

The little women were in the kitchen doing womanly things. But they kept getting louder and louder; I could hardly concentrate on my game for their chattering. Bits and pieces seemed to float into the den.

"And Michael shoots for three and he—"

"You know it's just hidden racism. That's all it is," Rosalyn said. "I'm telling you, that's *exactly* what it is."

"Did you see that shot—un-be-liev-able!"

"Why does everything have to be hidden racism?" Sister said.

"Foul on Toni Kukoc—"

"So J. M.—what do *you* think about it?" Rosalyn asked.

"...Pass to Scottie Pippen for the lay up and it's—"

"I think there may be some merit to your concern Rosalyn, but I don't know if I'd go so far as to categorize *that* as hidden racism."

"Dennis Rodman for the rebound—"

"Oh you're just taking Sister's side."

"Did you see that pass? That one will go down in the books—"

"No. No I'm not taking anyone's side. I admit it's something to be concerned about but I can't fathom a bunch of starchy white men sitting around some conference room saying,

"Well Jim, how do you think we can discriminate against the African-Americans on this one?" Johnnie Mae's voice was nasal as she mimicked a '*good ole boy.*'

"Then Jim saying: *You know, I hear the Ne-groes...oh I'm sorry, I meant African-Americans...I hear those people—especially the females—all have 'big...old...butts.' So, I propose we make our regular kind, shorter. Then we can keep the longer ones, but decrease the total inside the packages...possibly even charge a tad bit more for them. Now the Black—oh I'm sorry... African-American women, would have to buy the more expensive package because, of course, if it is true that they all have big old butts—'Oh yeah'—then they will have no other recourse* but *to purchase the package of longs. Thereby giving less in each package for about the same, or maybe a little bit more money, and upping our bottom line in the process. J. B. that's my take on it,*" Johnnie Mae said laughing after she finished.

"Yeah," Sister said, "then J. B. says: *Jim, you're a freaking genius! Write me up a proposal and have it on my desk by tomorrow. And remind me to promote your narrow butt—'Oh yeah'—and give you a big fat freaking raise next week.*"

They all laughed except Rosalyn. "Y'all are *sick,*" she said. "This really isn't funny. That probably *is* just the way it happened. They know most black women use their product. That other stuff—packed and jabbed—oh no, I don't play that. The crap might end up lost in me one day...so nope...I ain't down with the alternative. And those other companies just don't seem to get it yet, so they know there's nothing left for us to do *but* buy their brand. And we're sure not gonna get out and be protesting about it in the streets. Not something like *this.*"

Johnnie Mae said, "Well I do admit to having tried the shorter kind that are supposed to be good for heavy days, but I had no peace the whole time I wore them."

"Me too," Rosalyn said. "I was afraid I'd had an accident; I was checking every five minutes just to be sure."

Sister giggled.

"Sistah, it's not funny," Rosalyn said. "Now you know how that can be."

"Well actually, I don't any longer." Sister lowered her voice. "Not since I've been having my *own...private...summers.* I don't have to deal with *that* problem anymore."

"Oh that's right," Rosalyn said loud, "just another something to look forward to."

"God women have it hard, don't we?" Johnnie Mae said.

I couldn't stand it any longer so I got up and went to the kitchen. As soon as I stepped foot in there, they hushed and stared at me like I was Lucifer coming to ask God if I could possibly move back into my old room in Heaven.

"So," I said casually, "what are you little women talking about?"

They exchanged looks—one to the other. Sister started smiling. She had this little shy sparkle in her eyes, then she looked over at Johnnie Mae as if she were saying, *You tell him, he's your man.*

Johnnie Mae turned to Rosalyn and must have told her—using telepathy—*You're not scared of no-body. Go on; blow him away,* because Rosalyn stood to her feet, looked just as serious right straight in my eyes...didn't crack a smile and basically...very calmly and without blinking, she said:

"Wings sanitary napkins and menopause." She cocked her head to one side like I was slow. "The change *So-lo-mon.* The cycle and the change!"

"Oh," I said, blinking enough for everyone in the room. "Well." I sighed. "I guess I'll just go back in there and...watch the game." After which I slithered right back into my little den.

"*Napkins* and *menopause?*" Sister said. "Girl, you're not sick...you're just plain nasty!"

Rosalyn Benefield's Journal

I met this cute man today. I didn't really meet him, just talked to him over the phone. I went down to put in an application hoping to get a loan approved for a car that will at least crank...hopefully run more than twice a week. The boss lady said if I drag into work late one more time, she is just going to have to let me go. The job ain't much, but it's all I got for now—I can't afford to lose it.

I tried to explain to her how bad I needed this job; she explained to *me* how bad *she* needed someone who could be here...on time...every day...to do it.

"Lady, I have four mouths to feed not counting mine," I said, but she wasn't hearing none of it.

The credit loop: Because I have bad credit, I can't secure a loan for a car. And if I don't get a dependable car, then I'll lose my job, I won't be able to pay my bills which only leads to, bad credit. What's *not,* to understand? Rocket science—it ain't.

"Look Ma'am, I can afford the note as long as I can make it to work, but I need a car to make it to work so I can keep my job so I can afford to pay the note," I told this one loan officer (a woman) at my bank last month.

The shrinking silver haired lady behind the desk just shook her head and said, "I do wish I could help you Dearie... but it's just out of my hands. Understand?"

No. Not really, I don't. I sat there wondering, *What's stopping you? It's not like it's coming out of* your *pockets, you old gray-haired biddie!* Now stupid—I ain't!

This girl who works in my section and knows of my situation, slipped me a card with the number of a place that's supposed to rarely turn anybody down. "Girl, I was in worse shape than you sound, and they gave *me* a loan," Janice said. "Why don't you give them a call...see what they can do for *you*. They guarantee you an answer within three days or less."

So I called and talked to a woman there who said I sounded like a good candidate for their program. The company is called, *A Upper Hand, Incorporated*. Honest to God, that's their real name.

"When can you come so we can get the process rolling?" a woman named Mrs. Wright said.

I left from work, hurrying to get there before they closed. Mrs. Wright, a tall white woman with dyed brown hair (I saw her gray roots) said (after I filled out the paperwork, of course), "I won't be able to tell you anything today. Your application is one of the *few* that's required to go to a higher level."

"It's *that* bad?" I said.

She smiled, but didn't say one way or the other. So I took that to mean—it was. She told me she didn't want to get my hopes up...they're not *100* percent guaranteed, but that she would forward it on and either she or someone else would get back with me in the next day or two. *Yeah...right, Mrs. Wright.*

So I was surprised as soon as I stepped foot in my house and answered the phone to hear this man with this d-e-e-p *sexy* voice. Sure, I've heard many voices like his before—and never has even *one* matched the body I had them in with the one God managed to stick them in (when I have gotten to see them, that is—God really has a great sense of humor!). But this one sounded like he *might*—could—be the exception. *Yeah, right!* He would have to be *TOO* fine!

"Miss Benefield," he said, after identifying himself, "your application was passed up to me, but I need to verify a few things with you first."

Five-thirty and the man's still working? Oh I *do* like that in my man. "You're working awfully late," I said proper, yet almost breathless (on purpose, of course!).

"Yes. I took an interest in your file almost immediately. I thought it would be to both our advantage if I didn't waste any time. I hope it's all right for me to call you now—this isn't inconvenient or a bad time for you, is it?"

"Oh no. You're doing me a favor—the sooner I get approved...the better." I tried not to sound *too* needy.

"Great, great. Now Miss Benefield—"

"Oh please...call me...Honey, why don't you."

He laughed a little. "Honey? That's...sweet." He proceeded to explain some of the problems my application had posed, and I thought for sure he was leading up to tell me there was no way even *they* could see approving me. But he could also tell you, with *that* silky voice of his, your mama just died...and you'd be so caught up in the way he was saying it, you'd just sigh and say, "Uh huh...I understand completely. That's life. Those things tend to happen."

"Now, this J. M. Taylor you have listed as one of your references—"

"Did I forget to put the phone number down or something—"

"Yes," he said with a slight chuckle. "And I was also wondering if there was a name associated with these initials?"

"That's what she goes by...her initials."

"Oh, so J. M. *is* a she?"

"Yeah, she's a good friend of mine. Are you planning to call her?"

"Possibly. I just wanted to be sure about...J. M. Taylor." He was quiet as he wrote down the number I gave him. I've not even had a chance to tell her I used her as a reference yet.

It struck me that he was getting ready to get off the phone and I hadn't a clue *what* he had said his name was. "Excuse me, but what did you say your name was again?"

"George Landris."

"George, huh? Well George, I'm sure your wife...*or* girl-friend, can't get enough of that wonderful voice of yours."

"Pardon me?" He sounded like he was blushing.

"Your voice...it's...nice. I was just saying how much your *wife* or *girlfriend* must—"

"Oh...I'm not married."

"Oh *really.* What a...shame."

"Well thank you Miss B— Honey. You've been a great help. And someone will be getting back in touch with you soon."

"Thank you...George."

Ah...what I wouldn't do to see what the good Lord gave him for a body to sport around this earth in!

 J. M. Taylor's Journal

I got a call today. One that stopped me in my tracks.

"Veni, Vidi, Vici," a polished silky baritone voice said.

"*Excuse* me?" I said, trying to figure out why the voice was so familiar and why I was unable to put my finger on the identity of this phantom caller who spoke...Italian?...Italian I once told...oh my God..."George?"

"In the flesh—well, maybe not as far as you're concerned. But trust me...flesh."

"Trust you? Now where have I heard *that* before?"

"Johnnie Mylove...we're *not* going to go there, are we?"

"Suits me. I didn't call you."

"Yes, and that has been well noted. I did wait—believing I was giving you time to cool down...didn't know you were going to ice over completely."

"Listen...I'm really busy right now, so—"

"Hold up. I come in peace. I didn't mean to open up any wounds."

"I have no wounds; just busy is all. And if—"

"Too busy to play, right?"

"I told you from the very beginning, *Mr.* Landris—"

"Oh so you're going formal on me now; O.K. *Ms.* Taylor."

"Now *you're* just trying to be funny."

"Johnnie Mylove—you know me. And funny is *not* a word that goes well with the name...George Landris."

"Look...why are you calling?" Just hearing his voice was bittersweet. I wanted so bad to talk, but then I hated talking to

him. "So what would you have done had my husband answered instead of me?"

He smiled—I know he smiled, because I actually felt it ooze
all the way across the line or the airwaves or however his voice
was traveling right now. "Then," he said, "I would have asked
for you."

"And what if I had not been here?"

"*Then* I would have left a message. Just like I used to—in
the old days." He smacked, like he was eating something tart.
"You do remember the old days, don't you Johnnie Mylove?"

The old days. Of course. How could I forget? Where the
bitter joined the sweet. Except, he found legitimate reasons to
call me back then and leave messages—created a cover. "Well,
you know what they say about the past?" I said. "It passed.
Now, if you won't think me *too* impolite, I *am* busy—"

"So am I, woman!" he said strong, then softer, "However,
I took it upon myself mind you, being the person that I am,
and I'm trying my best to get a loan application approved for a
certain...Honey—"

"Degrading women I see. So what in your wildest fantasies
made you think I might *even* care about what you're trying to
do for your *women* friends?"

"Whoa! Stallion! Give a brother a break why don't you! I
thought you would have mellowed a bit in the last...what's it
been?"

"I don't know. Maybe I should check my *George*
calendar."

He laughed a hearty deep laugh. "Johnnie, Johnnie,
Johnnie Mylove...you still have that certain bite I see."

"It's J. M. I told you before, I prefer being called J. M."

He stopped laughing. "And I told *you* before what *I* prefer-
red. So I suppose neither one of us gets any satisfaction, huh?"

"So what were you saying about your little *honey* trying to
get a loan? What? You thinking about hitting me up for a few
dollars? Is that why you called?"

"Not just *any* honey. *Your* Honey."

Now *I* had to laughed. "Oh good one. And to think you actually believe that George Landris and the word funny don't go together. But you also know...I don't swing like that."

"Woman—will you direct your mind out of the gutter and off sex for just this one minute. At least, long enough to allow me to do my job."

I almost laughed...again. "You mean sex *isn't* your job?"

"Oh, better one. Below the belt though, so we'll have to deduct one point from your score. Sorry." He paused. "Let me try *one* more time here. And if you'll just button your sweet pretty lips..." he was quiet for a second. "What color lipstick are you wearing right now?" he said with a smack.

"George, I'm about to hang up now—"

"Benefield," he said, "Honey Benefield. She listed you as a reference...on her loan application."

"Honey?" I laughed. "You were talking about *that* Honey." I continued to giggle and he let me. "I am so sorry Landris..." I said still laughing. "Rosalyn—"

"Landris? You called me Landris."

I stopped laughing and only a smile remained. "Don't make anything out of it. It *is* your name you know—"

"Johnnie Mylove called me Landris. All right then! Landris is back on track."

"*George...*"

"Nope, it's too late; you said Landris."

"*George*, what do you need from me—"

"Well now, *this* is more like it—"

"What do you need *from me*...for Rosalyn's application? What do you need for her application?" I tried to hold my mouth tighter. He does have a way of making me smile...even when I don't want to.

"How about we discuss this over dinner tonight?"

"I don't think so."

"A late supper?"

"No-o."

"A drink...or what about coffee at Joe Muggs...Cappuccino...a Granita maybe—"

"Landris—no! Are you deaf?"

"Only when it serves me," he said.

"George, ask what you need—"

"All right now—"

"...for Rosalyn's application and only for Rosalyn's application. Ask now or I'll forget you *and* this little game you're playing. I told you I'm busy."

"She's already been declined."

"*What?*"

"They declined her already."

I sighed. "So why are you bothering me?"

He sucked his teeth and made a couple of clicking noises. "I have the power to override their decision. *If...*I deem it applicable."

"Oh...big man. You've got the power—"

"Power? Power?! I'm not the one on a power trip. Look in the mirror Mylove. 'Call me J. M. My name is J. M.' Your friend Rosalyn wants to be called *Honey* and since you and I have been talking...you've done nothing but try and correct *me*. But *you*...want to crack *me*...about power?"

I wanted to argue my point...I did. But I was speechless. "Are you going to give her the loan?"

"I'm not sure. It could go either way at this point."

"Rosalyn really needs a car. That's what this loan is for, right?"

"That's what her application states."

"So *are* you?" I was impatient; I wanted to know.

"Depends—are you interested in discussing this matter with me further. Face to face? And as always...no strings attached."

No strings attached. Now where have I heard *that* before? *Veni, Vidi, Vici. Oh yeah—I came, I saw, I conquered.*

Rosalyn Benefield's Journal

I got to meet George Landris today! When I picked up my letter. My loan—it was approved! And Mr. Landris? He's a hunk, a hunk, a hunk. Did I mention he's a hunk?

When my eyes fell upon his gorgeous face, hazel nut eyes, long Jamaican styled hair en-route down his back; I couldn't control my mouth. "Damn!" I whispered or at least, I thought I whispered it. Mrs. Wright jerked around like she had caught it or something. But I mean that brother is *too* P-H-I-N-E...fine!

I almost didn't get to meet him. I had to insist on thanking him myself...in person, for all the help he had given me. And for being so...so...wonderful.

"When you locate the vehicle you want," George said, "all you'll need to do is give them your letter and they'll take care of the rest."

"Thank you so much," I said in my sexiest voice. "You won't regret this."

"Oh," he said smiling. "I'm already certain of *that.*"

I stood gazing at this...this...hunk of man chiseled by God himself.

"Miss Benefield? Is there anything else I can do for you?" he said with almost a grin.

I wanted to scream, *Hell yeah there's something else you can do for me! You can help me out of these clothes, then help me get you out of yours!* Damn, that man is fine! Just thinking about him rocks, vibrates, and shakes me in places he ain't got *no* business being...not just yet, anyway. (Oh Lord...I slipped.)

And if I hadn't been so shy, I would have asked him out-right then and there. I think he might be interested in me. He had that look...like he wanted to say something but was too afraid I would turn him down. And since I had been crying earlier on (he had to get me some tissue, all the while saying some of the most complimentary things to me), I was simply overwhelmed.

But it didn't take me long to finally pull myself together.

"No," I said to his question, "everything is...PHINE (fine). J-u-s-t phine!" I smiled and then shook his hand, almost not able to let go. "Thank you...again," I said, then I walked away with my special—highly perfected—walk. I know he watched as I walked away. I just know he did. Look out now!

Pearl Sue Hunter's Journal

Honey called; just a babbling. I thought for sure she had finally lost her mind. Her voice sounded excited at times, but it was hard to tell whether she was happy or upset.

"He said I was Fat," Honey said real fast, "and that my face *and* hair were Beat! Just mentioned it casually...in the middle of our conversation."

I didn't know what to say, so silence filled the space where I should have been supportive.

"Sistah! Did you hear what I just said? He is tall and gooood looooking, and *he* said...I was Fat and both my face and hair were Beat! Exactly what he said."

I took a deep breath. "Well now Honey...who cares what that jerk has to say? What does *he* know?"

"What?" she said like she was dumfounded. "What exactly are you trying to say? That I'm *not* fat? That my face is *not* beat? That my hair is not beat either?" She sounded like she was mad with *me*.

"So you *want* to be called fat and beat? Are you so desperate for a man that he can call you up—out of nowhere—and say things like that to you before you've even gone out? Who is—"

"That's the other great news!" she said. "We're going out Friday night. And he didn't call me, I called him and asked."

"You did what and you're doing *what*?"

"Going out? I wish it were Friday night right now!" She sighed. It was impossible to tell whether she was disgusted with him...herself...or with me. "Sistah gurl...which part of this are you *not* getting?"

I laughed. "Maybe the part where a tall, sounds like good-looking guy you only just met, immediately comes on to you by calling you fat...although I think you carry your extra pounds quite nicely; and not only that, but he thinks your face *and* hair are both beat...although I've grown rather fond of your tiny little afro leftover from the seventies; however, I do feel you could go a little lighter on the makeup...personally, I think it makes you look much too much like a...a—"

"Cheap floozy?" she said.

I smiled. "No. That's not what I was going to say at all. Now Honey, you know me...lipstick is all the makeup I feel any woman ever needs." I stopped and thought for a second. "Hold up here...why are *you* upset with *me*? I didn't call you fat *or* beat in your face and hair."

Honey started laughing. That's when I knew with assurance she had tilted too much to the edge. Those children of hers, working those long extra hours hoping to supplement her income...not having had a date in a while (that I know of); the pressure has catapulted her over the edge. Things have finally caught up with her...I predicted as much. Only a few months back, in fact—

"Sistah!" she said trying to catch her breath. "Sistah, gurl... you're gonna have to get out of the house more! You're too far behind the times." She was starting to get her laugh more un-der control, only speaking in spurts. "Fat," she said, "is spelled P-H-A-T, and it stands for Pretty, Hot And Tempting. And, Beat...B-E-A-T...is Beautiful, Elegant And Terrific!"

I felt about two inches tall after she told me that.

"So," Honey continued, "what Dreameo actually said to me was...he thinks I'm a pretty hot and tempting woman with hair and face that's beautiful, elegant, and terrific. See—I'm P-H-A-T (fat) and my face and hair are both B-E-A-T (beat)." Then she burst out into her deep laugh again.

I laughed too. "Oh," I said, "...my bad."

"So I told him I thought he was P-H-I-N-E...fine, and then suggested maybe we could catch a movie some times."

"And what, pray tell...is P-H-I-N-E.?" I was almost afraid to know.

"Powerfully, Handsome, Intelligent, Nevertheless Ex-tra-D-naire, of course! I think he really likes me. We seem so relaxed together."

"Oh you t-h-i-n-k?" I said teasing. "So tell me...what's his name?"

"You're not going to believe me when I tell you."

"Will you tell me already!"

"He's really smart...suave, debonair, and he's got a J-O-B!"

"*No!* You're kidding! You're saying you actually met and will be going out, with a guy who has—let me brace myself now—a J-O-B?" I began to laugh. "Wait until J. M. hears about *this!* So cut the suspense and tell me...what...is this man's name?"

"George Landris. The guy who approved my loan, no less! You know, for my new van."

"Well you go girl! He sounds delicious!"

"Yep. J. M. can't help but to approve of this one! Sistah, I think I've finally found H-I-M. My *H*usband *I*nthe *M*aking!"

 J. M. Taylor's Journal

"Green green the crab apple tree. Where the green grass grows tall," a young woman's voice seemed to sing sweetly inside my head. Was it only a dream? Why did it appear so clear then? What does it mean?

I sat up straight in the bed...awaken by a laugh. The young woman's laugh and that song, "Green green, the crab apple tree..." Sweat seemed to trickle from every opened pore of my body.

"What is it?" Solomon said, first grabbing, then holding me. "What's wrong? Was it a bad dream?"

"I don't know. Maybe," I said. Yet, it felt so real. I laid down and tried to drift back to sleep.

* * *

Words I had spoken to my mother when I was about ten, hauntingly rushed back to my mind when I held up the shiny silver piece I had stuck inside my jewelry box. I came across it again while searching for the necklace I had promised Pearl. "Did I tell you about my powers?" I had said to Mama that day.

"Powers?" Mama said with a strange look on her face. " *What* powers?"

I smiled, proud I had gotten her attention so quick and easily. "Well, seems I make light bulbs blow out."

"Do what?!" Mama said, putting both hands on her hips.

"Either I walk in a room with a light already turned on and it blows or shatters to pieces, or I turn on the light switch and then it blows."

"Johnnie Mae—what are you talking about child? Are you trying to tell me I've got two blown bulbs I need to change? Is that what you're saying?"

I smiled. "No Mama. Now you got three!" I pointed to the room beside us. "That one in there just blew while you were talking!"

Mama turned and look. "Well I'll be, it sure did, didn't it?" She shrugged. "Lord child," she said shaking her head as she headed for the cupboard to get new bulbs. "Powers!" She started laughing. "Ain't no powers blowing these bulbs. They all temporary things—they make them like that at the manufacturing place. That way, they are sure you must come back and spend some more money."

But I knew the truth. It was more than that. There were times when I *knew* stuff. I could feel things before they even happened. And if I concentrated on something long and hard enough, I could—most times—make it come to pass. The problem with the light bulbs blowing must be too much energy leaking out when I'm not paying attention. I just need to be more careful, that's all.

Mama had finished unscrewing the bulb in the bed and bathroom and was now headed back to the front room to change that one. She looked at me and shook her head again. "You know," she said like she was going to let me in on a little secret, "folks used to say when bulbs flickered or blew like that, it meant a spirit was trying to let you know something."

"A spirit?" I said opening my eyes wide.

Mama turned the mop bucket upside down and stepped up on it. She glanced from the ceiling back down to me as she spoke. "Yeah, but I don't think I believe in such things. I probably should, but I don't."

"Wow!" I said. But I was actually thinking—powers and a spirit too! The next time old Hip Cat yanks my pony tail, I'll have a few surprises for him. Mama says he only pulls my hair 'cause he likes me. Ain't *that* much like in the world. I'd rather he *not* like me at all if that's the way *like* feels. I'd hate to know what he does when he falls in love. I could end up bald if he ever took a notion to love me too hard. No, Hip Cat's just mean! So if he messes with me again, he's going to find himself up against my newfound powers—and a spirit to boot, provided this spirit can go to school with me. She probably can— She? How do I know it's a she? It just *feels* like a she.

I grin now as I think back to that time. It's hard to imagine I actually believed something that bazaar. But as I rotated this golden silver dollar in my hand...a hole bored clean through its top...a delicately stitched piece of green cloth strung unhindered; I can understand why I probably did. All those tales Mama would recant to us as children the way Great-Grandma Nam-o told them to her—it's no wonder.

"*This*," Mama said, holding the coin while it twirled on the string in mid-air, "once belonged to *your* great-great-grandmother called Nam-o." Mama had taken it from a velvet pouch packed neatly inside the old trunk in the back room.

"I really should have gotten rid of a lot of these things a long time ago, but I just can't bring myself to do it," Mama said taking other stuff from the trunk. But then she stopped, picked up the silver dollar, polished it using the tail of her apron, and handed the strange medallion to me.

"This is old," I said. "Can't be worth much now." I flipped the coin over and noticed the woman who seemed to float in the air.

"And why do you say that, missy?"

"Because people are always gittin' rid of their *old* stuff. It ain't worth much."

She looked stern. "What have I told you about chewing up and mispronouncing your words?"

I swallowed hard. "Yes'm. I mean...yes ma'am."

"Better. Now what were you saying about old things not being worth much?" She sat straight before leaning over to retrieve a few other things.

I decided it best I choose my words and take care in pronouncing them properly, "Well...we throw away old shoes, old clothes, old food, old people—"

"Old people?!" Mama stopped pulling things from the trunk and stared. "Are you saying old people aren't worth much and should be thrown away?"

I knew from *that* tone, there was only one right answer, and I would do well to find it. "No ma'am; that's not what *I'm* saying at all. I was just making an *observation*." I hoped a big word would help calm her.

Mama started putting the things back in the trunk. I did *so* want to see what other treasures were hidden...buried, inside this black "*Keeper of the Past*" as Mama put it. "Well, we don't throw away *our* old people! No ma'am! That's one thing we can be proud about. Got that from our ancestors in Africa. Older people were respected and cherished in Africa; it was an honor to grow old."

Mama took back the coin. "This thing, this little piece they call a silver dollar. Did *you* know this has gold in it?"

I shook my head so she turned it to the side so I could see the golden band.

"Enough gold that people are now going back, digging up, and pulling out their buried and hidden money to cash in their older silver dollars. Did you know they're offering fifteen dollars for every *one* of these old things you bring to the bank?"

My eyes lit up. "*Fifteen* whole dollars for *one* of *these?*" I thought of all the jawbreakers and six-lets (at two for a penny) I could buy if I had just *one* of *these*.

"Yes." She put the coin that hung from the green string back into its black velvet pouch and carefully tucked it inside the trunk.

"What? You mean you're not going to trade it for fifteen?"

She closed the lid of the trunk and pressed both sides to clasp, causing two separate clanking spring-like sounds. "No. I'm *not* going to sell *that* one." She sighed. "They probably wouldn't give me fifteen for *that* one anyway."

"Why not Mama?" I asked. "Because it once belonged to a slave?"

"No Johnnie Mae. Because..." she looked away and suddenly a smile crept over her face—like she had been told a joke only *she* heard. "Because...it has a hole in it."

So the other month when Mama pressed that silver coin in my hand...the one with the lady (Liberty seated holding a flag, thirteen stars, 1854) green string threaded through a hole bored in its top; she told me that secret joke.

"Do you remember when you asked me when you were a little girl...the day we were in the back room looking in that old trunk for something and I pulled out this coin, if the reason I couldn't get fifteen dollars for *this* one was because it had once belonged to a slave?"

"Vaguely," I said, although I did remember...every word. Knowing the year now, I knew its value was more than fifteen—even back then. "What about it?"

"I laughed or rather, tried *not* to laugh after you asked me that."

"Yes, I wondered what was funny at the time."

"After I thought about what you had asked, I realized the truth really *was* because it had once belonged to a slave."

"Oh Mama, that's not it. Money is money—no matter whose hand it's in."

"Most times I'd agree with that. But you see, only a slave who had once been free...with a culture of her own that she remembered so well, although she was six when captured and forcibly brought here in 1856, could change it. One who would strive to hang on to ceremonial things...hoping to pass them on to her children's children.

"Because *that* slave who called herself Nam-o...refusing the name Peggy, had owned this piece...this piece she placed in my hands having herself pounded and driven through its hardness...proving to it, she was tougher; strung from a piece of cloth whipped from her body, then sewn together by her hand...a coin worn against *her* often sun-beaten sweat glossed black skin.

"Because she passed it to me, for me to pass on to mine, and mine to some day pass on to the next one...this is our link...our connection to a woman who never forgot who she was and what it was to be free—she changed it. Great-Grandma Nam-o rubbed her hand over this; I, mine; and as I sit here with you now..." Mama smiled.

I looked to see what was drawing her attention and found myself unconsciously rubbing my hand over the silver dollar.

Mama continued. "It may appear it is worth less now because it had once belonged to an African made slave. But she left something much more valuable than money...more valuable than anything we could exchange for it. And to think, one day this piece will make its way down through our family—the Lord be willing—and *my* great-great-great grandchildren, when I'm dead and gone, will be able to touch this same piece I have touched.

"Somehow, this piece of metal connects us—even beyond death. A piece an old slave made to *some* worthless, to us...has become a legacy—a link to each other." Mama lovingly touched the trunk. "There are many, many stories—both written and unwritten—inside this old trunk...this *Keeper of the Past.* Stories I hope someday will find new life."

Mama got Solomon to bring that trunk to our house since we have space to store it. But she had taken out that old silver dollar...on the green cloth string, and pressed it into the palm of my hand herself. Like a family ritual. So I placed it around my neck in appreciation for the responsibility of taking care of it...for now. However, as soon as it touched my skin, there was this strange feeling to come about me. I can't explain it, but I took the necklace off as soon as I stepped foot in my house and placed it in my jewelry box with my better jewelry. And that is where it has been...until I came upon it again today.

Today. There was something about it today that drew me to place it around my neck. And for reasons I can't begin to explain, I feel as though I know things I have no business knowing. I have even—at times—found myself laughing for no good reason other than...I just felt like laughing.

The Plains of Jericho

Now Jericho was straitly shut up because of the children of Israel: none went out, and none came in. And the Lord said unto Joshua, "See, I have given into thine hand Jericho, and the king thereof, and the mighty men of valor. And ye shall compass the city, all ye men of war, and go round about the city once. Thus shalt thou do six days."   Joshua 6:1-3

 J. M. Taylor's Journal

"Green green the crab apple tree where the green grass grows tall..."

I had that dream again. Children playing in a circle singing a song I've never heard before—not that I recall having heard. But every time I have this dream, the song is sang in the exact same way, yet all I can remember upon awaking is that same small part.

The first time I dreamed it, was a night right after I came from Mama's house...the day she gave me Great-Grandma Nam-o's silver dollar necklace...the one tied with that green string. I had put it on, just so Mama could see how much I did appreciate her having given it to me to keep. It was strange, running my fingers across that piece of metal...realizing my connection to this African...this one who was enslaved...my past...this link to my ancestors...an ancient one who had also run her fingers over this piece well before I was born.

Mama has told us many tales about Nam-o but I have more questions, it seems, than answers. Why did the Doctor Master put out her eyes? What was she really like? Why didn't *they*—those who were slaves—not do more to become free? Who was this woman from Africa whose blood flows through my vein?

"Nam-o was a griot. At least, she was from a line of griots," Mama had said. "Her grandmother in the old country, held and recited, the history of the people—much like a walking, talking, living, breathing encyclopedia. Words imprinted in the mind and the soul. Nam-o recalled stories her own grandmoth-

er told her when she was a young child—before those who came
and stole her away from home and family. Before being held in
a dark and cold dungeon—waiting for, who then, even knew
what. 'Before the big boat that did float on water.' Before she
had cause to tremble inside her own skin—wishing if only she
could just slide away...disappear...without being noticed. Before the huge pot with boiling water...before the forced feeding
of her and so many more."

"These people, the color of light pink blossoms, they mean
to cook and eat us?" Nam-o said in her native tongue of
Ghana.

An older more learned man with rock muscles who also
spoke Nam-o's language, said, "There are tales about these
spirits that have taken us. Spirits called *whiteman*. These
spirits bad. They steal, will kill at times. Take pickens from
mame and pape...take pickens (symbol for the stars) from their
mame (maternal symbol for the moon) and their pape (paternal
symbol for the sun). Take 'way native tongue...take 'way name
if you forget and let them."

"By what authority do they these things?" Nam-o asked
with strong focused eyes.

"In the beginning, they say for a holy cause—in the name
of Christianity." The older one frowned. "Juba! Little one
speaks well for such a young age."

Nam-o's eyes searched to and fro of this horrible place
where she was held against her will. "Nam-o six...almost seven.
Got history in *here*," she pointed to her temple, "and in here,"
then her heart. She stared at the huge pot of water boiling.
"Whiteman gonna *eat* us?"

He stared ahead. "They not eat us. But get sick, and they
will feed you to the ocean."

"This Christianity...what is it?"

"Religion. I have been taught and have learned Christianity. But Christianity teaches equality and brotherhood."

"Still, they take us? Stars from our own moon and our own sun? The whiteman do this, by the authority of this Christianity? That's what you say?"

He nodded. "They with the help of our own who either capture us or allow it."

"Then I no like this Christianity!"

"But they say we savages. Take us from here to another place suppose to save us. Whydah! Take us to the new world. Savages, they say—to be converted to receive Jesus Christ. A holy cause. Yet, it's more about money now."

Nam-o began to cry. "Don't want to go! Don't want to leave mame and pape and other stars. Don't want to go to Jesus. Bring Jesus to us!"

"Juba!" the older African said in a deep voice. "I am called Olaudah...(which is to say—fortunate...one favored and having a loud voice). In my tribe I am known as well-spoken." He shook the chains that bound his wrists and ankles. "Sailors, it is told, first bought slaves, beads, and cloth then exchanged them with Africans farther west—Ghana—for gold dust."

"I am Ghana...I am called Nam-o."

He continued. Focused. "There is such an abundance of goods being traded, Guinea coast now named for chief products. The Pepper Coast, the Ivory Coast, the Gold Coast, and the Slave Coast." He leaned back against the wooden plank. "We Juba, are *now* viewed as mere products. Products from the Slave Coast."

"Maybe if we tell them we got religion. Got temples and ceremonies. Nam-o still got rattle my mame gave me that her mame gave her. Use rattles to invoke the spirits. We worship. If it good enough for mame, pape, and nana the griot...it good enough for Nam-o." She began to cry again.

He reached forward with his chained hands, wiped, then threw her tears to the wind. "Save your breath and tears little one. It is yet a long journey. The only deliverer to freedom you will know once you reach Whydah will be, most likely, death. Still, never forget who you are...the soil you come from. Find a way to *keep* Nam-o. Learn, and do not perish little Nam-o."

"And we be savages? Whiteman call us savages?" Nam-o cried.

"Juba. There is none to hear your cry. Save strength for a new and better day. Should you survive the middle passage, there is whole-nother life you must then learn to survive. I read and speak English...will teach one as smart as Nam-o as we sail. But the rest...Nam-o must learn and do...for Nam-o."

Mama smiled. "And Nam-o decided right then and there," Mama said squinting her eyes, "...that she *would* survive. She learned. And the oral literature she kept inside—received from the griot of which she was born—the supernatural tales...moral tales...all the proverbs, poems and love songs; she wrote or got others to write down. All she owned she felt important, is stuffed inside that old black trunk."

"I am the griot who will tell my children so they can tell their children's children," Nam-o said. "Olaudah, you say there is no way back now that we have sailed many moons. We go to America...home of free...and brave. I free...I brave. And I vow to keep home close inside here," she tapped near her heart, "as much as possible. That's a promise I make before you...and before God."

Countess W. Gates' Journal

Johnnie Mae came to visit today. I was shocked; she hardly ever comes on a Saturday. I was even more surprised considering everybody will be here next week for Easter dinner (except Christian and his family stationed in Germany). Mr. Gates' eyes just lit up as soon as she stepped foot in the door.

"Hey there, Baby Girl!" he said grinning and pulling out his unlit pipe.

"Hi Daddy...Mama." She leaned over and planted a kiss on both our cheeks.

"O Jay, O Jay," Mr. Gates sang, "it's so good to see ya. You want to come see my new rose plant? This one's a dilly! Yep, this one is certainly one for the books all right. The books."

Johnnie Mae touched his hand barely and smiled. "Maybe later, okay."

"All right." He giggled, almost to himself. "O Jay. O Jay," he said, as he smiled then pulled out the white handkerchief from his back hip pocket and wiped his nose. "Busy Jay. O busy Jay." He shuffled out the room and the back door squeaked then slammed back shut.

"He's looking better," Johnnie Mae said smiling. "So Mama...how's he doing—really?"

"He seems fine physically," I said. "I just worry sometimes about his mind. There are days when I think he's sharper than his razor. Then there are days...when I just don't know."

Johnnie Mae smiled. "Well I'll say this, even *I'm* not as sharp as I used to be." She took off the thin coat she wore. "It's a little cool still for April." Johnnie Mae's attention seemed more drawn to the back of the house as she continued to glance that way several times. "What does he *do* out there all day?"

"Piddle. That's exactly what he does...piddle! Just like my granddaddy when he got up in age," I said as we walked back to the door to watch him. He was out there pulling weeds by hand. "I tell him over and over, 'Mr. Gates, we got a fellow to take care of the yard now so you don't have to pull weeds like that.' He just looks at me and smiles. 'Well Mama...' he says, 'you know idle hands are the devil's workshop. Besides, that fellow don't ever do it like it ought be done. You got to get weeds up by the *roots*. He don't get 'em, so I make my hands useful. Keep the place from looking so scraggly.'

"So I just leave him be; as long as he's not hurting himself or anybody else."

Johnnie Mae laughed as she watched.

"Why don't you go out there so he can show you his garden? His winter vegetables came up real well—we eat from what he's sown almost every day...collards, turnips, broccoli, peas, cabbage. The cabbage are gorgeous! Get him to pull you up a few to carry home and cook."

"It's only me and Solomon, Mama; it would take us a while to eat a few."

"Then just let him give you a little of everything. He'd love that—if you carried something home from his garden." I smiled. "He's getting it all ready for spring planting. Seedlings already started down in the basement."

"Waiting for Good Friday to plant them," she whispered, to herself mostly.

I smiled. "You *do* know your father."

"I do, don't I."

"Go on out there—it would just make his day. It's the first time in a long time, I've seen him appear so...at peace."

Johnnie Mae turned and looked at me. "You mean at peace when *I'm* around?" She turned back and stared outside. "I've not made it easy on either of you lately, have I?"

I smiled and followed her eyes. "I just wish you'd tell me what happened between you two. You were always like overcooked rice—stuck so close together. Like peas in a pod. Then it was like somebody ran a finger down the middle and all the peas fell to the ground. Why won't you tell me what happened...what was it? You've said it wasn't anything he did to *you*. I never thought he did...but I was relieved to know for sure. I see on television how some of these fathers...with incest ...child molestation...and you never want to honestly believe your own could or would do anything like that—"

"Mama, you know Daddy would *never* do anything like that. Never! I remember how he'd say he'd kill a man—*dead*—if he even attempted to violate any one of his children. No, Daddy was the best when it came to us." She smiled as though her mind had traveled farther than she had intended.

"Then what was it? Please tell me."

Johnnie Mae continued to gaze outside...such a strange look on her face. She watched Mr. Gates like a parent watching a child doing something that every other child before it has done, but the parent acts as though it's the first time it's ever been accomplished in the history of the world. That was exactly how she looked, like she was watching him take his very first step or form his first words.

"Johnnie Mae? Johnnie Mae?" I said, pulling her back to *this* place.

She shook her head as though she really had been some-where else. "Mama, it's hard to explain what it was exactly. When I attempt to put *my* finger on the one thing I felt changed things, it seems trivial and stupid, even to me." She turned and smiled at me.

"Yet whatever it was, it still affects you today. So it can be neither trivial nor stupid. Maybe if we talk about it—together, we might be able to make it better."

Johnnie Mae continued to smile as we watched Mr. Gates piddle and pick. Shuffle, piddle, hoe, pick. Pick, shuffle, hoe, piddle. "Mama, there was a time when I believed *my* daddy could do anything—could move mountains."

I drew closer to her and laughed as I took her arm. "*My* Daddy can do anything!" I said, imitating the way she always said it as a child. "*My Daddy can do anything!* You would sing his praises for miles and miles around—for all to hear."

Johnnie Mae laughed, but then, just as suddenly...it turned into a whimper as she held on to me. "What is it, Baby? Tell me. What is it?"

"*Why* Mama? Why is this world so cruel some times? It's not fair!" And it was while I held her in my arms...rocking her gently, that I noticed the silver dollar around her neck.

"Shhhh, Baby. Hush now. You know Johnnie Mae, when *they*—whoever *they* are at the time—pluck out your eyes..." I lifted up the silver dollar, "you just have to find another way to see...better and clearer...than even before. You must see what others can't or—moreover don't—who profess to have sight. You can't allow *them* to take from you; you just can't. *They* win when you give up or give in to them and their tactics.

"When *they* say you can't, you must say, *Watch me*. When *they* say you won't, you must say, *Try and Stop me*." I rubbed her hair while hugging her more. "Not always with your mouth either. *Action*. Action shouts volume! People can't help but hear you then. But Baby...you don't cut off your finger just because the fingernail gets brittle or breaks. A nail can only grow when there's a finger there waiting on it."

Johnnie Mae looked at me. "I expect too much, don't I? I try too hard."

"Nah! Expecting and trying is a good thing...as long as either leads to intend and do. We're all spiritual beings—old folks in my day used to say, '*Just pilgrims traveling through this barren unfriendly land.*' Spiritual beings housed temporarily in human containers—not perfect—yet, human *BEings*. And eventually, all things do go back to where they came from. Dust to dust...spirit to spirit. Still, we must strive to do what we came here to do or heck!...all the troubles we've gone through and the joys we've shared...are for naught."

Johnnie Mae started grinning as she held her head up. She wiped away any lingering tears and said, "*Naught.*"

I smiled too. "Yes! Naught! Nothing...zip...nada...zero. A big fat goose egg!"

She hugged me. "I love how you phrase things. Like, *'I'm not sure she's here or no.'* or *'aught from aught leaves aught.'*" She became suddenly quiet. "Mama...?" was all she said.

I looked in her eyes. "Why don't you go on out there. You don't have to resolve everything in one day. But you should live each day as though it were the last—yours...his...mine. Ask yourself: Will I have any regrets later regarding my action, this decision? Whatever you do in life, just ask yourself that one question and answer it honestly each time. There, you will find everlasting peace and true rest."

"I know, Mama. And you're right I know. But—"

"*Butt* is what you *sit* on! Now go on out there and let him show you that ugly plant he calls a rose. Though I'm gonna tell you up front...it looks more like a tumbleweed if you ask me."

Johnnie Mae leaned against the door jamb. "Maybe later."

Mr. Gates sang to himself as he pulled, shuffled, piddled, picked...hoed.

"My children my children I call you," he sang. It wasn't even a song but a game we used to play when we were little. "We don't hear you," he answered himself back. "My children my children I call you," he sang again.

"We don't hear you!" I yelled out the screen door. He stopped and looked up, then smiled.

"I'll send my shoes at you," he said.

"We'll walk in your shoes," I yelled back.

"I'll send my car at you," he said grinning.

"We'll drive your old car." I then nudged Johnnie Mae. "Come on," I whispered, "you remember this game."

"I'll send my house at you." He was hobbling back toward the house; the gout in his knees slowing him down tremendously from moving like he used to.

Johnnie Mae started to grin. "We'll live in your house," she said. We took one step back as he came closer to the door.

He pulled the handle, and opened the door. "I'll send my-y-y..." a signal that the game was about to change, "...*self* at you!" he shouted.

Johnnie Mae and I both screamed and yelled back, "We'll run from yourself!" Then we laughed. The only part of the game to cause major reaction, was when the person declared to give of him or herself. Good message, huh?

Mr. Gates started to cough. He coughed so hard, blood was on his handkerchief. "Calm down, Mr. Gates. Come on now. See...you did too much."

"Your new rose bush, Daddy," Johnnie Mae said, "tell me about that new plant of yours."

He smiled as his cough began to calm. "It's just 'bout one of the ugliest things—so says your mama—but it's *so* beautiful to me. You got to see it, Baby Girl. How it can curl up when it needs to and flatten down at other times. Ugly as sin, some folks say—like some folks would say about me."

"What color is it?" Johnnie Mae asked.

"Color? Ain't no true color. Gray is all. Called...Rose of Jericho."

Johnnie Mae started to laugh. "Are you serious?" She looked over at me and I nodded. "Daddy, you mean they finally named a rose after you?"

He laughed a little, but laughing made him cough so he cut it short. "Some say it's an ugly thing," he cut his eyes over at me again, and I just waved him off, "but that's its secret weapon. It don't have to show all its beauty up-front. It has a hidden beauty...hidden treasures—you understand what I'm trying to say here, Baby Girl?" he said.

Johnnie Mae smiled and squeezed his hand slightly. "I'm trying, Daddy. I promise...I *am* trying. It's just hard, I won't lie to you—you've always known that."

"Well, in time...I pray you do. It would hurt me to my heart to know you never did understand. And that you still hold something against me because you don't."

I'm not sure what they were saying, but I'm sure it's about what ever had come between them. I was just glad they were actually talking...maybe not like in the past, but they were at least, holding a conversation. I caught Mr. Gates gazing into Johnnie Mae's eyes; and I was certain then...he knew whatever he needed to know. He'll make whatever is wrong—right. I've seen him fix too many things too many times with me that Lord-God-Almighty *knows* I shouldn't have ever forgiven him for. Yes, Mr. Gates has a gift for peering deep into the soul. He'll fix whatever needs fixing between him and Johnnie Mae. I know that now.

But I do wonder, what was bothering Johnnie Mae so that it caused her to visit us on a Saturday. I'm not complaining about it—just wondering. It's been years since she's been here... just for a visit...on a Saturday.

 J. M. Taylor's Journal

I drove down to Edgewater to visit with Mama and Daddy. Daddy's lost weight, though he still sports all his more gray than black hair. I don't know why, but something made me look him in the eyes today. Then I knew he knew, what troubled a part of my soul. I never meant to hurt him, but it's hard to forget. One day...was all it took—that one day. When my eyes saw, and I didn't like what they saw. Consequently I shut them tight...so tight, that in the process I must have closed off my heart as well. It's not natural, just not natural for a child who positively adored her father to feel this way. Yet feelings can't always be controlled—only reactions. And I did control my reaction; just not my feelings.

Today, Daddy really reached out—trying to teach me something no less. I'm sure that's what he called himself doing...it's what he does best—teaching something when you don't even realize he's teaching you something. Forever using nature...like gardens, plants and animals were his own private textbooks.

"See Baby Girl, how each one different—like folks," he had said pointing to the whole garden when I was only twelve. "Can't treat 'em all the same way either. Take this 'un here... it's partial to full sun. Yet this 'un...only thrives in shade. Some like a lot of attention; some don't care to be bothered. And *some* just gon' do what they gon' do no matter what *you* try to make 'em do."

"Which plant am I most like Daddy?" I said as I swayed from side to side.

He stood and pointed off a distance. "I reckon you most like my strawberries over yonder."

"Strawberries?" I giggled.

"Yeah...strawberries. Just give you what you gonna need and let you gon' and do what you gonna do. Just better not ignore you for too long, cause if you do, you liable to find you done took over every thing in your path."

"Daddy!"

He laughed and puffed on his hand-carved black pipe. Oh how I loved its sweet fragrance. A smell that danced in the air like a snake being charmed.

" 'Course now you as sweet as you wanna be," he said. "When you get enough sun. Otherwise, you can be a Blue Jay. O Blue Jay—tweet, tweet."

Daddy showed me his new rose when we walked to his garden later in the day. "It's called Rose of Jericho," he said. "Named just like me. I *laughed* when I saw it. You see how gray it is? Gray like me too."

I looked at the plant; Mama was *right.* It wasn't pretty by any means.

"It's also called Resurrection plant. Kind-a strange ain't it? Seeing that the walls of Jericho are about tumbling down, and resurrection is about rising up."

I smiled at him and the plant. "It's nice Daddy."

"I used to wonder why my Ma named me Jericho—something most famous for its walls that fell down. So right before she passed over to the other side, I asked her."

It was unusual to hear him speak of his half-blooded Cherokee mother—my grandmother. "Why? Did she say?" I said.

He looked at me and smiled. "She said, 'Something have to come down some times before something better can take its place." He glanced down at the gray plant. "You see this Rose of Jericho here? It curls its branches—its seed pods—inward. Protecting them during the dry season. Look just like a ball then. But as soon as moisture touches it, it just spreads out—

look just like a fern. This one's a foot wide when it spreads. But this what I want you to understand. When it's dry—and the Rose of Jericho is in a ball—it can be stored for years. Years, you hear? But there gonna come a day of moisture...and when it comes, the Rose of Jericho gonna be ready to s-p-r-e-a-d. Spread, I say!"

I laughed. "But Daddy...it really *does* favor a tumbleweed."

"That's what Mama say too. But looks ain't always so. This *tumbleweed* as you call it, bears little white flowers. Guess how many folks miss *that* particular sight completely just because they judge the thing wrong." He started walking away.

"Jericho's a good name for that old tumbleweed looking thing," he said. "Looks can be deceiving. Like that J. M. you go by...how many folks mistake you for a man?" He stopped and smiled at me. "Ain't no mistaking when they hear Johnnie Mae though. You're a rose, Baby Girl. The rose of Jericho."

I looked at the plant again, smiled, then headed back toward the house.

"Oh," he said, "And will you please tell your mama I ain't getting senile no such a thing. Tell her. 'Cause she don't want to hear me. Also, tell her my eyes are working just fine. I know pretty, when I see pretty! Tell her my eyes and mind in fine working condition. Just fine! And she's still fine to me." He laughed. "Old, *nothing!*"

"Daddy!" I said, not believing he had said that. Not *my* daddy!

"Tell her I heard what she said to Rachel. And I do too know what year it be! She act like a man can't reflect sometimes. I know what I like..." Then his talk became more mumbles to himself.

I went back inside and told Mama exactly what Daddy said.

She just laughed. "Pray tell, Mr. Gates said *that*, did he?!" She laughed even more. "Johnnie Mae, listen to this." She pulled out a paper and her reading glasses. "This is so cute; I found it the other day in this local paper and just had to keep

The author's unknown; it's called *Older Folks Are Worth A Fortune.*"

I really *didn't* want to hear it, but Mama was going to read it regardless of what I said, so I sat down and listened with a smile. Mama began to read aloud.

"Old folks are worth a fortune," she said. "With silver in their hair, gold in the teeth, stones in their kidneys, lead in their feet and gas in their stomachs. I have become a lot more social with the passing of the years; some might even call me a frivolous old gal. I'm seeing five gentlemen every day."

She paused to see my reaction. I grinned; she continued.

"As soon as I wake, Will Power helps me get out of bed. Then I go see John. Then Charley Horse comes along, and when he is here, he takes a lot of my time and attention. When he leaves, Arthur Ritis shows up and stays the rest of the day. (He doesn't like to stay in one place very long, so he takes me from joint to joint.) After such a busy day, I'm really tired and glad to go to bed with Ben Gay. What a life!"

She smiled and looked over the top of her reading glasses, then her eyes dropped back down to the page. "P. S. The preacher came to call the other day. He said that at my age, I should be thinking about the hereafter. I told him I do all the time. No matter where I am—in the parlor, upstairs in the kitchen or down in the basement—I ask myself, 'Now, what am I here after?' " Mama laughed.

I smiled. "Cute Mama."

"Cute? I don't know what you're talking about...that was *Da' Bomb!*" she said.

I laughed. "Okay, Mama. It was *da' bomb*...all that...and a bag of chips!"

"I'm sticking this right on my refrigerator so everybody can read it time they come in."

And that's exactly what she did!

Rosalyn Benefield's Journal

I talked with J. M. today—told her about me and George.

"Rosalyn, I don't believe George Landris is one you should get involved with. But hey...you're going to find the right person for you one day soon; I just know you are," she said.

"What do *you* know about George? What? Do you think somebody like me is not good enough for someone like him? Just because he's a high level company exec who wears expensive clothing and drives that cute BMW?"

"Rosalyn, that's not what I'm trying to say at all—"

"And just how do you happen to know George, anyway?"

She cleared her throat. "I did some consultant work for A Upper Hand once, and prior to that...well, I sort of met him when I worked at the phone company."

"He worked for the phone company *too?*"

"No...he worked for...another company, and he and I sort of...worked on a project the phone company put me in charge of that he requested specifically be done."

"Then you really *don't* know him." I heard her sigh hard. "J. M., George has been nothing but a perfect gentleman with me. We even have plans to go out again. Next week—"

"Rosalyn just—" J. M. started then stopped. "Look, I just don't think he's the right man for *you—*"

"Dag J. M.! What is it? You think you're the expert on every man around? I'm telling you, George is the man for me!" I paused a second. "Say? Do you hear that?" I said.

"Hear what?"

"Bells, gurl. Wedding bells! I do believe I hear wedding bells in the distance." I exhaled. "Isn't that something! I finally ᴊ decent car that runs and run up on me a decent man to ᴏot. Thank you Jesus! for finally hearing my cry!"

Oh well...J. M. wasn't so excited. A touch of jealously maybe, though I've not the faintest idea why she should be.

I don't believe he actually shaved his head though. All that Samson hair...gone! He looks kind of like Solomon now. When I happened to mention Solomon's shaved head, I had no idea he was thinking about doing that as well. But people, especially in the work place, do judge folks by their outsides. If you don't look a certain way, they'll try to hold you back.

But that George *is* fine now! And Lord, it's been awhile since...well, you know.

Now I'm fully aware you have rules about these things...and I certainly don't want to burn in hell over a little thing like this...but Lord—in all fairness—you ought not have made sex so good!

You know what you said about everything you created—the heavens, the earth—that it was all good? Well, when you created love...sex, let me say it here (as opposed to when I usually just scream it out on certain occasions), Oh God! It's *good!*

 J. M. Taylor's Journal

Oh if I were able to take a snapshot of my feelings inside right now; it would be much simpler than trying to explain or put them into words.

I don't know what he saw in me. What can one see in those first few seconds that would cause minutes to stretch into hours...days...weeks...months...years...? What happens to cause another to say, "I want to be with *this* person."

It certainly couldn't be my looks because my chest is flatter than even I care to think. My butt's not all that. I've never considered either my face or hair enough to grab even fleeting moments of attention let alone another in passing. And yet— there he was...trying to talk me out of a few more minutes of my time.

He said it was my smile. But other people smiled, and I didn't see him walk up to them...make a move on them. No. There must have been something else I missed on that lovely sunny Friday—June 11, 1993.

I don't know; maybe I looked easy. He told me not to ever put myself down like that—not ever did he want to hear me say anything like that again!

And upon the conclusion of our first conversation, he asked two favors of me. One, for me to tell my husband what a lucky man he was *(yeah...right!* like I'd really tell my husband a thing like that! "Oh Darling, this good looking charmer of a gentleman told me to tell you what a lucky man you are." Yeah, I can just see *that* all right).

The second thing— You know, I just realized, he never told me the second thing. But that's okay. I didn't tell him my last name either. The last thing I need, is for some strange man showing up one day asking for me. No, just my first name was enough. Johnnie.

Later that day though, he made up...gave me a middle name. "Mylove," he said. That's what he began to say. "J. M.?" he said after catching my initials when I spoke it to another. And "Johnnie Mylove" is what he began calling me because I refused to tell him anything more.

And he has called me that—every since. Johnnie Mylove. Like my whole name were truly Johnnie...My...Love.

Men...I don't know. He said once that he wished he knew what went on in *our* heads. "We're pretty straight forward," I said. "You men are the ones going to such great lengths to protect yourselves because you're afraid you might end up hurt. We usually just lay ourselves out there and take our chances."

But I did tell him, at the end of that first day, it was best this way. That he go his way and I go mine. I said for him to take all the passion he claimed he felt for me and adorn his wife with it. That's the problem with marriages; people feel all lovey-dovey-got-to-have-you-near-me-every-second-every-minute-or-I will die in the beginning stage, but lose fire soon into the I-gotcha-now-so-what-do-I-do-with-ya? latter stage. Then someone else comes along, fans the smoldering ashes, a fire catches hold only now, with the one who fanned the flames last.

The other thing I said was, when he wasn't feeling so pleasant toward his wife, to remember how he said he wanted to treat me and lay it on *her* instead.

My, my...that was *some* counseling I gave on those sandy white beaches as the waves crescendoed in the background like a symphony I was conducting.

"Is this beach taken?" was what he had said when he first walked up to me.

"No," was all I said back. And from that *No*, came all of this...and more.

 J. M. Taylor's Journal

Under the water, he grabbed my hand, brought it up to his mouth, and kissed it. As we floated separately in huge sun-glow orange inner tubes, he refused to let me out of his sight. More than once, he grabbed both my feet and brought them gently to his mouth—kissing them. My *feet*. He actually kissed my *feet!* But why? What was it about me that would cause him to kiss both tops of my, otherwise, undesirable feet. Like a mother bringing forward her own little one's feet...he did *that* to mine.

"Stay," he said. "Stay the night with me." Over and over, again and again he asked.

"Please don't," I said knowing my answer would not—could not—change.

"I'd like to take you out to dinner. Take you dancing—"

My eyes widened. "Dancing?" My favorite thing in the whole world, and this man...this man who calls me Johnnie Mylove is volunteering to take me?

"Please," he said, "don't make me have to beg." His hazel nut eyes danced in the glow of a full moon. "Because I will."

He was determined to persuade me to stay—with him—the night. I had to get away. But he wouldn't let me out of his sight—not again (that first time after he told me how lovely I was, I slipped away from him); so no...he was determined not to let me out of his sight again. Though I knew sooner or later I'd manage it in... *The Lazy River.*

It was a forked place, and yes...I knew exactly what I was going to do. I pretended to get bumped, then mixed up in the crowd...he went one way; I the other. When I was some distance away, I ran...like a fugitive from the law, I ran. But there were still five days left of my vacation. I knew I would not be able to hide from him forever—providing he hadn't already gone.

The second I saw him with two friends, I felt criminal again...hiding out...watching him as, apparently, he searched for me. All three guys looking for me? They stood at entrances to places as though I might emerge at any time. As the waves beat against the beach's swelled breast, I watched them search the faces of those who bobbed near and around the water.

When the beach was quiet and practically deserted, I felt safe to stroll alongside the cool breeze of the waters. Standing near the edge...close enough for the ocean to nibble at the tips of my toes, I relaxed in the eve of the night.

"Mylove," a deep sexy voice whispered in my right ear. "Where have you been? I've searched all over for you...all the day long."

"Oh I'm sorry. You were looking for me?" I looked and acted surprised.

He grabbed my hand and I felt fire ricochet within me. "Walk with me."

I pulled my hand from his. "No. I don't think that's such a great idea."

"I would never do anything to hurt you," he said. "A little walk—no strings attached." He held his hands out, showing me there were indeed...no strings.

I looked, then turned as though I needed something more than his word.

He smiled, licked his forefinger and held it in the air. "Cross my heart and hope to die," he said as he made a cross on his heart. "I'm George Landris...in case you've forgotten already," he said then waited, I suppose, for my *full* name.

"Only a walk, Mr. Landris?" I said instead, as I found myself smiling back.

"And a little conversation." He looked at me. "*If* you deem it appropriate."

"With no strings attached?"

"No strings." His smile felt like the wet sand squeezing up between my toes...cool, warm and squishy. "I believed I had lost you forever," he whispered. I tried not to smile.

"I thought I was having fun *before* you came, but afterward...your smile lit up this whole island for me. I didn't want to lose you. So me and my two buddies looked all over the place for you. I was just about to leave when I decided to come back...I had to try one more time. When I saw you standing here...I was ecstatic. Please, stay with me tonight. I don't want to let you go."

"But you're going to have to," I said. "Whether it be today or tomorrow; I've already told you...I'm married."

"Then where is he?"

"In Alabama...working," I said. "He's a dedicated worker—my husband."

"He's a fool."

I laughed. "*Excuse* me? You know neither me *nor* my husband."

He stopped walking and looked at me with those piercing brown eyes. "I know that *if* he is *there* instead of *here* with *you*—then he's a fool! There is no way, were you mine, I would ever want you out of my sight for too long. That much, I do know. I would want to be wherever you were every second of the day. And still, I'd wish there were more than twenty-four hours to each day just so we could have even more time to spend together. I do know *that* much."

I started back walking. I did want Solomon to come...so much I did. I asked him over and over, but he...we...don't...do much of anything together anymore. He does his thing and I've had to find something in the meantime to occupy the time.

"Johnnie Mylove, one night. Please. I would be all right if I could just spend one night—just you and I. Dinner...dancing, whatever your heart desires."

I laughed. "Do you really believe a night like that would make it any easier?"

He lowered his head, then back up. "I don't want to let you go just yet. Okay?"

"Trust me, this way *is* best." I should have said for both of us. For both.

"Johnnie Mylove, why won't you tell me your last name?"

"George...Landris—" I did like hearing his name.

"I'd love to visit Alabama and see you some time. Give me a second reason to come...I already have the first. Johnnie."

"Landris, please...just let it go." I meant to say Mister Landris...let it go.

He looked down at me and gathered me up by my shoulders. "How can I?" he said. "I'm sorry, but I can't help myself."

"Now I want *you* to do *me* a favor," I said pulling back. "The next time you're with your wife, treat her to all the things you say you wanted to treat me to. And the next time you get frustrated or upset with her—remember how frustrated and upset you are with me right now. Be as persistent with her, as you've been with me. In that...both you *and* your wife win."

He took my hand and kissed its back. "Johnnie Mylove. If you only knew how much I want you right now." He looked up at the starry night sky. "All right. *You* do two things for *me*."

"What's that?"

"Make sure you tell your husband he is one lucky man." He smiled and shook his head as he bit down on his bottom lip...scanning me from head to toe. "One *lucky* man indeed." He leaned closer. "Just one night to talk more. That's all—talk."

I shook my head.

"Then...may I kiss you on your...cheek?"

I laughed. "No. But we can shake hands...like two new friends would do."

"A hug, too?"

"Promise you'll behave?"

He nodded, shook my hand, hugged me...and the next thing I knew, he had kissed me. And I...

"No strings attached," he whispered. "Veni...Vidi."

"What is that?" I asked feeling as though I were in someone else's dream now.

"Italian," he said with a smile. "It means: I came...I saw."

Pearl Sue Hunter's Journal

Tornado watches and warnings are out all over Alabama. I was working on my income taxes when Honey called to see if I was going to Bible Study. She wants me to meet George, and she thinks he might come to church tonight. I told her I was skipping tonight trying to complete my taxes before next week.

"You, J. M., and y'all's stupid taxes. That's what *she's* doing. If y'all were like me, you wouldn't have so many forms to have to complete," Honey said. "I don't have all y'all's income and deductions to have to fool with."

"Yeah," I said, "and you *still* end up getting more money back than any of us." I laughed. "So...J. M.'s not going to Bible Study either huh? Maybe *you* should sit this one out too. You know, J. M. doesn't miss a Bible Study unless she's out of town. No telling what God's either told her or plans to do since *she* won't be there."

"Now, Sistah—you know you need to quit! J. M. has missed Bible Study before without being out of town, and you know that."

"I know. I was *just* kidding. And I'm sure I'll have another opportunity to meet your new *friend* some other time."

"He is *so* nice. I am serious! So polite...a gentle man...and everything."

"What did J. M. say when you told her about him."

Honey made a puffing sound. "Oh you know how she is— worse than somebody's daddy. You'd think there's not a man alive good enough for me."

"Did you tell her how cute and fine he is?"

"She already knows. Or, at least, she should anyway."

"How?"

"They worked together at one time on something or other. She won't say much about him, but he's all the time asking me about her. I don't think he likes her all that much...based on the things he's said..."

"He talks about her?"

"Just things like how some women want to be in control of everything. And how some women be on power trips," Honey said. "Doesn't call her specifically by name per se...but we all know who he's talking about. He asks questions about her every-now-and-then...nothing major. Even though they worked together, I get the impression he's totally in the dark about her. He's probably curious about what makes her tick."

"Like *most* folks," I said.

"Well, I've gotta run. I need to call George and see what he's planning; then make my way to McDonald's Chapel. You know how Pastor is about folks being to church on time."

"Yeah, and Pastor *will* start if nobody is there but him to start it."

"Yep. Then he'll teach on how the only thing you can truly give God is your worship, and how tacky it is to be slothful in that department of the service."

"Well you take care in this weather now."

"Oh, it won't be about nothing! You know how the weather folks are. Get folks all riled, and it won't turn out to be half of what they predicted," Honey said.

* * *

I called J. M.'s house around nine o'clock as soon as I saw where a tornado had reportedly touched down near Edgewater.

"Have you checked with your folks? The people on the news just said the tornado hit over their way," I asked, when she picked up on the half-ring.

"No," J. M. said with a slight panic in her voice. "I haven't been able to get through. Not to Mama, not Donald or Marie."

Another report was just coming in: *A church has been hit by the tornado in McDonald's Chapel. We don't have any details but we'll get more information to you just as soon as we can. Again...a tornado has touched down in the McDonald's Chapel area...*

"Oh...my...God!" I said.

"*What?*" J. M. said, holding her breath.

"Honey went to church tonight. They just said a church was hit in the McDonald's Chapel area."

"Did they say *which* church?" J. M. said.

"No—they didn't."

"Let me call Rosalyn's house. She may have changed her mind. And if she didn't—her children; I need to check on those children."

J. M. called back in less than five minutes. Honey did go to church. The kids were, shaken, but all right. J. M. still hadn't been able to get in touch with any of her people, so she wasn't sure what had actually happened or whether they were okay.

"I'm going to get Rosalyn's children; they're scared and I don't know what else to do," J. M. said. "Call me on my car phone if you hear anything before I get back. I'm going to keep trying to find out what's happening in Edgewater."

She then began to babble—obviously shaken. "But I'm sure they're okay. I just know they are. I may even drive over there after I pick up Rosalyn's children. I'm sure it wasn't *that* bad. Couldn't be. Not with praying Countess over there. She probably prayed half heaven's angels down; got them working overtime tonight."

"J. M., now I can run get Honey's kids. I'm much closer than you are—"

"No, it's okay. Like I said, I'll probably drive over to Edgewater...since I'll be out anyway. You know."

 J. M. Taylor's Journal

Such devastation from the tornadoes that touched down in Alabama. At least two of them were said to have been Force Five—the strongest grade a tornado can be rated. They figured—by the way the bark was literally stripped from trees—the tornado was moving at 260 mph...at least!

"It looks like a bomb went off," one man said who stopped me from getting anywhere near any of my folks.

Cars were strewn in ravines; they looked like crumbled up colored aluminum cans. Trees were frozen in the midst of falls...like loose teeth held only by a strand.

I had Rosalyn's children with me, and they were terrified... mainly because they weren't sure whether their mother was safe. It took me three hours to find my way out of that maze of ruins. Sirens filled the air. Pearl called on my cell phone and said Rosalyn had gotten home and was almost hysterical. She was grateful to learn her children were safe with me.

I took them back home, but I still hadn't heard a word on the condition of my family surrounded by all this catastrophe.

"Thank you so much J. M.," Rosalyn said as she rushed to the door. "Are y'all all right?" she said, hugging each child tight.

"We saw on TV where a church got destroyed and we were *so* scared," Darryl LeDale said as he clinged to his mother's leg.

"It's okay. I'm all right now." She looked over at me. "Thank you again J. M.! I just don't know what I'd do without you." She hugged me. "We heard the tornado siren just in time. They huddled us into the hallway, and that's where we stayed until it passed over. It sounded like a train outside—it was loud and quick. I hear it tore *up* that church one street over from ours."

"What took you so long to get home?" I asked.

"Trees down all over the roads...we had to find alternative routes out. There weren't any lights—poles were down. You literally had to feel your way out of there. I was shaking so bad...out there by myself...feeling my way home. Thank God, I had a dependable ride and gas in the van for a change."

"And you're safe."

"I heard it hit near your folks' place. Have you talked with them yet?"

I shook my head. "No, and I thought I could get through there but they've called out the National Guard and everything. You can't get anywhere near those areas. The phone lines must be down too, because I haven't been able to get a call through to anybody over that way yet."

"Well I just know everybody's fine. So don't worry none, okay? Call me and let me know when you get word." She hugged the children again, individually; then me good-bye. "Thank you so much for checking on them for me. You are a *true* friend."

I smiled, but my mind was still on Edgewater. Please God...let all be well with them. *Please.*

Solomon Taylor's Journal

Cars looked like toys thrown in a pile. Trees looked like toothpicks. Homes were blown to pieces, some only the foundation marked whose house *might* have been there...once.

The debris on the roads hampered the search and made it harder for survivors to be found. Houses were flattened. The National Guard was called out to keep people from looting; it looked like a crime scene.

Under the cloak of the night all this devastation had been hidden as the twisters rolled and spun. Jumping just some twenty minutes from hitting the downtown area all the way to the other side, to tear up and devastate other communities.

There was an entire house picked up—in tack—and almost sat down on a lake. Blown completely off its foundation, it sat about 100 yards from where it had originally been erected. The death toll kept climbing as now people could see what the night held secret. Several churches were hit, as many were in Mid-week Services, Prayer Meetings, or Bible Study.

Johnnie Mae stayed up all night trying to reach her family. Finally about six o'clock this morning, the phone did ring. Yes!—they were all alive. Her parent's house sustained some damage, but they would be able to stay there when it could be repaired later. Yet with so much damage all over, who knows when *that* might even be. Donald's house was totally demolished, though he and his wife had been spared as they huddled inside a single closet.

"The only thing left standing," Countess had said, "was *that* one closet they huddled inside. An angel's hand was surely holding those walls together. So don't nobody even *try* and tell me there's no God!"

Marie's house had been touched, but they too, only sustained minor damages. Yet so many weren't so fortunate. I always hate when people say the hand of God was on them, especially when so many others do lose *their* lives. I just figure it rains on the just and the unjust. I don't believe in people having a set time to die, but I do believe that things can happen no one can foresee.

A whole family of five did precisely what everyone is told to do in a tornado situation. They went to the basement, but even *that* was not enough for the Force Five tornado. I personally believe an angel was with them too...even though none of the five made it out alive. Lord, who would have imagined all this could have happened in one night. I saw it on the news, rode by some places...and still it's hard for me to comprehend. And to think, some people lost everything—except their lives. *Except* their lives.

"I'm still having Easter Sunday dinner," Countess said. "And I expect to see everybody here too. We got much to be grateful for...a real Passover. We are still having Easter Sunday dinner. The death angel passed over us one more time; we got too much to be thankful for!"

"The ironic thing," Countess told Johnnie Mae, "is the place where that old trunk was...well, it was totally demolished. Thank the Lord we got that trunk to your house when we did."

After Johnnie Mae knew all was well, she laid on the couch and fell fast asleep. She looked so sweet...I couldn't bring myself to disturb her so I just covered her—and let her sleep where she lie.

Shout With A Great Shout

And it shall come to pass, that when they make a long blast with the ram's horn, and when ye hear the sound of the trumpet, all the people shall shout with a great shout; and the wall of the city shall fall down flat, and the people shall ascend up every man straight before him. Joshua 6:5

 J. M. Taylor's Journal

"Green green the crab apple tree. Where the green grass grows tall. Miss Johnnie, Miss Johnnie, your true love is..."

What's the rest of that song? I keep having this dream, but I can't remember what the children say at the end. Why can't I recall the whole song? These children stand in a circle singing *this* song...why can't I remember the rest of what they say?

It's been two weeks since the tornado. Vice President Al Gore came but President Clinton ended up still having to visit. And yet—there were people crying about him not visiting their area. My God, they lose almost everything and they're mad because Gore or Clinton didn't visit them? I just don't know sometime.

Solomon invited company over after church today. "Impromptu," he said. "You'll like this. And I'm picking up something to eat so we can all just hang out."

What could I say? I didn't have to cook; the house was clean. What was there to say? "Who did you invite?" I asked him for a third time.

"You'll see!" was all he said.

So when they arrived (all at the same time), and I walked into the living room where they had gathered; I could not believe what he had done.

"Well now—" I said blinking real fast, "What a...surprise."

"Solomon said he thought it would be nice considering all the stuff that's been going on lately, if we all got together and just hung out," Rosalyn said.

"And I promised not to smoke...in the house anyway," Flick said.

"I think this was a wonderful idea!" Pearl said. "And Pastor *know* he preached today!"

"Oh, oh—" Rosalyn clapped, as she stood next to this tall man...'a refreshing drink of spring water.' "Solomon..." she said looking his way, "and J. M., I know you two already know each other, but I want to introduce my friend just the same. This is my *new* friend—George Landris."

"Good to see you again," Landris said reaching and taking hold my hand.

"Yes," I said fast, almost yanking my hand from him.

"Nice to meet you Solomon," he said smiling. "I've heard so much about you...when I worked with your wife some time back. And, Honey speaks so lovingly of the two of you."

"Well!" I said, now clapping my hands once as I tried to smile. "Solomon was nice enough to do pick up, so all I had to do was situate the food—which I completed prior to your arrival and you all can...pretty much just knock yourselves out!"

Landris looked around the room and then smiled at me. "Lovely home you have here."

I glanced quickly. "Thanks," I said then turned away from his fixed gaze. *His shaved head...all his long ropes—gone.*

"*Very* lovely indeed," he said again, this time burning his eyes totally on me. He turned to Solomon. "You're a fortunate man, Solomon. Very. I hope you don't mind my saying so."

"No—and you won't get any arguments from me. Come on inside Man and make yourself at home. The kitchen's this way. We're going downstairs to the activity room and watch the play-offs on the big screen. Maybe shoot a game of pool."

"Well, if you *think* you're going to stick us off in a room somewhere," Rosalyn said, "while you guys are off watching some kind of basketball game, then you got another *think* coming! I like basketball as much as the next one!" she said.

"Baby, you going to watch?" Flick said to Pearl.

"Sure."

"This should be good," Rosalyn said.

I searched the cabinets. No hot sauce. And everybody seems to want some.

"I'll run to the store and get a bottle," I said.

"Oh please, allow me to take you," Landris said.

"That's okay, it'll only take me a minute."

"Oh but with all the cars, you're blocked in. Please, it's no trouble at all. It's the least I can do to show my appreciation for your gracious hospitality. It certainly would be my pleasure."

I fixed my mouth to object again.

"Johnnie Mae, let him take you," Solomon said. "We're ready to eat! You could have been there and back by now."

So Landris took me to the store. I didn't say much to him the whole way there or back. He must have gone inside before I came out, because when he came around to help me out of the car, he handed me one yellow rose. "For you," he said.

Everybody had fixed their plates, and were already downstairs—fully into the double-header.

After about an hour of sitting there, I leaned over and whispered to Solomon, "I'll be back." I just felt so uneasy in that room; like I could scarcely breathe or sit in the right position. Upstairs, I began to put the food away. I figured I might as well do something constructive.

It wasn't a good ten minutes, before I felt a touch on my hand and jumped.

"You look good enough to eat," the silky voice whispered in my left ear.

I turned and looked in his eyes. "Landris," I whispered as I stumbled away from him. "I didn't hear...I didn't know anyone had come in."

He brought both my hands up to his lips and gently kissed them on the bend. "If you'd like me to leave, I will," he said. "I didn't mean to make you uncomfortable, but I did *so* want to see you. And you haven't exactly cooperated as I had hoped."

I pulled my hands out of his. "Why aren't you downstairs with Rosalyn?" I said casually.

He shooed her name away. "Who, Honey? Please! I know you don't think for one second I'm interested in her. Do you?"

I looked up at him. "Then what *exactly* are you doing?"

"The woman *is* persistent if nothing else. She says it's okay if we're just friends; she already knows my heart belongs to... another."

"Did you—"

He laughed and grabbed my hand back and kissed it again. "No, I haven't said a word."

I relaxed. "Don't you hurt her, you hear? She's known too many jerks already in her lifetime; she doesn't need you messing around too."

"Look. I've told her I'm not interested in pursuing a relationship with her...I have things I'm trying to work out."

He pulled me up to him and looked as if he were about to kiss me on my lips. I pulled back. "Landris...please don't—"

"Say you'll meet me later...come to my place. You remember where?"

I started putting things in the refrigerator. "No, I don't think—"

He grabbed the bowl and my hand and was just about to pull me closer to him when the kitchen door swung open hard.

"Well, well, well. Ain't this a cozy little sight!"

"Thank you," I said to Landris, "I don't know what caused me to almost slip."

Landris came in right on cue. "I don't *see* anything on the floor that might have done it. I guess it must be your shoes. You just need to be more careful."

"I came for a wine cooler," Flick said grinning, "and a smoke...outside...on the deck. You know J. M.—can't smoke in *your* house. And looks like I might owe you an apology."

"For what?" I said wondering what he was up to today. The day I took Pearl that diamond necklace, Flick tried to push up on me. She wasn't home, and he was awful.

"Oh," he said puckering up his lips at me as he scanned my body up and down, "seems I may have misjudged you *after* all." He smacked, smiled, then left.

"*Now* look what you've done!" I said to Landris.

"Who him? He's a jerk if I ever saw one! And the way he looks at you...I'd watch myself around him if I were you."

Landris stepped back from me. "Come see me tonight. I've got something I want to show you."

"What?"

"Come see."

"I couldn't come tonight anyway."

"Okay, then when?"

"I don't know," I said.

He took out a business card and flicked it taunt in his hand. "Here's my car phone number—just in case. When you decide, call me. You promise?"

I smiled, afraid someone else might come in at any minute. *Say yes and he'll go on back downstairs.* "Sure...okay," I said reaching to take the card. But instead, he gently pushed it down inside my bra and kissed me lightly, delicately, and quick on my lips.

Thank God after that, he went back downstairs. And I could finally breathe a sigh of relief. Or a sigh of *something.*

Rosalyn Benefield's Journal

I really think George enjoyed himself today. I don't know
what it is, but he and J. M.—there's something deep going on
between those two. It must have been difficult for them to work
together.

George keeps telling me he's not interested in anything too
heavy with me. I told him that was cool, but I know he's just
saying that. It's evident the man wants me. Why he's trying to
fight his feelings for me, I'll never understand. But then—I
don't understand the way men think anyway.

I asked George if he wanted to stay over a while, but he
said he had to get home. He was hoping for an important call
tonight. I told him I didn't mind going to his place...

"I'd love to see where you live anyway," I said.

"Oh it's nothing grand; just a simple little place. You'd
probably see it and begin to feel sorry for me or something."

I placed my hand on his. "I'd never do that."

He slid his hand away carefully from mine. "I'm not all
that hot about having certain females come there. It's just my
own space. You know?"

"I can understand that. But maybe...one day you'll change
your mind."

"You plan to see to *that*, I'm sure."

"Oh, of course!"

"As long as you understand..."

"I understand that you're not leading me on...that you and
I are friends."

"Good," he said as he kissed me on my cheek. "I'll holler
at you later."

"Sure George. And thanks for deciding to come go with me on such short notice. When Solomon asked, and I learned Sister and Flick were coming—"

"That's Pearl right? I heard J. M. call her Pearl."

"Yes, Sistah is Pearl. She likes being called *Sister* though. Anyway, when I found out she was coming *and* Flick too; well, I just didn't want to be the only one there without *somebody.* You know, always the spare tire in the trunk."

"It was no problem. I rather enjoyed myself."

"You're not just saying that are you? I mean...I saw the way you and J. M. were together."

He cocked his head to the side. "What do you mean by *me* and *J. M.?*"

I sighed. "George, it's really not a secret you know."

" *What's,* not a secret?"

"You and J. M.—you don't really click so well. That's the impression I get. Like the two of you don't care for each other."

He smiled and licked both lips before making a smacking sound. "I have nothing against...J. M. She just needs to loosen up a bit. Just my opinion of course. But Solomon appears to be happy with her—my impression anyway."

He said it like he was asking a question so I said, "I *think* they're pretty happy. And even if she *was* having problems or *wasn't* happy, she most likely wouldn't let anybody know it."

"I kind of felt she was one who liked keeping to herself. Oh well, maybe she'll find what she's searching for...or know it when she *does* find it. I do admire her work." He smiled. "I think I might contract her services again...for A Upper Hand."

"You're amazing," I said. "Do you know that?"

"How so?"

"You just look past your own feelings about things; you're just so professional and everything. I do love that about you." He opened the door to leave. "Again, thank you so much for going with me..." I walked alongside him. "...to their house."

"If you ever need an escort to visit with them again—just let me know. I must say, I truly did enjoy myself."

He is so fine! I think I'm in love. I just wish he'd wake up and see we could make some beautiful music together...if he'd let go of whomever he's still carrying that old *tired* torch for.

Honey and George. Honey Landris. Rosalyn Landris. Mrs. George Landris. Oooh I like the sound of that!

Oh, and Flick was so nice to me today. He said he heard all about the deal with Oprah and the book club.

"I never *did* like Oprah," Flick said.

It's something with how supportive everyone's been about the Oprah letdown. But it doesn't really bother me. I tried—I didn't make it. That's life, right? You fall off, you get back on. And I still love me some Oprah now! I don't care how much I looked like an idiot afterward when I didn't get picked. Next time, I'll just keep my little phone calls from her show...to myself.

Wonderful day today. An absolutely *wonderful* day! Thank you God for a possible HIM!

 J. M. Taylor's Journal

Landris called me at my office early this morning. The company where he's now Operations Manager (A Upper Hand, Incorporated), contracted me again, and he was calling to confirm our appointment. Or should I say, calling to see if we could change a few things.

"I'm sorry to have to do this on such short notice, but the President of the company is happening in today. He learned you were scheduled to give the presentation and—having heard so much about you—he wants to meet you," Landris said.

"He wants to meet *me?* But why?"

"I probably shouldn't be telling you this but, apparently he did some checking up on you *and* your company...and he's—let me see...how do I put it—highly impressed? That's what he told my boss. But I believe he has a position in the company he would like to talk with you about filling. He wants to see you in action, firsthand. And the only reason I just happen to know all of this, is because no one realizes the true nature of our relationship."

"Landris, how many times must I tell you—"

"I know. I've heard you. And, honestly...there's no sense in repeating it again today."

"You hear me, but you don't seem to understand as well as you hear."

He laughed. "Oh I understand better than you think. I would also venture to say, I believe I know and understand *you* better than anyone on this earth—including your little hubby."

I started to ask, how so, but this was business and I wanted to keep it as such. "So, what time were you thinking of changing it to?"

"Mr. Bijur is due to arrive here from our office in Atlanta around one this afternoon. I was thinking of three o'clock. That would give him time to get here...get squared—"

I flipped my calendar fully aware there was a conflict. "I have something scheduled for four already. There's no way I could do all I have to do in an hour."

"Johnnie My...Johnnie, this is big. Can't you reschedule your four o'clock? Look—even if you're not interested in his job proposal, the man is connected all over the U.S. Just consider the impact he could have on your own company...by word of mouth...of your unique talent." He paused, like he was reading my temperature on a glass thermometer. "This could be big...I'm telling you. I know you; I know how important this might be for you."

I thumped the head of my mechanical pencil on my desk several times.

"Hey," Landris said, "but it's your call." He paused. "As usual," he added.

"Okay. I'll reschedule my four. The president, huh?"

I heard the smile in his voice. "Girl...you stomping with the big dogs now."

I cracked a smile too. "Cut it out, will you!" I teased.

"You like this—don't you?" He didn't even wait for my *yes* answer. "Now aren't you glad we hooked up again? I keep telling you...I'm good for you. I'm always doing things for your own good."

"Yeah...right. If I recall correctly, that's what my mother used to say when she was whipping my butt. 'I'm only doing this for your own good.' "

"Oooh—Johnnie Mylove," he said with a long breath, "now don't get me started. It's going to be hard enough watching you do your wonderful presentation today—and I know it's going to be wonderful—but it will be even harder if you get me stirred up in advance. I'll be just like a volcano, ready to—"

"Is there anything else about the meeting today I should know?" I said.

"Yeah—I hope you're wearing red. You always look hot and powerful in red."

I smiled. "Anything *else?*"

"Yes. It is possible this meeting may cross over now; we may end up being much later than you think. I've met with Mr. Bijur before...you probably should call the hubby and let him know—so he won't be *too* worried about you."

"Cross over? What do you mean cross over?"

"I mean...Mr. Bijur might want to take the meeting into a late supper. He likes good food and it's nothing for him to think everyone else is at his beckoning disposal—no other life. Now *you* know how some of these execs can be."

I held the phone. That much, I did know. Some of them visited places on the pretense of business while mixing too much fun on the side. Like this one exec I knew who felt the dog track was the perfect place for him to conduct company business. Said it got his juices flowing. Yeah, got his juices flowing all right; I ended up winning ten dollars and losing twenty. And twenty was my limit!

"Jay?" Landris said, sounding much like my father. "What's wrong?"

"Oh nothing. And don't worry about me; I'm a professional. I'm aware meetings bleed into my own time, at times. It's not a problem for me."

"Great! Then we're all set? I sort of told my boss, when he called in a panic after he got the call the President was making this unexpected visit, that you'd work with us. We owe you... big time."

"Sure. Oh and don't worry, you'll *all* get my bill. I'll see you at *two* then?"

Landris laughed. "Two? Always the perfectionist I see. Get there early and give things your best. That's one of the things I love about you."

"Well thank you—"

"One of many things—"

"The meeting's still in Conference Room C?"

"No. As a matter-of-fact, we had to change it. Seems the President's announced attendance has sparked more than a few former declines begging for inclusion. So now it's Conference Room A. And before you ask, yes the computer and projector are already set up *and* waiting for you to test upon your early arrival."

"Thanks," I said wondering if I was really *that* bad. "Then I'll see you...at two."

I hung up and smiled, spinning myself around in my high-back executive chair. I then went to the closet door where a full length mirror hung, and played with my hair long enough to ensure it was set. I tugged and straightened the new suit I had bought especially for today. A new *red* suit, although this one did fit me a bit tighter than my usual seven/eights. I suppose they must have cut this one a little smaller than normal.

"Great!" I said to the image in the mirror. "You knock 'em dead, girl! They'll never know what hit them!"

Solomon Taylor's Journal

Johnnie Mae works almost as much as I used to—years ago. Seems like when I finally got the revelation that this wasn't great for a budding relationship almost falling apart, she picked up where I seemed to have stopped.

I would be so busy back then, I would hardly take time off to go on vacation with her. No matter how much she pleaded or begged, got mad or cried; I didn't budge. I've never been one who cared for traveling to other or exotic places. I'd rather hang around the house any day than visit some island or whatever hit Johnnie Mae's fancy at the time.

Most of my vacation time, would be centered around Mudear and what she might need done. Johnnie Mae finally came around and left me alone about it. She learned to go on vacation by herself, and things really worked out well.

We both had what we wanted—I think. Except now, she works harder than *I* think she ought. I would consider taking off a few days to vacation with her—nothing long—but a few days, would be all right.

"You're just not romantic!" Johnnie Mae had said once when we were discussing something (I don't even remember what it was).

"Who needs romance...we're married now," I said.

"Solomon...oh, just forget it! Why keep banging my head against a brick wall?! I try and tell you what I need while you keep telling me what I don't. Now what's wrong with *this* picture? I...*want*...romance! I...*need*...romance! I want you to hear me Solomon. I would like for you to truly respect me and what I'm attempting to do—"

"I respect you," I said. "Are you saying that I don't?"

"You see? Do you see? Now that's exactly what I'm talking about. I said more than just respect, but all you seem to have heard was that one thing!"

"I heard you Johnnie Mae. And I love you."

She sighed. "Yeah. I know you do."

So I don't understand our problem. Why is it that she and I never seem to be in the same place at the same time?

Maybe it's just a woman thing. Maybe men aren't suppose to understand. Because even when we try, women just seem to change the rules; ensuring that we don't get it. Sister tells me that's not how it is with women at all.

"It's you men who don't seem to even want to get it!"

Well I'm trying. Although it would help if women didn't make it so much like...a full-time job with mandatory overtime.

Johnnie Mae asked if I'd like to go see a movie on Friday.

"Friday? Not really," I said.

"Then what about dinner or maybe dancing? Something."

"Johnnie Mae, I'd really much rather stay in. You see, there's this play-off game on Friday night. But we could rent a video, order something in, put a few golden melodies on the CD player—just the two of us. We could be real romantic, right after the game," I said. I smiled, using my most romantic game face, opting to put on hold any suggestions regarding a practice session for that baby we've been putting off forever.

"Fine," she said gravely. "Fine. Just forget I even brought it up. I'm sure I'll find something to do. Maybe work on a few proposals. I have some unfinished business that needs my attention anyway."

 J. M. Taylor's Journal

My presentation today went well. Mr. Bijur shook my hand firm upon our greeting and grinned as though we were mere reacquaintances as opposed to meeting for the first time. After the presentation, he came and shook my hand again.

"That was something!" Mr. Bijur said, glancing occasionally at Landris and smiling.

Landris was right about things going over. Mr. Bijur insisted a select few of us continue the discussion of my ideas and suggestions over supper; and of course, we dined at the most upscale establishment in town.

After supper, Mr. Bijur approached me about possibly discussing other opportunities within his company. He gave me his card with his direct number and asked me to call in the next few days to set up a date and time convenient for both our busy schedules. Meaning, he'd either fly back here or I'd have to fly to Chicago since that's where his office is located.

Landris smiled as we stood talking in the parking lot. "Woman, you showed up and showed out!" he said. "All day and all night long! You had them eating out of the palm of your hands!" He smiled. "Even *I* didn't realize you had all *that* hidden in that little body of yours!"

He looked down at me and smiled, locking me with his eyes...oh God his eyes...they seemed to call my name. I tried turning away, but he gently touched my chin and softly kept me in the embrace of those eyes. "I just love your mind," he said.

I smiled. "Well that's a first for me," I said. "No one's ever fallen in love with my mind before."

He licked his lips, like...like somebody eating something good or else they want you to think it's good just so you'll want some too. That's how he licked his lips. "You still haven't come to see what I told you I wanted to show you."

"Landris, I just don't think that would be wise—"

"Why so? You already know I'll never make you do anything you don't truly want to do. I know you know *that*."

"What's going on with you and Rosalyn?"

"What is this with me and Honey again?" he said, like he couldn't believe I had the nerve to bring her name up right now...at this moment. "Shoot! I already told Honey there's nothing going on...happening...*going* to happen—between me and her. I like her as a person...she's lots of laughs—but she knows my heart will never belong to her."

"But I—"

"What? Thought she and I have a thing going on? That's what she'd like to believe, but you of all people know how I like my women." His eyes began traveling the length and breadth of my body as he leaned back breathing me all in. He shook his head and said, "Oomph, oomph, oomph. Have mercy." Then he sighed long, loud and heavy.

"I told Honey, she's a little fat—kind of like on the chubby side—for *me* any way. That first day when she insisted upon 'thanking' me, before she called that next day suggesting we catch a movie on Friday," he said. "The girl's face was beat looking too. Mascara was smeared all over her face since she'd been crying, I suppose because she got the loan...thanks to you actually. But she looked like a piece of paper someone had scratched up with a black marker and dripped water on."

I put my hand on my hips—an automatic response really. "What?" I said.

He continued. "And that tiny 'fro of hers was all out of shape that day. I teased her about it...told her *it* was beat as well...all matted down in spots. Probably happened when she mashed the sides of her head together while screaming, 'Thank you Jesus!' I thought—if God didn't hear *that,* then He doesn't hear anybody!"

"Landris...you didn't. You didn't say that to her."

"When I told her she was sort of fat, and her face and hair were beat...she acted like I had paid her the highest compliment. Surprising, she was quite receptive about it." He took my hand and started to swing it. "Johnnie Mylove...now you know me; you know how straight I am with folks. I don't play games. And that's the way I like folks to treat me. But like I told her and I just told you, she's lots of fun. Just not the woman for me." He licked his lips. "You of all people, know what I want."

"And you, of all people, also know...you don't always get what you want."

"And *you*...also know...I'm not one to give up so easily either." He was still holding my hand and now softly caressing its back with his thumb. "Not when I *really* want something."

I tried to pull my hand away. "Landris, I really must be going. I've been gone all day, and I'm really kind of tired. But I do want to thank you for everything."

"Then why not thank me properly. Come to my place. Just for a little while. We can sit back...kick off our shoes...unwind, have a nightcap...if you like. Come, stay fifteen minutes and after that; you can leave if you want."

"Not tonight. I really need to get home. I've got a lot to do tomorrow."

"Okay, then...tomorrow is Friday; I'll agree to drop tonight if you'll agree to meet me tomorrow night. There's this Christian nightclub in 5 Points West called Zamirs (pronounced Zimirs). Why not meet me on neutral territory."

"A *Christian* nightclub?"

He smiled. "Yes. I hear it's a nice place...a wonderful relaxing atmosphere. This I've heard from some who've been there before, of course."

"*You* at a Christian nightclub? You? George Landris?...at a Christian *anything?*" I smiled and cocked my head to one side.

"Yes!" he said, first tapping my nose with his index finger, then he smiled like a shy little boy.

"So you're telling me...*you* would meet *me* at a Christian nightclub...tomorrow night, if I will say *Yes?*" I bit down on my bottom lip and held it a few seconds. "Maybe," I said as I wrenched my mouth. "I mean...I'll have to let you know later. Solomon and I might have plans or something for tomorrow night. So...we'll see."

Why I didn't just say *no* I'll never understand. Instead, I left him with a pretty solid...*maybe.*

I asked Solomon about going out tomorrow night. Begged him, actually.

"Friday night?" he had said.

In a nutshell...he'd much rather spend his night at home with...the TV.

Pearl Sue Hunter's Journal

I called Honey to see what she had planned for Friday night. Neither of us, it turns out, had anything to look forward to.

"What's with your new man? The one with the J-O-B?" I said.

"Who, George?" Honey said. "He's not really *my* man; we're more like friends."

"Oh—friends, huh? So what's the scoop on this one?"

"No scoop. We're fine. It's just...he's—he's somewhere else other than where I am right now. So friends is...good."

"I don't suppose you have anything planned for tomorrow night either then?" I said.

"Not one single bless-ed thing. What you got?"

"How about a nightclub—"

"Sistah! Girl, you've finally seen the light I see."

"Hold up...this is a Christian nightclub—you know me."

"Yeah, I know you. Shoot! Well...I'm gamed. But I still can't picture you going to a nightclub."

"A *Christian* nightclub."

"Do they play church music or what?" Honey said.

"Contemporary gospel...by a live jazz band. Virgin drinks. Dinner if you like. It's just a real nice place. I went last month to this ball they sponsored, you remember. I really enjoyed myself. It's a serene kind of atmosphere...something for the older generation to do to get out."

"Look, I said I'd go. So do you want me to pick you up?"

I laughed. "*You* pick *me* up? Yeah, that will be nice. Why don't you pick *me* up."

"Want to see if J. M. would like to go?" Honey asked.

I thought a second. "She's been working late these few weeks; she probably won't feel up to it."

"Yeah, you're right. I haven't talked to her since that Sunday we were over there last. Wasn't that fun!"

"It was. She's been so busy *lately,* she hasn't even had time to review any of my stories. Maybe after she slows down a bit, we'll go again."

Honey and I decided—since we didn't want to appear *too* needy, arriving *too* early—that eight was a good time.

"So I'll pick you up around seven-thirty?" Honey said.

Great! Friday night...Honey and I...Zamirs!

Solomon Taylor's Journal

Johnnie Mae called today from work. Said she was going to work late tonight...at the office.

"On a Friday night?" I said.

"Why not? You don't have any other plans—do you?"

"Other than the game, we could watch a video if you want," I said pausing to see if the proposition appealed to her yet. She was silent. "Johnnie Mae, are you all right?"

It sounded like she almost sighed. "Yeah," she whispered, "fine. Just...fine."

"Okay. Then I'll see you when you get home?"

"Solomon?"

"Yes?"

"I...may...catch a movie or something...later. Might even grab a bite to eat while I'm out. I might be late getting in."

"After all you said you ate last night?" I laughed. "Sure. That's fine. Now don't worry about me; I'll order a pizza or some Chinese. Oh—and Johnnie Mae?"

"Yes."

"Call me when you get ready to leave the office...so I'll know you left okay."

Again, it sounded like she sighed. "Sure. All right."

"Johnnie Mae?" It sounded like she gasped for breath. "I love you," I said. I hoped she knew how much.

She laughed a short laugh. "Yeah," she said, "I know. Yes, I know."

She called about seven-thirty saying she was leaving and had decided to meet up with a friend. She'd be late getting in.

"A friend, huh? Who? Sister? Rosalyn?"

"No."

"Oh, so you *do* have other friends? I thought maybe you did." I paused. "Well enjoy yourself. Better them...than me."

Thank you God! She has someone *else* she can drag to these places...other than myself!

Rosalyn Benefield's Journal

Hell yeah, it was a shock...what I saw! And hell *no*, I couldn't believe it! But there she was right there. Wasn't something I heard through some damn grapevine either; I saw this myself! But J. M.? *No*, I still find it hard to believe! Yet, I saw it with my own two eyes!

"Honey?" George said with a slight frown scrawled across his face. "What are you doing here?"

I smiled. "Sistah and I didn't have any big weekend plans so she suggested we visit this Christian nightclub. And you *know* me!" I said, patting my hair, hoping it hadn't mashed down...too bad, anyway.

"All right...so you and Sister decided to go out. That's nice. But still...my question is—what are you doing *here?*" He pointed at the floor.

My eyes followed his finger and began to work their way up...noting first his gorgeous black spit-shined shoes, shined to a *'T'* as always; then upward to the black pants he sported... perfectly pressed, razor sharp creases, pleats near his waist...his powerful waist belted tight, pressing firmly the silk, slick white shirt tucked solidly in his pants and against his divine physique. God! if only I could trade places with that shirt tonight! I worked my way up to his chiseled, freshly shaved face and head (those gorgeous ropes gone now, although roped or shaved, he looked good!). Our eyes met, he was staring at me now. I laughed and attempted to clear my head.

He just stood there with his door partially opened. "Well, aren't you going to invite me in?" I said. He opened the door wider and stepped back—allowing me entrance into a light and spacious area. Oooh *such* a cute be-hind! I thought as I glanced over briefly.

"Only for a moment," he said. "I'm expecting company in about fifteen minutes; in fact, I thought you were...they."

"Oh I apologize. But who arrives to a place *early* anyhow?"

"This person, generally does."

"Well I didn't mean to interrupt. I just wanted to check out where you hang out. And besides, it's been awhile since we've actually sat down and...chatted—"

"Honey—"

"I know you said you didn't care for ladies coming to your place, but it's *so* nice. And I got your address from the phone book." I scanned the place—clean, orderly, appropriate. "I love this. I could come here and simply *never* leave."

He glanced at his watch. "Listen, I really don't want to be rude, but as I said...I'm expecting company any minute now."

"Yes...right. Would you mind if I used your little men's room? I *really* have to go," I said. "It'll only take a minute—I promise. Then I'll be out of your hair." I twitched as I glided toward him. (I really wanted to checkout more of his wonderful home since he seems determined to keep it all to himself. Him and—of course—the little hoochie-mama he must be afraid I'll run into.)

He let out a sigh and pointed—obviously somewhat ticked I had even managed to find my way this far inside his little fortress. "It's down the hall; to your left."

I twitched and switched more, allowing him a grander view of my staples and wares from behind (giving him a taste of *what* he's *really* missing). "No peeping or listening in at the door now," I said smiling, effectively halting his following me.

Locating the bathroom was easy, but snooping into rooms while watching out for him, was a bit more tricky. I hurried, finally finding what *had* to be *his* bedroom. There—stretched a king-size bed, an old-fashioned dresser, a baby blue sofa looking deal without a back (only arms, a seat, and four legs) that matched the width of the bed it nestled against. And all this time, I pictured him as some helpless bachelor, buried beneath clothes, dirt a foot high, and dust the size of bunnies. One who wouldn't recognize a home-cooked meal if it came and bit him on those luscious lips of his.

But like the rest of the house, the room was immaculate. Positively spotless! I've never met a guy who kept a house clean. *That,* was just about the time I happened to glance up and could not believe my eyes. J. M.?

"I see you found it all right," George said, causing my whole body to jump as he pulled the bedroom door shut.

"Huh? What?" I said trying to be sure what I had just seen.

He gestured with his head while holding fast the knob. "The bathroom, I see you found it okay."

"Oh...yeah. The bathroom. Yes I did...and thank you so much. Whew! Boy, was that ever a relief."

"Great, then if you don't mind..." He grabbed me by my left elbow and lead me back down the hallway.

"I apologize for any inconvenience I may have caused stopping by like this," I said, trying to steady myself on two blocks a woman at the store had sold me on the pretense of them being shoes, as I was officially being escorted out. "George, when I happened by your bedroom...was that J. M. I just saw? J. M. Taylor?"

"*J. M. Taylor?*" he said, halting to grin as though to make fun of me.

"Yes. That woman; I'd swear that was J. M. I just saw."

"Now what would *I* possibly be doing with...J. M. Taylor?" He smiled. We had reached the front door, and he cheerfully held it opened. "Well Honey, it—"

"So I suppose you want me to believe that woman only *looks* like J. M.? Same hair, same facial expression—in fact, the very same face?"

He smiled and started to close the door while almost shoving me out of it. "I'll be talking with you Honey," he said. "Now you make sure you drive safely."

"George?" I said putting my hand up to the door, denying it to shut totally in my face at that moment. "Then who was it?"

He started shaking his head then pinched the narrow part of his nose. "Well now, let's see. I *could* tell you it's none of your business, but why don't I just say good night—instead."

He smiled, though apparently not for me. I could see it all now; it wasn't even about me. He had to be smiling about *her!* I know he was.

"Good night," I said stumbling away as he promptly closed the door—almost before I was safely out of its path.

Well I know what I saw. And that *was* J. M., in living *damn* color! It was J. M. all right; I'm sure of that much! Just as sure as my name is Honey (hell!...all right then, Rosalyn!).

 J. M. Taylor's Journal

Rosalyn called really upset. She was talking strange and horrible at the same time. Solomon told me she had called twice before I got in last night.

"Rosalyn was anxious to talk to you," Solomon had mumbled barely waking from his slumber (probably doesn't even remember telling me). "She called...twice...after I had fallen asleep." He yawned.

I wonder why she's so hot and heavy to talk to me. What's so urgent, it would cause her to call twice...so late?

I didn't have long to wonder; she called early (six-o-five to be exact!)—waking me dead out of some much needed sleep.

"J. M.—I don't believe you!"

"Rosalyn? What's wrong? Do you have any idea what day or what time it is?" I said, having told my friends a long time ago not to call my house on weekends ever before eight unless it was a matter of life or death.

"I don't give a damn *what* time it is! I haven't slept all night, so your ass can certainly wake up and hear what the hell I got to say, heifer!"

Oh no...she...didn't! "Look, you're not going to call here talking that way to *me*...not me—"

"What's the *real* deal between you and George Landris?"

"*What?*" I said sliding out of the covers...quickly gliding my feet inside a pair of fuzzy slippers.

"Heifer, you heard me!" she said.

I looked down at Solomon who had only stirred enough to reposition his body. "Just hold on a minute," I whispered as I tip-toed out of the room.

"You'd better not hang up on me—" Rosalyn said as I reached the kitchen...finally.

"Now what is your problem?" I said.

"Problem? It seems *you're* my problem, damn you! You see, I went over to George's place last night. Yeah...that's right! Uh-huh. After Sistah and I left Zamirs, I dropped her off at home and decided to see what George's little hide-a-way looked like...surprised him...stopped by *unannounced.*"

"Yeah?" I said, wiggling to get better situated on the bar stool. "*So?*"

"So? *So?!* So hell! Would you like to know what I happened to see all *dolled* up in his bedroom?"

"Frankly Rosalyn, I really don't care what you saw—"

"Well you'd better care!"

I sighed, tired of this tit-for-tat charade she was in charge of. "Rosalyn...*what* are you talking about? Will you please make sense for once in your life?"

"You, J. M.! I saw you damnit! All right?! You satisfied?"

"You saw m*e?*"

"Yes, you! And before you try weaseling your ass out of it like old slick George, save your breath. Sitting there...all innocent...in some cheap *virgin* negligée—"

"*Cheap?*" I said, "Negligée? Rosalyn, *what* are *you* talking about?!!!" I was seriously contemplating hanging up on her right about now. "Are you experimenting with drugs or something? *You,* of all people, should know that mess will fry your brain cells."

"No I ain't using no *damn* drugs! You the one tripping!" Rosalyn said.

I didn't doubt she was upset...but her cursing was starting to wear on my nerves. It's been a while since I've heard her roll off words and phrases like this. She's been doing so well.

"Rosalyn, look—I don't know just what you saw...or *think* you saw...but you didn't see me."

"So now I'm crazy too, huh? My eyes are playing tricks on me? Oh it was you, J. M. all right! In living color...it was you!"

"At *George's* place? Last night?" I laughed. "Rosalyn, why don't we talk about this a little later? After you've calmed down a bit. You're not making any sense. Give the light of day time to settle in...I'll come over so we can talk calmly and rationally—face to face."

"What's there to talk about? Why didn't you just tell me you and George had a thing going on. I'm a big girl. Obviously, I'm even bigger than I thought. But clue me in on one thing. Is this why I ended up getting the loan? Did you arrange that for me J. M.? What did it cost you? Or was *that* one for services already rendered? Tell me J. M.—did you? Are you the reason my loan got approved?"

"As a matter of fact—yes I was!" I said it before I could even stop myself.

Rosalyn was quiet.

"Will you just let me explain—"

"Explain what? What's to explain? I'm the one who made a complete fool of herself. Thinking a guy like George Landris? might possibly be interested in somebody like me? I bet the two of you have had great laughs about this. At my expense."

"And just why wouldn't a guy like him be interested in somebody like you? Rosalyn...you've got a lot going for yourself. Beauty...smarts...you're talented—"

"Yeah, but you know what J. M.?...I'm *just* not you."

I laughed. "And you should thank God you're not, too."

"Why? You have it all. Solomon, a job you love, a wonderful home...even George." She started a laugh unquestionably on the verge of a cry. "How fair is *this*? I can't get *one* decent man to look at me long, and you've got...at least two!"

"Rosalyn, let's talk about this...over a cup of coffee...tea maybe—"

"J. M., what's to talk about? I don't really know what I should have expected you to do. I was the idiot—flinging myself at him like that. What do I expect you to have said? *Oh Rosalyn, I'm so sorry...but you can't possibly talk to George.*

You see, George and I had/have/might have this thing going on." She laughed. "I don't even know which one it is! No J. M., you couldn't have possibly come out and said anything like that to me. Could you? You couldn't tell *that* to anyone. That's the part of your world you keep locked tightly away from the rest of the general population. You can't even tell your friends something like that...not *your* friends. Can't share anything *that* deep, can you? How am I doing so far J. M.?"

I rubbed my temple, catching each and every word she had hurled my way.

Then Rosalyn laughed. "Yeah...I understand what's going on. You want to have your cake and eat it too! You're right J. M.! I *wouldn't* want to be you!"

The next thing I heard was the dial tone, then the honking sound alerting me the phone was still off the hook. I snapped back and clicked the off button of the phone.

Solomon stumbled into the kitchen rubbing his head. "Johnnie Mae?" he said. "Who was that calling this early in the morning? Johnnie Mae? Is something wrong?"

I looked up at him and couldn't help but wonder...what *was* going on in my life?

Countess W. Gates' Journal

"Go down Moses, way down in Egypt's land," I sang loud while straightening Johnnie Mae's kitchen back. I had no intentions of even coming here today; but as things turned out, it appears this is exactly where I was supposed...was meant to be.

Mr. Gates was the one who insisted we had to go to Coffee, Alabama—today of all days.

"We have to go to Johnnie Mae's *today*," he said.

He had bought plants for her and maintained we had to take them up *this* weekend. I told him I had plans—big plans (the church's annual bazaar which he knows I've not missed since they began it thirty years ago) was today. He smiled and said it was okay.

"I'll just drive myself there then," he said.

"You'll do *what?*" I almost laughed. "Drive yourself? Do you realize how long it's been since you've even *sat* behind the steering wheel of a car let alone mashed the pedals?"

"Been ages since I rode a bike too, but I believe I can still manage it just fine," he said.

"Well go on then. This I've got to see myself." I knew he would cower to my bluff. "Now Mr. Gates, I'll be happy to drive you up next week; next week is a better day for me. That would just be May the second. Next Saturday."

"Too far off. I got to get these to her now. She needs to have them, at least in the ground, today." He held up several individually wrapped packages.

"They already look dead," I said. "They can't get no deader than dead. Those there look like a bunch of sticks. And you know already what I'm going to say about those tumbleweeds you have in the other bags."

He shrugged, then shook his head. "Now Mama, you know I usually try not to bother you. I've always been pretty independent. I tell you a long time ago—you cook my food and leave it on the stove; I can fix my plate myself. I tell you—you wash, iron and put my clothes up; I can pick out what I want to wear...I know what color I like. But I tell you today, I got to carry these plants to my little Jay. Blue Jay needs help being O'Jay again. I *got* to go today. These plants gonna help her see; she still don't quite see yet. I got to help her, I got to." He walked over to the door. "You see Mama—one plants...one waters... but only *God* gives the increase. But there must be some planting done first."

"You talking about the plants—or Johnnie Mae?"

"One in the same...they one in the same," he said.

"Well," I said, "both will keep another week. I'll carry you bright and early *next* Saturday—May the second. And if you could hold off until the week after, she'll be here for Mother's Day. You know she always comes down on Mother's Day." I watched him as he situated plants in the crook of one arm, while holding the others with the hand of the other. "Mr. Gates, it's a long drive up there, even when I drive fifty."

"Won't keep I tell you." He looked serious at me. "Mama, I got to go today."

"Okay, next week. I promise, bright and early. Probably get there too early for her, just as long as it's not before eight. To-day she might not even be in town—"

"She in town." He grabbed the car key from the hook next to the door. "I'll run these up to her and plant them. I'll be fine...it's just like riding a bike."

So I ended up missing the bazaar for the first time ever to drive him to Coffee. I'm sure he might have been all right...but I didn't want to be worried the whole time. Not with him having to drive so far...not with his coughing spells, and especially, not with the way I believe he mind travels sometime. I don't care what he told Johnnie Mae to tell me. What if I'm right...and he forgets where he was going? He could be wandering around God-knows-where! And there are far too many crazies out there...no telling what somebody might do to him if they find him in a wrong state of mind. I couldn't look myself in the eyes if something were to happen to him when I could have taken him. So when he took the key, I knew he had effectively called my bluff. Old man! Picked a fine time to decide to do it!

I was right; we should have called and let them know we were coming. But Mr. Gates was fit to be tied for us to get down the road. When we arrived, Johnnie Mae wasn't even home. Sol was there, but it appears we slipped up on him and Johnnie Mae's friend—Sister is what she prefers being called.

Yeah, both of them there...alone. Mr. Gates waited awhile, but then he asked Solomon for a pick and shovel. Solomon smiled and volunteered his help. Mr. Gates took his bags of sticks and tumbleweeds, and shuffled in the lead of Sol right on outside. Seems Johnnie Mae had bought ten flats of flowers she was intending to set out, so of course Mr. Gates was now in hog heaven! Pick, shovel, hoe, plant...piddle, piddle, pat.

"We'll just knock these out *too* while we're at it," I heard Mr. Gates say to Solomon when I took a notion to peep out there on them.

It was taking Johnnie Mae so long to come home, I decided to fix lunch. I have medication to take, seeing as I'm diabetic now. And Mr. Gates would likely be starving after working himself up an appetite out there in that blazing sun.

Sister and I had a nice little chat. She was telling me all about her plans to become this famous author one day soon. I smiled, but I really wanted to tell her how my Johnnie Mae could be a wonderful author too—were she to pursue it.

Johnnie Mae won all kinds of writing contests and awards. She reads like most folks eat barbecue ribs. The phone rang just as I got my hands deep into the lunch preparation, so Sister got it for me. (I could tell she intended to answer it anyway, she just wasn't sure what I would think about it. She acted like she was waiting for me to ask her to get it...so I did.)

It's just as well she got it; from the little bit I overheard, it was that other friend—Honey. Sister glanced at me a couple times, (I saw her out the corner of my eye)...like she was trying to supervise what she was saying and seeing me reminded her I was still within hearing range.

Finally, she decided to change phones and asked if I would hang that one up for her. I smiled, of course, and said I would though I do think that's awfully rude (spit in my face and tell me it's raining). Why not just come right out and tell the person in the room, "I think you're nosy and even if you're not, I don't want you to hear a word I'm going to say." Now *that* would be a more honest way of handling it.

After I cleaned my preparation mess, I was on my way to tell the men-folk they could come eat, and I just happened by the room where Sister had gone. I would have figured she would have been finished with her conversation by now, but Sister sounded deep into it still. She laughed and spoke loud at times; low at others. I wasn't really eavesdropping, but I did happen to catch a few words here and there.

"You did *what?*" Sister laughed. "Girl, you are being too bad now. J. M.'s going to have a *fit* if she ever finds that out."...Pause..."I don't believe you. Well, you'll never guess what I did?"...Pause..."I said I wasn't going to tell anybody, but I suppose I could tell you since you've just spilled your guts about what *you* did."...Pause..."Something of mine is set to be published!"...Pause..."No, it's just a short story."...Pause..."I didn't say anything because truthfully I don't want anyone I know to read it just yet."

Pause..."I knew you were going to ask to read it. I don't know...I might let you."...Pause..."Because—if J. M. reads it, she'll want to kill me...or worse!" She laughed. "You know the law: For every action there is an equal or more power-ful..."...Pause..."There you go!"...Pause..."No. We're still friends; it's nothing personal."...Pause..."I don't know which of us is worse—me or you!"...Pause..."If she wasn't always so perfect," she whispered, "I'd tell her too. But my next work that gets published, I will definitely tell her."

My feet started back moving again. "Haints! Just two old haints, that's all they are! As much as my baby's done for the two of them. The ingrates!"

"Mr. Gates...Solomon! Lunch is ready!" I yelled off to the side.

They were trying to finish so they wouldn't have to go back. I really believe it was more Solomon wanting to finish than Mr. Gates. Mr. Gates would have been content to stay out there all day. All he was going to do anyway was eat lunch then shuffle his way right on back out there. Hunt some weeds to pull up or something.

Fortunately, this yard didn't have many weeds to spare him. Mr. Gates removed the red bandanna from his back hip pocket and wiped the sweat from his face and brow. Sol took the back of his hand and slung the perspiration he found dripping from him to the ground, as he caught his breath.

It hadn't truthfully occurred to me until I sat and began writing this, but...why *was* Sister here when Johnnie Mae obviously was not? *And* what was it she had published she didn't plan to show Johnnie Mae after all the reading and editing my Johnnie Mae has done to help her? I know Johnnie Mae did; both of them have said as much. And *what,* pray tell, has Honey done?

Oh heck! And I still walked right out the house today and left that package I had meant to bring Johnnie Mae. Well, I'll just have to make myself remember to give it to her when she comes up Mother's Day.

Rosalyn Benefield's Journal

I called J. M. and finally got to say just what I've always wanted. I admit I was too upset to think straight; she ended up coming over two hours after I hung up on her. She and I talked, and I still ended up saying stuff I shouldn't have.

"What *was* I suppose to say to you, Rosalyn?" J. M. said. "What?" She blew, then sipped her hot tea with caution. "I told you I didn't think George was someone you should get involved with."

"Well you could have told me about the two of you. I would have understood."

"Understood?" She again blew ripples across the top of the tea. "What was there to understand? My saying he wasn't someone you ought to be pursuing should have been more than enough."

"Why?" I slammed the sugar bowl down in front of her after she frowned for the second time. "Because you think you're smarter than me...because you think you know who and what's right for everybody...*else,* that is?"

"And what exactly do you mean by *that?*" she said, holding the cup in the air without bothering to either put it to her lips or spoon in the needed sugar.

"I mean...you're Miss-Know-Everything...think you're so smart! 'I read this; I read that.' Is there not one thing you don't know something about?!"

"I do not—"

"Yes you do! Well, seems you're not the perfect little somebody everybody thinks you are. At least, not the woman *I* thought you were anyway."

"I never claimed to be perfect. I'm human just like everybody else walking around on this earth."

"No. No, you're not *just* like everybody else. You've managed a special anointing the rest of us still pray to receive someday."

J. M. took another sip, frowned again—then hesitated. "Honey?" she said.

I fell back against my chair. "Oh, so *now* you can lower yourself to call me Honey. After all these years, today you can adjust your mouth to say Honey? Well ain't this a bi—"

"Rosalyn, I was asking if you *have* honey—for my *tea*. I prefer to sweeten my tea with honey." She smiled, though it was apparent she was trying not to.

I smirked as I went to the cabinet to locate a jar of the sweet sticky stuff. "Sorry," I said plunking a little bear container in front of her.

J. M. smiled and shook her head while stirring a stream of honey into her cup of tea. "No problem," she said sitting forward. "Now tell me again what you *think* you saw—"

"Not *think*...saw."

"Okay...saw last night at Lan— George's place."

I sat back, tearing pieces and stuffing into my mouth a large cinnamon roll I had heated earlier in the microwave. "I *saw* you...in this lovely white negligée, poised on that long sofa-looking thing...the thing without a back...pushed up against his bed—"

"Bench."

"What?" I said peering hard back at her.

She waved it off. "Forget it. But you saw me?"

"Yes...*you.* "

"Rosalyn, I'm going to tell you the truth. That was *not* me you saw; I was at the movies last night...I still have my stub to prove it."

"Not saw you like that..." I chewed, my mouth now full of a sweet doughy substance. "A portrait. And from what little I was able to see, you were gorgeous! Frozen in time. Captured on canvas...colored with deep fine oils...surrounded by an expensive gold frame."

"A portrait?"

"Yes."

"Of me?"

"In this magnificent white negligée."

J. M. started laughing as she held her hand to her chest. "It was not me."

I stared at her and sat forward. "J. M. believe me—it was you." I got up, took the phone from the hook, and stretched it to her. "Ask him for yourself then." She first wouldn't take the phone so I shook it in her face again. "Go on, call and ask him."

She took the phone and pressed in the number. I didn't even have to tell her his number—she knew it by heart. She pressed the buttons and dialed without a second thought. That's when I knew I was right about one thing, there was *something* between them. Something other than business, too. You see...that was his home number!

Countess W. Gates' Journal

Mr. Gates and I stayed over to Johnnie Mae's longer than either of us had intended. Or maybe I should just speak for myself. As usual, it appears Mr. Gates had known something was happening out this way.

Johnnie Mae came home awfully late last night. She said she had an emergency she had to attend to, but never said exactly what it was even after Solomon told her how we'd been there pretty much all day worrying about her. Nothing anyone said seemed to be registering with her. Nothing mattered. She walked almost like a zombie to her bedroom and just laid across the bed. Like someone had poured her out but had forgotten what order to put her back in. She laid there like she was desperately trying to fit a puzzle together so she could see the whole picture.

"Baby?" I said as I knocked on the half-opened door.

She glanced only slightly my way. "Mama," she said, "you and Daddy don't need to drive back tonight. It's too late for either of you to be out. Stay, and get a fresh start in the morning."

"Are you all right?" I said dragging into the room. "What happened today?"

She sat up and forced a smile, but her pain was so visible. "I'm fine, Mama. It's all going to be fine. It always is. However it is...it always is."

I took her by the hand, noticing the birthmark up past her wrist now. "Your Daddy insisted we come up today. He brought you some plants—flowers. He and Solomon planted them earlier, along with those flats of impatiens and petunias you had already bought."

Johnnie Mae smiled. "I'll have to take a look in the morning."

"Do you want to talk about it?"

"What's to talk about? It's just life. Some things you have to deal with all by yourself. Sort them out...pray you end up doing the right thing....make the right decision when all is said and done."

I smiled and gazed at our inter-locking fingers. "Well, we can always talk later if you like. Now why don't you close those pretty brown eyes of yours and get some rest."

So I left her. Praying mightily myself. Praying she would be all right. By morning, I do hope she's all right.

Solomon Taylor's Journal

Countess and Johnnie Mae were both up early...in the kitchen up to their wrist making homemade rolls. Fresh homemade rolls. But one thing I've learned from this family is, they never ever really *just* make rolls or *just* plant a garden. There's always some lesson being taught—something to be learned.

So seeing the intent on Countess' face, told she was doing more than *just* making rolls (although the by-products of this lesson was fine with me. Hot fresh rolls!). There's something mystical about women and kitchens; I haven't figured it quite out. But I have learned to keep my nose out of their business and leave them to their "cooking" and their "kitchen talks."

I'm still unsure what exactly happened with Johnnie Mae yesterday. I do know I've never seen her in such a state in all my years of knowing her. Apparently, I'm not the only one. Countess was even more concerned. After Johnnie Mae came home, it was as though she were still wherever she had come back from. I'm used to her working odd days and hours, but she's never acted anything even close to this afterwards.

Come to think of it, all this started with Rosalyn's call on yesterday morning. I was too sleepy to hear anything and by the time I dragged myself out of bed, Johnnie Mae was sitting there holding a dead phone. I asked Johnnie Mae about it last night, but she didn't want to talk about it. I told myself she was exhausted; but I know that's just an excuse I'm creating *for* her.

I felt funny when that big old antique Lincoln Continental pulled up in the drive yesterday—especially with Sister being here. I started to explain to Countess why the two of us were here alone, but then I felt guilty. Like some crime had been committed, and I decided it best not to say anything—just better left unsaid. Countess probably didn't give it a second thought; she knows Johnnie Mae and Sister are friends. If I had attempted to explain, it just might have planted a few seeds that didn't *even* need to be earthed.

Sister did hang around for a little while—I was grateful she had the foresight to do that much. At least it made it *appear* as though she were waiting for Johnnie Mae, although the truth is, Johnnie Mae had just left when she called. I told her Johnnie Mae would probably be a while, so she rushed over. She had fully intended to be gone before Johnnie Mae returned. Which, as it turns out, she was still able to do (though not before the Gates pulled up in that *bus* they call a car).

Sister said Honey had called so she was headed over to her place to see what was going on. From what I can piece together, Johnnie Mae went over to Rosalyn's, then she left. But no one knows where she went from there. Nearly eight hours after even Sister leaves, and Johnnie Mae finally comes home. Some time after ten o'clock that night...with no apology, no explanation, no nothing.

"I had some business to take care of," is all she said. Drained? Refreshed? I don't know which she truly was.

Yet—the only sign my wife still resided inside the body she came home in last night is the way she looked as her mother made her world-renowned, homemade rolls.

Good old-fashioned, fresh, homemade yeast rolls! Hot, out of the oven, buttered rolls that would later be the source of the most delightful smells dancing through the house like Chubby Checkers doing the *Twist!*

Countess W. Gates' Journal

"Mix it. Blend it. Stir it. Knead it. Stretch it. Beat it. Caress it. Hold it. Fold it. Roll it. Cut it. Mold it. Shape it." Words I spoke as Johnnie Mae sat patiently listening and watching while I made my famous yeast rolls. "Then," I said to her, "it takes time to rise, yet still must go through the fire—in order to set it just right. Time to rise...heat to hold."

"Mama, you don't understand."

"Try me."

"How long have you loved Daddy...always and forever?"

"And—?"

"And, and—I don't know."

I dusted my hands from the white flour. "You asking if I've ever looked at another man? If my eyes were so singular they never wandered not even for a fleeting second? Well in the words of your dear father—every shut eye ain't sleep; every good-bye ain't gone!"

She looked up at me. "No," she almost whispered, "I wasn't asking."

I shook my head and shrugged. "Human. We're all human. Not perfect. Things come, you deal with it the best you know how. Just know...each decision carries its own consequence. You make one decision, you get one consequence—make a different decision about the same thing, you get a different consequence. So—you feel like talking about it now?"

She shook her head. "I don't think it's something I'm at a point I can talk with anyone about."

I kissed her lightly on her forehead. "Can always talk to me. I may not always tell you what you might care to hear, but I love you more than words can relay. I wouldn't deliberately steer you wrong."

"You think Solomon thinks anything is wrong?" she said.

I thought a second. Catching him and Sister here yesterday all alone and him not even bothering to give me one attempt at an explanation... "No, I don't believe so." I rinsed my hands after covering tight the rolls. "Let those set awhile. You want to tell me what's bothering you, Baby?"

"It's not what you think Mama. Just forget I even said anything." She smiled.

"I'm not *thinking* anything. Just trying to help. Oh, did I tell you Sister was here yesterday when we drove up?"

"Yeah...or maybe Solomon mentioned it; I'm not sure."

"That other friend of yours...Honey—she called too."

"What did *she* have to say?"

"Oh, she didn't speak to me or Solomon. But Sister talked to her for a good long while. I don't know if Sister left a message with Solomon or no...she didn't leave one with me. I do know that much."

"No...she probably didn't. Most likely she was looking for Sister so she could tell her—" Johnnie Mae stood up to leave. "Oh...forget it."

"How well do you know those two? Sister and Honey I mean?"

Johnnie Mae smiled at me. "Apparently...not as well as I think." She came and kissed me on my right cheek. "Thanks Mama."

"For what? Doesn't look like I did you any good."

"You have. Believe me, you have. I have to get ready for church now."

"Johnnie Mae?" I said before she was too far gone. "You look worn. Tighter than a nine day clock. Why don't you go get back in the bed and get some more rest."

"What?...and miss church? I don't think my *mama* would allow such a sin...and on a Sunday at that?" she said with a grin. "Actually Mama...I've been having this dream off and on for the past two months or so."

"What kind of dream? You know how I am with dreams."

"There are these children playing in a large circle. You know, like we used to play various games. They're singing this song, but all I seem to be able to remember upon awakening is the beginning of what they sing. *Green green, the crab apple tree. Where the green grass grows tall. Miss Johnnie, Miss Johnnie your true love is...* And that's as much as I can recall."

"Dead," I said barely above a whisper. "Miss Johnnie, Miss Johnnie your true love is dead. And he wrote you a letter to turn back your head." I looked hard...deep...with more questions than the simple answer I had just given her.

"That's it!" she said already walking back toward me. "That's the rest of what they say! But how do you happen to know that?"

"Great-Grandma Nam-o taught us that game...when I was a little bitty girl. The question is, how do *you* happen to know it?"

She laughed. "I don't know; I can't remember ever hearing it before."

"You didn't...I *never* taught y'all that one. Never knew no one else to teach it to you either. I didn't like that game. Didn't like the song. Who wants to play a game where your true love ends up dead? Then you turn away from everybody else until everybody's true love is dead only to end up doing it all over again...turning back eventually to the place you first began." My eyes fell upon the silver dollar resting on her chest. "Nam-o?" I whispered under my own breath.

"*What?*" Johnnie Mae said. To which I breathed, not another word.

Pearl Sue Hunter's Journal

I don't know why I even told Honey about that short story that's being published. I know she's like an old run down refrigerator...can't keep nothing! But as upset as she sounded with J. M., she probably won't mention it, yet anyway. Not until she and J. M. make up. I got a contract back in February; before J. M. gave me that surprise birthday party...before the gift of that necklace.

I didn't truly think my story would be the grand prize winner, and sure didn't expect *that* one to be published. But it was too late to renege after it won. My check should have been here though...wonder what's keeping it. Well, at least I was smart enough to use a pseudonym, in case someone does see it. They can't necessarily tie it back to me.

Honey never did say exactly what J. M. had done that had her so riled. But she was P.H.A.T. (Pretty, Hot, And Ticked-off!). She questioned why we even bothered being friends with someone who was sealed up so tight inside.

"What does she share with us? Does she ever confide in you anything personal that goes on in her life?" Honey asked. "No, but we spill *our* guts, don't we?" Honey was so mad she was cussing, something she had stopped doing—largely thanks to J. M. who didn't see the value of such words—long ago.

"It's not that they're more powerful," J. M. had said. "Just words used for shock value if you want my opinion. What's the difference in Shoot and well, you know? Nothing. Just one is more taboo. Dog and damn? See, mere words. It's the *meaning* behind the word. So when I say *Dog,* I'm just as mad as when you say, *Damn.* In my opinion, there's no true purpose in cursing."

And if J. M. happens on a subject, she can go on for days. Truth be told, Honey probably quit cussing so much because she couldn't take those long drawn-out sermons J. M. dished out afterward. The same reason I shut up about how Flick—at times—treats me. But J. M. hates to hear Honey cuss with a passion. So their conversation must have been good!

"What kind of an environment is that for children to grow up in? What kind of an example are you setting for them to follow?" J. M. would say to Honey.

Now, here was Honey calling J. M.'s house searching for me. Maybe she thought J. M. might tell me what had happened—her side of the story. Right! Like that would ever truly happen. Maybe when hell freezes over. J. M. doesn't talk to anyone about anything. From all I've concluded, she doesn't even tell Solomon all she should.

I don't know what happened between Honey and J. M., but if Honey's telling the truth about some of the things she *says* she said, Johnnie Mae might not *ever* speak to or forgive her again. You can't un-ring a bell! Among other things, Honey said she told J. M. she was a selfish, greedy, egotistical, power mad, hungry witch (I'm saying witch, but actually she called her the 'b' word). Of all the things Honey said and could have said, the 'b' word was the one she should have bit back and swallowed hard as soon as it surfaced. But I'm sure J. M. won't ever admit Honey called her that.

J. M. hadn't come home before I left, so I have no idea what's going on. I believe she was more upset than anybody realizes though; I know I would have been. I didn't tell Solomon what Honey had said, so if J. M. didn't tell him (and I doubt she did), he's probably completely in the dark even that Honey's mad and how she practically blasted J. M. I still can't help but wonder, where on earth *did* she go to cool down.

Rosalyn Benefield's Journal

I called George. Thought I'd get him straight while I was cleaning house. Just getting everybody told. Man, was he ever pissed—it wasn't even funny!

"What the *hell* did you say to Johnnie My...J.M.?" he said.

"What the *hell* business is it to you?" I said flopping down on my bed. (J. M. might not like my cussing, but he was the one who started it.)

"Look Honey, I told you from the very beginning there wasn't a thing happening between me and you. I didn't mislead you about nothing. You hear what I say—nothing! I also told you I didn't like people all up in my business."

"Your business? I come to your house to see you—"

"Who invited your fat ass up here? Certainly not me!"

I blinked several times. "Excuse me? But did you just call me fat?"

"I don't think I stuttered when I said it."

"Fat as in f-a-t?" I said.

"Very good. You get an A+ for spelling and vocabulary."

I sat up on the bed. "Now you look here Mister-You-Really-Ain't-All-That! I don't know who you think you are or who you think you're talking to, but—"

"Honey," he said, "all I have to say to you is—stay *out my* business! This doesn't concern you in the least. It never has. I was doing fine before I met you, and I do believe I'll be doing just fine when you leave me the hell alone."

"So why do you have her portrait hanging over your bed?" I said.

"Not your business," he said.

"Are you and J. M. sleeping together?"

"Not *your* business."

"What do you plan to do if her husband—Solomon—somehow finds out?"

"You planning on telling him?" He said it more like a statement than a question.

"That's not *your* business," I said with a smirk he could only hear in my voice.

"Tell him! See if I give a *good* damn!"

"J. M. will. What about her?"

"Honey, look...I don't know what part of not your business you don't understand, but I'm going to say it again—it's none of your *damn* business!"

"Tell me this...why was my loan approved? The loan for my van? Why was it approved?"

"Say what?"

"Was it because of her? J. M.? Is that why I got approved? Did that slut...that whore...make some kind of deal with you to get my loan approved? Did you make wild and passionate love to her—"

He started laughing. "Oh this is good. This is *so* good! First of all, let me correct you on a few points. She's neither a slut nor a whore!—that's first off! Let's get that straight from the jump. Secondly—yes! J. M. was the true reason behind your getting your loan. Your credit record was in such a mess, there wasn't even a way *A Upper Hand* could see to help someone like *you* up."

"So why did you approve it then? Is the whore that good?"

"Because, my dear little *Honey*. J. M. made me an offer she knew I could not—or would not—refuse!"

" *What* George? What was the offer?"

He was suddenly quiet. "She backed your loan with her own money! J. M. Taylor put up the collateral for your loan," he said. "Now, are you satisfied?!"

It was my time to be solemn now. "She did *what?* But why?! She doesn't even co-sign for anybody." I laughed. "You're lying. Why you got to lie so much—"

"Now *why* would I have a reason to lie to you?! You're over there trying to put J. M. down while all she has tried to do—from what I've been able to see anyway—is try to help you do better. So *now,* who's the whore? Who's the sell out? Looks to me like you just played your own self!" He then, hung up.

J. M. did that for me? Backed the loan for my van? Something she vowed never to do for anybody—sign her name on a loan for another person? Yet, she had done it for me? And I pay her back by calling her all kinds of names...every thing I could think of? Every thing that is, but a child of God!

Oh Lord, please forgive me! I don't believe she did something like that. Not for me.

Rose Early

And it came to pass on the seventh day, that they rose early about the dawning of the day, and compassed the city after the same manner seven times: only on that day they compassed the city seven times. And it came to pass at the seventh time, when the priests blew with the trumpets, Joshua said unto the people, "Shout; for the Lord hath given you the city."

Joshua 6:15,16

Countess W. Gates' Journal

Solomon came over with my Mother's Day present but Johnnie Mae couldn't make it. There's been only one other time she's missed wishing me Happy Mother's Day in person; she was out-of-town then too. She did call bright and early, although it's not quite the same, I don't care how much a person calls themselves reaching out and touching.

I received a wonderful gift, as always. Though I'll never be able to sashay all the name-brand clothing my children purchase for me, dazzle all the jewelry they try to adorn me with, or strut all my designer pumps. Still, I can't get them to quit.

Not even when I say I have more than enough; they are dogged to buy one more thing. They will not allow *this* day gone without my owning one more thing I didn't own the day before. I received so many flowers one year, I told them my house looked like a funeral parlor.

Rachel reminded me how I'm always preaching about folks giving folks their flowers while they yet can see and smell them. But that was just *too* many flowers for one body (dead or alive). I went throughout the community handing out bouquets to all the elderly. They thought I had started my own floral shop!

"Has Johnnie Mae called you yet?" Solomon said time he stepped foot inside the house. He was carrying a large box that appeared alongside him to be floating in mid-air.

"Yes, she called early this morning."

"She hated she couldn't be here, but she didn't expect to have to go out of town like that. Then to end up having to stay until Tuesday." He sat the box down in my lap once I was comfortably in my swivel rocker they bought me last year this time.

"Well, I know she'd be here if she could."

Sol sat on the couch...rubbing his hands together like he was warming them by a fire.

"So," I said sitting back smiling at him, "how is she?"

He laughed. "She's better I think. Still not talking much. Kind of staying to herself. And I believe she must have gotten a touch of food poisoning; she was throwing up quite a lot the last few days." He smiled. "But she got better *real* fast after Mr. Bijur called her to come meet with him. She was supposed to meet him on Wednesday and be back by Friday...but something came up after Johnnie Mae arrived and he had to reschedule their meeting. He's paying for her stay through Tuesday now."

"That's great. What exactly is she gonna do for this man in Chicago?"

"Oh, I believe Johnnie Mae said he's got offices all over the country and she might get quite a few contracts in helping to shore many of their offices up. Might be just the break-through she's been working so hard and long for." He smiled.

"That would be wonderful. Then maybe she'll settle down and—" I looked at him and saw his smile widening, "maybe you and she can start on that family?"

He had this huge grin now. "Hope so. I know I'm ready. But of course, you already know that as well."

I nodded. "Of course."

"She has a doctor's appointment this coming Friday, so I'm hoping she'll talk with Dr. Richardson about...you know...about it."

"Yes," I said smiling to relieve his discomfort. I opened my gift and thanked him with earnest for his part. "I'll talk to Johnnie Mae when she gets back. I have a package here I've meant to give her the past few months or so—"

"Would you like for me to take it back and give it to her for you?"

"Oh no. I'm sort of looking forward to seeing the expression on her face. But thank you just the same." Sol is *such* a thoughtful man.

"Well," he said as he stood to his feet. "I have to be going. I told my mother I'd be to her house no later than three. My sisters are fixing her this big Mother's Day dinner."

"And how is your mother?"

"Doing better, thank you."

"Tell her I asked about her."

Such a nice person. I'm glad my daughter married him. Yes, they gonna have some mighty fine children all right. They can't miss! Not with a mama and daddy like Johnnie Mae and Solomon!

Pearl Sue Hunter's Journal

J. M.'s not talking much to anybody it seems. I wanted her to look over my latest story, but she told me she couldn't. I told Honey I don't know what she did, but she needs to fix it. Honey says J. M.'s not talking to her either even though she's tried to apologize.

When I asked Honey what exactly happened, she's too ashamed to tell me now. She just keeps saying how wrong she was, and how she wish she could turn back the clock and set things back right.

Sugarman said she went to the doctor's on Friday, and he doesn't know what happened; but when he came home, he found her going through stacks and stacks of old notebooks. Her journals. Just sitting on the bed flipping pages one right after the other. When he told her I was on the phone, he said she told him to just take a message. She hasn't called back *yet*. It's not like her. I wonder if she knows? But how could she?

Besides, she'd be happy for me. If it wasn't for her, I'd never have gotten *anything* published right? She supports me.

"Honey," I said after that first day when I called and J. M. didn't feel like talking to me, "you didn't tell J. M. about my story that's being published, did you?"

"No, I haven't told her a thing."

"Are you sure? You know you were awfully mad at her."

"Even if I had wanted to tell her, she's not talking to *me* I tell you. I called her right after I hung up with George—"

"You talked to George about J. M.? Girl, you'd better not be putting her business in the street."

"It's not like that. I had to ask him something. Anyway, as soon as I hung up from him, I called her. She wouldn't come to the phone. I finally told Sugarman to tell her I was sorry. *Really* sorry. He told me she said it was okay, but she's definitely *not* herself."

"Well, I don't want you to say a word about my story, you hear?"

"I read that story, she probably won't even recognize one thing about it."

"You just make sure you keep your mouth shut. Don't say one word about it, okay?"

So I feel sure Honey didn't tell her. I just don't understand why she's not talking to *me.* After some of the things Honey said to her, I can understand J. M. fuming a while at her. But I don't understand why she's not having much to say to me.

Oh well, I'll try calling her again...see how she's doing. I hope the doctor didn't have bad news for her. It would be just like her to keep something devastating all to herself—opting to bear it alone.

Rosalyn Benefield's Journal

I called J. M.—again. Solomon picked up.

"I'm so glad to hear a real voice," I said. "Your answering machine should be full by now."

"It is," Solomon said.

"Is J. M. there?"

"Hold on," he said. Then he came back on the line. "She says she's busy. I just told her to call you back whenever she gets a chance."

"She's not going to," I said.

"What happened between you two?"

I sighed hard. "I was an idiot. Ran my mouth more than I should have. God, Solomon, I wish I could take it all back."

"Oh Rosalyn, you're not the cause of *all* this."

"You didn't hear what I said and what all I did. I wouldn't blame her if she never speaks to me again."

"So—how are you and...what's his name...George? Yeah, he seemed to be a really nice fellow."

"I'm fine and George is fine I suppose. We're just not fine together. I called him over the Mother's Day weekend to see if he and I were still friends, but he was out of town. In Chicago. On business. I left a message for him, but he's probably not going to ever call me again." *Either,* I started to add.

"Well you never know. You just have to keep believing."

I smiled. "Yeah, you're right. I'll keep that in mind. In the meantime, should you happen to come across someone single, cute, and available...don't forget I'm still in the market."

Oh yeah, I messed up...big time! And although when I *was* able get a message to J. M., she said it was okay—for me not to worry about it; yet she's had nothing more to say. Just quiet.

And Sister's over there worried about some old story she wrote. J. M. won't care about that stupid thing! She'll probably be happy for Sister. Nobody's encouraged her more in her writing than J. M., and for sure nobody else ever took the time to read and comment on most of her little stories.

I hope J. M. gets okay soon. I sure do miss laughing and talking with her. I never knew how much space in my life as a friend she actually filled, or the void that would be left were she ever not there.

God I wish I could take all I said back!

 J. M. Taylor's Journal

May 18, 1998

I called New York today about that published article I, by some miracle, happened upon (it took me all of Friday just to locate what I had written in my journal). Three days of wait, only added more fuel to an already raging blaze.

"Yes, my name is J. M. Taylor and I'm *trying* to find out the name of the person who wrote an article in your June edition titled— Yes, I'll hold."

The young woman came back in seconds. "Sorry. Now, where were we? Oh yes!—an article. Are you an agent, editor, a book publisher or something?"

"No, I—"

"Wasn't the name listed with it? At the beginning—"

"Sort of; it says J. T.—not exactly a name in my book," I said. "The article is called *Moroccan Rose*." I could hear clicking as keys were being tapped fast.

"An article, you say?"

"Yes."

"In our *June* edition?"

"Yes. June. *Moroccan Rose.*"

"June of *this* year?"

I let out a sigh. "Yes, this year. June. Mailed out in May. It was dated the following month."

She began to spell quickly, "*M-o-r-o-c-c-a-n?*" she said, "*R-o-s-e?*"

"That's correct."

She sighed hard. "Sorry. *Moroccan Rose* doesn't show up as one of our articles. Are you sure it was our maga—"

"I'm sure. I'm holding it right now...in my hand...as we speak. It's on page twenty-seven, the June 1998 edition. It says, *Fiction—*"

"Fiction? Oh it's, *fic*-tion? Then it won't be under articles, it will be listed under fiction. Hold on just a second please." There was music then, "Here it is! Oh I remember this...this was really a good piece. A little deep for me though. Now... what is it you say you need again?"

I took a deep breath and spewed the words in one collective stream. "I need the author's name and if at all possible—"

"The author's name is...J. T.," she said.

"Yes. I can see *that* much for myself. Listen, maybe I should explain the problem a little better. This story is actually mine—"

"You mean, *you* wrote *this?*" She sounded impressed.

"No...I mean yes...I mean— What I *mean* is, I *wrote* this but I didn't send it in to be published—"

"So what did you *think* would happen when you sent it in?"

"Please hear what I'm saying. *I* did not send it in. Some-one stole it from my personal things and apparently *they* sent it. Only it's not fiction—"

"But it says it's fiction," she said.

"I'm trying to tell you, that's why I want to find out who had it published—"

"Look..." she said lacking any semblance of patience now, "it sounds to me like someone wrote a great story. It touched on something so close to your life that it appears to have *echoed* your voice...your sentiments...as though it were some-thing you yourself *might* have penned. Which is *precisely* what great fiction should do—if it's done right, that is."

"Okay—I'll tell you what. Why don't *you* transfer *me*...to someone else...higher up...if you don't mind." I started to say someone who knows what they're doing, but I held my peace (as best I could under the circumstances).

She didn't speak for what seemed like a whole minute, then she sighed hard. "H-o-l-d...on," she said, emphasizing the word *hold*.

"Excuse me, what is your name—" but it was too late— music played...music I didn't *even* care to hear or have time for. Held hostage on hold.

Three *long* songs, five repeat recordings of "Thank you for holding; someone will be with you shortly"(s) later, and, "All right. Are you still there?"

"Yes," I said through clenched teeth, "I'm *s-t-i-l-l* here."

"No one's available to take your call at this time, but I can take a message and have one of our managing editors get back with you...providing you *still* wish to speak with someone else," she said in her rather thick New York accent.

"Fine—and I do." I massaged the silver dollar clutched in my right hand.

She asked my name—again, then took down my address and phone number. "So what's the J. M. stand for?" she said as though she were grinning.

"J. M.," I said.

"All right then," she said, pronouncing '*i's* like long '*a's*, hence sounding like *rat*...not *right*. "Well now, I *right* do declare if somebody won't be gittin' back wit-cha short-ly there in...Coffee, Alabama." Clearly a jab at my Southern classification and a testament of her ignorance as how all people "down South" usually talk—(I know of only a handful myself who actually *do* talk that way).

I hung up, only to remember I had forgotten to "git" and "wrat" down her name. I stared at the coin I held in my hand.

"I'm going to find out who did this to me," I whispered, "and when I do..."

* * *

It's been two days now, and no one has called me from that magazine company *yet!* I've run out of patience. I want to know my Judas *now*. So tomorrow—I get ugly!

 J. M. Taylor's Journal

May 21, 1998

I hung up the phone more confused now it seems than before I began having finally spoken with this editor in New York about that article. Yet, what I learned makes no sense. No sense at all. Has *everyone* gone mad—or is it just me?

"Look," the man who identified himself as Mitchell said, "I don't know what kind of game you're playing, but I'm much too busy to play along with you."

"*Excuse* me?" I said, attempting to dilute my own already fermented anger. "Apparently you must have me confused with someone else. You see—"

"You did say your name was J. M. Taylor right?"

"That's correct. But—"

"From Coffee Alabama? You called and left a message on Monday, about some fiction piece we published in our June edition entitled *Moroccan Rose?*"

"Oh so someone *did* get my message, just didn't have the decency to call—"

"Yes—I got your *urgent* message all right. Then I took it upon myself to promptly have the piece pulled to determine what exactly happened."

"And? *What* did you find—" This conversation was not going well at all. Maybe the message got mixed up somehow; I do hate I failed to get the woman's name I spoke with on Monday. "Did *she* explain to you the problem?" I said. "My problem? How someone seems to have stolen—"

"Yes...*she* explained the problem just fine."

I had just about had enough of his shortness and lack of professionalism and was about to put an end to it. *I* call over three days ago, end up having to call back because no one has bothered to even return my call, and now *he* wants to have an attitude with *me?!* I don't think so. Obviously, he has no idea who he's talking with. "So...*what*...did you find out?" I said in a harsher tone.

He sighed. "Look Ms. Taylor—I believe you already know the answer." For some reason, he continued to sound like *he* had some right to be upset.

"Pardon me, but if I *knew* the answer I *definitely* wouldn't be wasting my time with—" I almost said *a moron like you,* but instead; I took a deep breath, stilled the silver dollar that hung from my neck, and calming myself I said, "...I wouldn't be wasting *my* valuable time trying to find out. And please explain to me Mitchell, exactly what kind of a company is this anyway where no one returns calls, yet you have the *nerve* to be as rude as you've been with me so far?"

"All right. Why don't I put it like this," Mitchell said. "I received your message and I will admit, I was a bit concerned also by the theft implication. So I rushed the file *on Moroccan Rose,* and can you begin to guess what I discovered?"

"No, and I want you to know—my patience is about down to its nub now."

"The name—J. T.—as you obviously know *is* indeed a pseudonym. The pseudonym belonging to..." There was silence as his voice just suddenly hushed.

"Hello? Hello? Are you there? Hello?" I said. I could hear a woman's voice whispering in the background.

"I'm sorry; I'm here. Hold on a second please." Music began to play as I held...waiting, finally about to learn the name of the person who had betrayed me. "Listen," he said, sounding more personable after picking back up, "let me make a few more calls—be sure I'm not violating some company policy here. Then I'll get right back to you."

"*What?* I do *not* believe this! Why didn't you check all this out those three days you had me waiting to hear back—"

"I'm sorry. I realize you want an answer, but it's the best I can do for now."

"Thanks," I said with a touch of sarcasm. "So I still don't know any more than I did when I called on Monday."

"I apologize for that; but I promise I'll get back with you—one way or the other."

Okay, so it's wait...then wait some more, and *soon* you will know all you desire to know. Six days I have already waited, yet I wait again as minutes—like a digital ballet—dance away.

I did work on a few important matters (in-between the wait); however, I found my mind did more wandering, trying to figure out who this J. T. was. This person...this someone who had to be close to me. This someone I apparently had trusted. One who not only could have done but did do something like this to me in the first place.

Playing with the silver dollar that hung down like a loose noose around my neck, at times swinging it before my eyes—as though I were hypnotizing my own self—I whispered, without regard to what I was even saying, "You're going to pay for this whoever you are. Believe me—you're going to pay!"

Mitchell was true to his word and called me back within two hours. "What's your fax number?" he said. "I'm having the secretary send you something now."

"Finally," I said, then I gave him my fax number and again waited—the last page not coming through fast enough for me. And when I did hold it in my hand, my legs quietly directed me to my chair, and with confidence, gave leave to my weight.

"No," I said, shaking my head as my gaze lingered on the black and white slick, curling paper gripped tight by my hand, "This can't be!"

 J. M. Taylor's Journal

I sat there holding that fax—the fax Mitchell had his secretary send me—in my hand, dated May 21, 1998 with its time stamped on the top as well. But I still could not believe it.

Yes, it was my handwriting—my signature at the bottom of that contract for *Moroccan Rose*. But how? I didn't do it! I'm not crazy. I'd know if I had sent something to be published. And I'd certainly recall signing a contract!

But I did sign this; it's definitely not a forgery. That's my signature all right.

No wonder Mitchell was so put out with me. I can see why he must have thought I was playing games. This is even worse than I first thought. Not only did someone steal words from my journal, they also tricked me into signing this contract.

But who? God, who did this?

I held the silver dollar on the string. *Who did this? Please help me find them. I must know.* And God have mercy on their soul, when I do. They will surely pay!

Oh my Lord! What else have they done to me?

Solomon Taylor's Journal

Everybody's asking me what's going on with Johnnie Mae.

"I don't know. She had a doctor's appointment last week," I said.

"So did she say anything after the visit?" Sister asked.

"No, just that everything was fine."

"Do you think she might be trying to keep some horrible news from us? You know how she tries to protect everybody," Rosalyn had said. "She doesn't like bothering folks with her troubles, but she'll listen all day long when it's one of ours."

"I asked her how it went; she said the doctor pronounced she'd live forever," I said. "But that was all she had to say about the visit to me."

Countess called. I told her the same thing.

"Well that sounds like it was good," Countess said. "I just wish I knew what's going on inside my baby's head. She tries to take on too much, *I* believe."

I don't know what to do. She knows I'm here for her. Whatever it is, we can work through it together. She was acting strange before she even went to see the doctor. Maybe she talked to Dr. Richardson about it.

I *am* beginning to think Rosalyn knows more than the rest of us. Her call that morning—that's when things started to spin. That's the same day Johnnie Mae came home like she didn't belong here anymore. I don't know, maybe I should take her on vacation—get her away from everything for a few days.

I admit I was shocked that she took off an entire day last Friday. She doesn't generally do that. But her trip to Chicago seems to have been fruitful, although she didn't tell me much about *it*, either. I suppose that's partly my fault. When she's tried telling me things in the past, she claims I wasn't listening or paying her much attention.

Yeah, I'll see if she might be interested in taking a short trip, two or three days—she and I both could use some time away from phone calls and things. I want to ask if she'd like to start that family, but I won't push her now. Not now.

Sister was concerned Johnnie Mae was thinking something about the two of us again. I assured her, she was fine with the two of us now. After that talk we had back in 1993, I think it was '93. Yeah that's when it was...the year she went on that seven (or was it a ten?) day trip to Florida? No, it was the Bahamas. Some place with sand and water I remember that.

She had begged me to go that year. But I was knee deep into my work and couldn't, no wouldn't, take off. She had even offered to shorten her stay to four days, but I couldn't even see staying for *that* long. So she went without me, though not before voicing suspicions of my and Sister's close relationship.

"Tell me, what's the real deal between you and Pearl?" she had said steaming mad.

"No deal. She and I grew up in the same community. That's about it," I said.

The only thing was: Sister would forget and touch me with such familiarity. It only happened when she became a bit too relaxed and wasn't thinking about what she was doing. I understood and so did she, but not Johnnie Mae. I didn't realize back then that Johnnie Mae was watching us with such scrutiny. Sister and I joked around and stuff; wasn't nothing to it— but I guess that's not how it appeared to my dear little wife.

"You two ever date?" Johnnie Mae asked one time (I had no clue why she was asking at the time).

"Who? Me and Sister?" I laughed though she didn't think it was all that funny.

"Yeah, you and *Sister,*" Johnnie Mae said with one hand on her hip.

"No," I laughed harder, "of course not!"

If I had been paying better attention, I might have known how much it bothered her. But then she went on that trip, and after she got back...we had it out about Sister and a lot of other things.

"Do you love her?" Johnnie Mae had said.

"Love her? Well, I guess you could say I do—but it's different than the way I love you."

It took me awhile to explain to Johnnie Mae how Sister had baby-sat with us sometimes when Mudear had to work all those jobs. Sister's much older than me, and she has always been like...well, a big sister. When she would come over and I wanted something, all I had to do was look at her with my sad puppy eyes and say, "Please Sister" and she'd give it to me. She would even sneak sugar to our house because she knew I would be singing, "Sister, I'm thirsty."

"Then drink some water," she would say.

"Will you make me some of your special water?"

She would smile, get down my favorite cup, use the metal dipper to fill it with water, put sugar in and stir until the water became clear again. I got to where I couldn't drink water unless it had sugar in it. She started calling me, Sugarman; and I called her Sister. Everybody else started calling her Sister...and me, Sugarman. The rest, they say, is history and herstory.

Johnnie Mae understood better after I explained things. But sometimes I believe she still thinks there may be something between us. Sister and I will always be close. There are things I can talk with her about that I just can't say to Johnnie Mae. But Johnnie Mae understands that now; I'm sure she does.

"No, Sister," I said, having ran my notes through my head, "Johnnie Mae doesn't think there's anything going on between us."

I just wish I knew what she's keeping locked so tight and hidden away deep inside.

 J. M. Taylor's Journal

I've thought a lot about that day—the day everybody thinks I lost my mind. The day Rosalyn called me early and I went to see her. I can't fault her entirely for being upset; suppose I would have felt the same way, had it been me. But what could I have said or done to have avoided all this? Tell her how well I knew Landris. Landris, my bitter and my sweet. Probably the only person who will tell me just how it is and care less how it finds me yet he does...care.

"You want to know why you never called me after that last time?" Landris said when I stepped inside his house...the place he had allowed Rosalyn into only the night before.

"Not really," I said with a snap. *I already know why—you confuses my mind.*

He locked his eyes into mine. "Because you didn't want to give up the feelings you have for me. See by leaving things the way you did, there would never truly be closure one way or the other. Then you'd never have to lose the feeling; never have to give the feelings up or over. You fled from dealing with it."

"You're crazy," I said. "Insane. You're just full of yourself, aren't you?"

"Oh I'm crazy all right. That's what they'd call somebody who loves someone as hard and as much as I seem to love you." He took my hand and held it inside both of his. "I'm in...sane...about you Johnnie Mylove."

"Landris...look, I came here to talk about—"

"Marry me?" he said looking deep into my eyes.

"What?" I jerked my hand from his; although he promptly took it back...holding it now, more securely.

"Marry me."

I laughed. "I don't think that's possible."

He pushed my hair that laid on my shoulders to the back. "Why not?"

"Well now let's see—there is the matter of my husband, Solomon. I *do* believe, at least the last time I heard, there were and are laws against having more than one husband at the same time. In *this* country, anyway."

"Solomon? Solomon doesn't understand you like I do. He doesn't give you the attention you need...deserve...crave even. See, I know what you need—you know I do. I understand where you're trying to go in life. And I don't wish to mold or make you into something you don't want or care to be either."

"Like?"

"Like becoming a mother for instance. He wants a baby. Frankly, I don't care. If that's what you want, I'd be right there. If you never wanted one, that would be okay with me too. You see Mylove, you truly desire to leave a mark on this earth—"

"I don't want to leave a mark," I said.

"Johnnie Mylove, you're on a mission. I don't know why, but I do know you are." He kissed my hand, pressing it into his face, then kissed places upward my arm. "I'd be there for you. Encouraging you every step of the way."

I closed my eyes and let myself melt in his mouth. Then I remembered why I had come, and took *back* my self. "Landris, the portrait."

He glanced up, then grinned. "Honey? *She* told you."

"Yes, *she* told me. Now you show me."

He took my hand and pulled me into his bedroom. I looked up and sure enough...there I was...in the most beautiful white, negligée, wedding-looking gown.

He went over to his walk-in closet and came back with a frame exactly like the one hanging on the wall. "This is what I was trying to get you to come see." He turned the picture to face me.

"It's...beautiful," I said as I looked at the portrait of myself in a dark blue velvet dress.

"Just like you," he said.

"But when did you do this?"

"When you would sit for spans at a time just thinking. I drunk every detail about you, and then I poured myself out onto these two. You were the best subject I've ever painted."

"But I thought...Landris...this is so nice."

"This one's yours," he said handing it to me, then looked toward the wall, "and that one's mine."

I looked up at the wall. "Landris, you can't...what if somebody sees that and thinks—"

"What? That you posed for it?"

"Well...yeah."

"Now since when have you known me to care what other people think?" He took my portrait and leaned it against the wall. "Now, after you called this morning, I figured you would be over quickly, so I took the liberty of getting a few things ready for you."

He criss-crossed my arms and marched me into the bathroom where the Jacuzzi oozed with bubbles...candles flickered light all around it, while their shadows African danced on the still walls. He picked up, then handed me a royal blue terry cloth bathrobe.

"No strings attached," he said, as he started to slowly unzip the front of my blue jean dress...smiling with his dancing eyes. "You need someone to pamper you Mylove. You need to relax, to rest a while. With me, there is no pressure."

"Landris, please—"

"No one you are to please—in any given moment," he said. "Except yourself. The water should be just about right now, and I'll be back with some other things in just a minute."

"Landris—"

"*And* if you plan to stand there and argue with me about it...having not found your way in there," he pointed to the black marble whirlpool, "by the time I come back; then I will *personally* put you in there myself. *With* or *without* your clothes. And MyLove...you know I'll do it. I hope I have made my position perfectly clear."

He kissed me on the cheek and was gone. I hurried and got undressed, hiding my nakedness in the bubbles before his return. And he brought back with him five perfect roses, a plate full of fruit and other things to eat...strawberries, grapes, melons, mangoes, kiwi, peaches, cheese, crackers...a cup of hot tea, and a glass of Chablis—*his* favorite.

"Tea?" I said smiling.

"With honey," he said. "Just the way you like it."

I could hear the stereo playing the song and the words, *"Love Me In A Special Way"* in the distance as he stirred my tea for me. He smiled while making a lovely clinking sound as the metal hit the ceramic.

"Now, have I forgotten anything?" he said, as he caressed my face with the soft buds of each individually stemmed rose.

The roses I understood...back when he told me before.

"Red means *I love you.* Pink...*Please believe me.* White says, *You are heavenly.* Yellow tells of *feelings of joy and gladness,*" he had said.

"And the brown?" I had asked. "What about the brown?"

"A Moroccan Rose...for you my Nubian princess. Brown means *You shall always know love joy and gladness is there.* You always know it's there."

I smiled and relaxed my head back.

You always know it's there.

Solomon Taylor's Journal

I was getting the groceries out of Johnnie Mae's trunk when I saw this huge gold frame pushed way up in the back. I pulled it out and couldn't believe my eyes.

"Johnnie Mae, where did you get this portrait of yourself?"

She took it from my hand. "Somebody I met paints and they did it," she said.

"This is wonderful! Did you pick it up today? How long did you have to sit for this? In fact, *when* did you have time to sit for it?"

"I didn't. And I've had it a few weeks now."

I frowned. "You didn't? You didn't have time or you didn't sit for it?"

"Didn't sit."

"It looks so life-like? It certainly captures the real you."

"He's just good I guess."

"Where did you have it done?"

"I'm sorry, but I'm really tired. Can we talk about this some other time?" And she did look tired.

"Dr. Richardson called again. She says she really needs to talk with you," I said as she dragged away. "Did you not call her back from Thursday?"

"I'll call her," she said. "Monday's Memorial Day holiday; I'll call Tuesday."

When I looked in on her later, she was leaning against the bed swinging that silver dollar on that old green string. All that expensive jewelry she owns and the only thing she ever seems to wear lately, is that silver dollar on a string.

"I put up the groceries. Do you need anything?" I said.

She looked up at me with such pain in her eyes. "No. I'm fine. Thank you though."

"Are you sure?"

She smiled. "I'm sure." Then she laid down and turned away from me...her head missing completely even one of the ten pillows that flanked the bed. That's when I decided I probably should call Dr. Richardson back myself.

Rosalyn Benefield's Journal

I talked with George. He appears to have calmed down. In fact, he was really quite congenial with me.

"Oh, and Honey...I really do want to thank you," he said.

"For what?"

"Just for being you. I said some rather unkind things to you. But I want to tell you what a wonderful person you are. I'm sure there's someone out there searching hard for someone just like you."

"Yeah. Sure," I said. "Look George, we've been kind of concerned about J. M. lately. Every since that day I, well you know kind of lost it, she hasn't been the same." I took my time...picking the right words so as not to cause him to become defensive. "I was wondering if you might know or have noticed anything. You know, since the two of you had been working together there recently."

"No, she seems perfectly fine to me. But you know how she is when it comes to work—truly a professional."

Look at him acting like all he knows about her is her work. "Well, I just thought I would ask," I said.

"Did she tell you she's been offered a golden opportunity with *A Upper Hand?* At the Headquarters."

"No, I hadn't heard."

"Funny, they asked her a few weeks ago. Mr. Bijur propositioned her with a vice president's position."

"Wow! Vice president, huh? That's something."

"Yes. And with the money she'll be making, she can easily replace the house she now lives in."

"I'd imagine so."

"She'd have to live more in the suburbs though...there are not a lot of houses comparable to what she has now near downtown Atlanta—"

"Downtown *what?*"

"Atlanta. The job's in Atlanta."

"J. M.'s going to move to Atlanta?" I felt myself panic.

"Hey, look. Now you didn't hear that from me. She hasn't said *yes* yet...as far as I know. And that's still between her and Solomon."

"Oh, of course. I'll not leak a word. It's none of my business anyway, right?"

"Yeah. Well, I did want to return your call...see how you were getting along...and to thank you—for everything."

"I wish I felt like I'd done something to deserve thanks."

"Trust me...you did. Oh...you did."

Then he was gone. J. M. may be moving to Atlanta? My God, I wonder if Sister knows? And if so, why hasn't she said anything to me?

Pearl Sue Hunter's Journal

Honey came over. She couldn't call with this...she had to tell it to my face. I don't know if she wanted to see for herself did I really know or what.

"Did you know J. M. and Solomon were moving to Atlanta?" she said.

"No. And I don't believe that either."

"Well it's true!"

"Where'd you hear that? Sugarman hasn't said a word about moving or Atlanta."

"I can't reveal my sources but I hear J. M.'s been offered a huge position...Vice President. Only it's in Atlanta. And unless she's planning on commuting, then she'll have to move there. I would assume Sugarman's going with her."

"Just because she's been offered a job like that, doesn't mean she's going to take it," I said as I turned up my bottle of Coca-Cola.

"Did you know a black woman actually invented the recipe for Coke?"

"Girl, ple-eze. You're full of it today."

"It's true. I read it just the other day somewhere. If we ever get to go to Atlanta, in Collonwalde, that's the mansion outside of Atlanta where they say there is this statue of a black woman in the foyer."

"A black woman? Then who is she?"

"Nobody seems to know...or will tell. You know, people try and act like black folks were so passive about being slaves, but you'd be surprised what some of those slaves did. The black woman who helped create the Coke recipe, I hear, was trying to dope her master...you know they *say* Coke used to have real coke in it...a long time ago. She probably thought she'd help make him a bit more pleasant to deal with."

"You're for real?"

"Yeah, I'm for real. Heck, some slaves used to grind up poisonous spiders in their master's milk and when they drunk it, they died. That's probably why they were much nicer to the house Negroes than the field ones. You could never tell who might be plotting to bump your tail off. I know if I had been one, they would have had to be *extremely* nice to me."

"No they wouldn't have; they would have stuck your old black butt out in the hot sun in the field and let you pick cotton or chop sugarcane. That's what they would have done with you!" I laughed.

"And I'll tell you something else I learned—J. M.'s mother told me this one time when she was telling me and my kids some tales about her Great-Grandma Nana or something like that. Did you know the words yam, goober, canoe, banjo, gumbo, tote, ninny, mame, pape, pickens...are all African words?"

"No, I didn't know that. So gumbo is..."

"Okra. Yam is sweet potato. Goober is peanut. Canoe is a boat. Banjo is a stringed box. Tote of course means to carry. Ninny is the female breast. Mame is what white folks took and made offensive to us now, but it's the maternal word for the moon which is what Africans equated the mother. Pape is pappy, which is the paternal word for the sun, I believe. And pickens, which were the stars—of course, white folks took *that* and made it sound nasty too...making fun of pickaninnies. But black folks have always been and will be resourceful. That's what Mrs. Gates say. See how they just *slid* those words in, even though white folks wouldn't allow them to keep their own old traditions."

"Umph. I probably should have hung around Mrs. Gates more often. I could write an interesting book—just from the stories she tells about her great-grandmother," I said.

"J. M.'s got a trunk full of that old African's things. Mrs. Gates said she thinks there's a book in there her great-grandmother wrote—before they put her eyes out. Even some things she told her grandchildren to write; things she would tell them so they wouldn't forget."

I turned on the faucet and got a glass of water to take my medicine. "I wonder if J. M. might let me look at that book one day...provided she doesn't move to Atlanta that is."

"What kind of medicine are you taking?"

"Blood pressure. It's been high lately so I've got to take these pills to keep it under control." Flick walked in just about the time I uncapped the top on the bottle.

"Hey baby," he said kissing me. "Honey." He smiled her way.

"Old Flick, long time no see."

"But is it *ever* long enough?" he said sounding like he was teasing.

Just as Honey was about to open her mouth I said, "Did you ever finish that job?"

"Yeah," Flick said opening up the refrigerator and taking out a can of beer. "You're never gonna believe this though."

"What?"

"You remember those two women? Carol and Maxine?"

"The two you said I should become friends with?"

He took a swallow of his beer. "Well forget that sh—"

"Flick, just tell us what happened."

"They're a couple of lesbians, that's what happened! Fine as those two bit—*ladies* are, and they turn out to be gay. A crying waste to mankind!"

"Why is that, Flick?" Honey said. "You weren't planning on trying your *man kind* out on them now were you?"

"No," I said quick. "But he thought they were more my type than you and J. M." I smiled. " '*Can spot one a mile coming,*' huh?" I laughed.

"Yeah well...you just stick with the two you're already with," Flick said. "At least I don't have to worry about either of *them* trying to take you away from me. We men have it hard!

Have to compete with other men and now with gorgeous other women. What's this world coming to? Lord have mercy!"

"That's who we need now," Honey said. "And while you're calling on him, you might want to ask him to excuse your filthy mouth."

Flick looked at Honey. "You're one to mother—" he looked up to heaven then back at Honey, "You're one to talk," he said.

"Well at least I'm trying," Honey said. "The Lord knows, habits are hard to break—good or bad."

"Amen," I said.

"Amen," said Flick.

Honey laughed and dipped like the preachers of old used to do. "Then let the church say Amen *again!*"

And we all said..."Amen!"

I talked with Christine tonight. "No, Christine. I don't believe now is the best time to tell your father. But don't worry, he really *can't* spot one—I don't care what he says. Not a mile coming...not even one right under his nose!"

Let the church say...Amen.

The Wall Fell Down Flat

So the people shouted when the priests blew with the trumpets: and it came to pass, when the people heard the sound of the trumpet, and the people shouted with a great shout, that the wall fell down flat, so that the people went up into the city, every man straight before him, and they took the city.   Joshua 6:20

Countess W. Gates' Journal

Solomon called today...to see if we were still planning to come for the weekend; I told him we were. I'm glad he called. It reminded me about that package I keep forgetting to give Johnnie Mae. I'm glad Mr. Gates is coming too. He wanted to see Johnnie Mae's face when she sees it. And well he should; it was his idea. I only did all that he couldn't do.

Solomon asked had Johnnie Mae said much the last time we talked, but I couldn't say she had. Just did the proper housekeeping sort of things "How's everybody" that kind of stuff. He said he was thinking about calling her doctor to see if she might be able to shed some light on anything that might help. I told him Johnnie Mae would be all right soon. "Just give her room to think things through. She's in deep thought."

So when we got there, we weren't prepared for all that was to take place.

"Who told you?" Johnnie Mae was saying when we walked in (we had to let ourselves in; thankfully, the front door was not locked since no one seemed to hear the doorbell).

"I just want to know is it true?" Solomon said.

"Look Solomon, I haven't made up my mind yet okay. I still have time. So give me some room, all right?"

"What's wrong?" I said, but Johnnie Mae just threw her hands in the air and walked away. So I turned to Solomon. "Solomon, what's going on here?"

"Your daughter!" he yelled more for her benefit than mine. "Your daughter here has a job offer in *Atlanta.*"

"Johnnie Mae?" I said walking over to her. "Is that true?"

"Yes Mama, it's true!"

"Tell her how long you've known," Solomon said. "Since the Monday after Mother's Day!" he said, not even giving her the chance to answer it.

I looked at her; she avoided my eyes completely. "I've not decided yet what I'm going to do," she said.

"Well do you think you might have thought of including me in this decision making process? Or were you planning on doing all this without me?" Solomon said.

"When I knew better about which way I was leaning, I was going to talk with you—"

"You mean, after you had decided what you were going to do, then you were going to let me know? And what if you decide to go? What about me then?"

"Solomon, I haven't taken the job yet. Mr. Bijur is being more than gracious; he's given me until the end of the month to let him know."

"Baby," I said, "you really should have told Solomon before now—"

"Ask him how he found out! Go ahead, ask him!" Johnnie Mae said looking at Sol.

I turned to Sol. He slapped his leg with his hand after it flew up in the air and came back down. "Sister *told* me," he said glaring back at Johnnie Mae.

"Sister? *Your* friend Sister?" I said looking back at Johnnie Mae. "What...did she slip and tell it—"

"Not just *my* friend Sister...Solomon's friend before he ever knew *me*. She just *had* to run tell *Sugarman* as soon as she found out! She couldn't ask me about it first. No. She just calls my husband and blurts it out to him—"

"Well she wouldn't have had to tell me if my own wife had done it, now would she? Do you have any idea how *stupid* I felt? Everybody knowing things I should know, but yet I never seem to have a clue."

"If Sister would just tend to her own business—"

"Well how did *she* find out?" I asked, to which both of them answered me with a strange look.

"I don't know. I think she said Rosalyn *told* her," Solomon finally said.

"Then *who*, pray tell, told her?" I said.

Johnnie Mae looked like she was going to be sick and excused herself to the bathroom. By the time she got back, cooler heads prevailed and the discussion was less heated.

Later I told Johnnie Mae she was wrong not to have told Solomon. I don't care how grown and independent she thinks she is. "You just can't go around living your life like you're an only...when you're not," I said.

"Mama, what am I going to do?" Johnnie Mae said as she cried in my arms. "Everything seems to be happening at the same time. I'm tired Mama. Just plain tired."

Just then, there was a faint knock on the bedroom door. Mr. Gates peeped his head in.

"Blue Jay? Blue Jay? What's the matter with my Blue Jay?" Mr. Gates sang. In his hand he held one perfect brown rose and the envelope I had left on the foyer table when I burst in earlier. "Look what's done gone and bloomed Blue Jay. Your very own Moroccan Rose...one has bloomed, just for you."

Johnnie Mae sat up immediately. "Moroccan Rose? I don't have any Moroccan Roses in my yard."

"Yes you do," I said. "Your daddy planted them when he was here the last time. He was on his head to get it in the ground that day...said it had to be done *that* day. Made me miss my bazaar to do it, too."

"And now look what we got Blue Jay," Mr. Gates said. His hand was trembling so bad as he shuffled forward holding the beautiful brown rose in the air.

"Daddy," Johnnie Mae said as she wiped her face with her hand. "Daddy, it's beautiful. But I thought you only planted that...that Rose of Jericho."

"Planted it too, but I remembered how you said you loved Moroccan Roses, so I searched everywhere till I finally found a bush. They are hard to come by. But now it done gone and bloomed. And just in time too!" He gave her the bud.

Mr. Gates stopped. He had a strange look on his face. Suddenly, he collapsed to the floor...still clutching tight the white envelope.

I don't recall all that happened after that. Not after I heard myself and Johnnie Mae screaming for Solomon to come quick. Then came the sirens and everybody pushing and rushing, and shoving, and asking all kinds of questions.

I do remember they pried that white envelope from his hand and tossed it on Johnnie Mae's bed. I do remember *that.* But most of the rest...is just one big blur.

Solomon Taylor's Journal

The ambulance got to the house rather quick. We were fortunate; there was one that had been called out this way already—barely missed getting to the scene before another service beat them to it. So they were only minutes away from our house when they got our call.

"An aneurysm," the doctor said. The swelling was keeping him from regaining consciousness, and Countess wouldn't dare roam from his side, not even for a minute. Johnnie Mae was almost beside herself. She called the rest of the family, and everyone got there except Christian and Denise (stationed in Germany; the Red Cross was in the process of contacting him as soon as they could get him word).

I ran into Johnnie Mae's doctor—Dr. Richardson—when I went down to the cafeteria to bring back a few cups of coffee.

"Dr. Richardson? Hi, I'm Solomon Taylor—Johnnie Mae Taylor's husband. I met you a few years back. I'm not sure if you remember me or not—"

"Oh of course! How are you? Johnnie Mae? She—" A look of panic came over her face as she reached and glanced down at her beeper. "Nothing's happened to the baby has it?" she said while pressing the button of the beeper.

"Oh no. That's not why we're here at all." *Baby? What baby is she talking about?*

She let out a sigh. "Good, I'm glad to hear that."

I almost couldn't think for dwelling on what she had just said. *A baby?* "No, her father...an aneurysm...trying to get the swelling down...unconscious..." I wasn't sure I was even making sense. I couldn't focus on a single word I was saying.

"Oh my, I am so sorry to hear that. So how is he now?"

"Not good. They don't think he's going to make it. The doctors aren't sure if he'll ever regain consciousness." *Baby? Baby? What did she mean by the baby?* "You know Johnnie Mae Taylor; she's about this tall...brown skinned...long black hair—"

She touched my hand. "Trust me, I'm quite familiar with Johnnie Mae, a.k.a. J. M. Taylor." She smiled. "I'm here with another patient who's due to deliver any time now. I've got to get back...just came down for a cup of mocha. Solomon...this is a good hospital. Your father-in-law couldn't be in any better hands."

"Doctor? Do you think all this stress might be harmful to the...baby?"

"With Johnnie Mae as its mother? I doubt it. But she should take it easy. And don't let her get too tired out. Make her rest, because you know she won't if you don't make her. And will you *please* tell her I would like to see her in my office early Monday. Tell her I'll get her in and out quickly. I need to check on her blood pressure too. That's providing she can, with her father and all. Tell her she and I still have unfinished business. She might be putting the baby in jeopardy by continuing to put it off. Will you do that for me Solomon?"

"Sure. Of course," I said shaking her hand. "Thanks, Dr. Richardson."

She smiled and left. I found I had to sit down. Johnnie Mae's going to have a baby? But why didn't she tell me? We're finally going to have a *baby?* How far along is she? I ran to catch up with Dr. Richardson, stopping her as she pushed the elevator button.

"Excuse me again, Dr. Richardson. Johnnie Mae wasn't too clear about the due date. You wouldn't happen to remember—right off the top of your head would you—the due date? I'm sure you're not walking *around* with this information—"

"Christmas," she said smiling. "I can remember it because I told her it will likely be a Christmas baby."

I smiled until she stepped inside the opened elevator. Then I counted to be sure I was coming up right. She's two months? Two whole months...and she hasn't said one word to me?

 J. M. Taylor's Journal

I had gotten home and heard Solomon in the bedroom. When I walked in, I saw the suitcase on the bed.

"Where are you going?" I said.

"I love you Johnnie Mae, and I know your daddy's real sick...but I got to get away for a while. I'll come by the hospital and check on you. And if you need me, you'll be able to reach me—"

"Solomon? What's going on? What are you doing?"

"Obviously, you and I want different things in life. We definitely didn't start out this way. In fact, I didn't think there were two people more compatible, other than your mother and father of course. I kind of thought you and I would be like the two of them when we reach their age."

"You're not leaving are you?"

"I won't be far. I just need to— Look, you obviously need your space."

I laughed a short laugh. "In this big old house? I have all the space I could ever need. Solomon, what's going on? Tell me. What's wrong?"

"I'll be over to my mother's. She's not so well herself. There are things, at *least*, that I can do for her."

"Meaning?"

He threw more clothes into the suitcase. "Meaning...I love you."

"*Love* me? How can you say you love me? My father's in the hospital, not knowing he's even in the world. And you pick *now* to...to leave? Now of all times? Okay, fine! Go! Whatever!"

He came over and held me tight.

"Solomon," I said, "....don't go."

He looked down into my eyes. "Give me one reason why not," he said.

I pulled away and looked down at both my hands then back to his waiting brown eyes. "I'm...I'm...pregnant," I said.

He came closer...hugging me first, then kissed me on my cheek. "Yes, I know," he said.

"You *know?* But how?"

He lifted the suitcase off the bed. "I saw Dr. Richardson in the cafeteria. She was afraid when she saw me that something had happened to *our* baby. You know *our* baby? The baby I didn't even know about? Oh, and you really do need to call her; better yet, she said you should come in as soon as possible. Wouldn't want to put *our* baby in any more jeopardy than you already have."

"That was why you never came back with the coffee." Tears began to roll down my face. "Oh Solomon—"

"If you need me...which I'm starting to take it, you don't— you can reach me over Mudear's house."

"But Solomon, you don't understand—"

He shook his head. "That's the problem Johnnie Mae. I truly don't." He walked out the door and I heard the door to the garage open and slam as it came back down.

I laid down on the bed and cried. What *is* going on?

When I awoke, I saw the white envelope and the withering rose Daddy had brought in to me. "Please God. Let Daddy be all right. There are so many things he and I need to set straight...I need to set straight anyway. I didn't mean to hurt him the way apparently I have. All he ever did was love me with all his heart. An agape kind of love—unconditional love."

I picked up the envelope laying on the bed; the return address almost surrendering me numb. New York? Addressed to J. M. Taylor, yet directed to Mama and Daddy's home address?

I unclasped it, and could not believe my eyes. *Moroccan Rose?* The printed short story, a signed copy of the contract, along with a $3,000 check, were all neatly tucked inside.

 J. M. Taylor's Journal

I went to the hospital; Daddy's still unconscious.

"It's not doing any good to just go sit in there. He's not going to hear a word anybody's going to say," Donald said.

"Oh hush Donald and leave her be," Mama said. "You never know what might get through." Mama smiled at me. She looked so tired yet so beautiful.

"Mama...I opened that envelope last night. But...why... what...how—?"

She smiled and lead me down the hall, away from Donald. "Your daddy found what you had written one day when we were at your house. He wasn't snooping or anything like that mind you...just saw it on the couch and picked it up. He didn't know whose or what it was. After he read those few passages, he showed it to me. Said it was too good to be sitting around in some old notebook."

She looked away then back. "He was so proud—what and how you had written it. You were busy that day. He asked if you mind him getting a copy of just those few pages. To keep." Mama smiled. "I don't believe you were paying enough attention to know what he had asked. But you said it was fine with you. When he told me you said it was okay to copy it, well...I saw it was your journal. I tried to tell you, to make sure you knew what he was saying. But you waved me toward the copier, later asking if I had gotten his copies okay."

"Mama...I don't remember any of this."

"I figured you wouldn't. Anyway, he read that paper over and over, and it touched him *so*. Lord it touched him! Then he saw in this magazine where they were looking for good short stories and he got this wild notion that his worn and folded copy would make a great story for them. All it needed was to change a name here a place there. He really thought your story would be picked. He asked me to type then send it off; he wanted it to be a surprise for you. He kept saying, 'My baby girl got talent, don't she Mama!' Oh he was so proud of that story. Well...I did type it and intended for that to be as far as it went; but then he walked all that way...carrying it to the post office."

"He walked?" I said.

"Yes ma'am. I had it fixed up like I was going to mail it...just to satisfy him that I had done everything. But I knew he'd never know why it never got published. I had typed it real nice, put it in an envelope, and sat it so he could see that I'd done everything since I knew I would be the one to take it to the post office some four miles away. And truthfully, there really shouldn't have been any more to come of it.

"But I came home one day and found him gone. I was worried—you know I was. I didn't know if he had wandered off or what. About an hour or two later, here he comes shuffling back in the yard. I ran out the door just-a-fussing. 'Where you been?' I said. 'I been worried sick!' He grinned. 'Oh, I just took Johnnie Mae's story to the post office. Didn't want it sitting around...thought you might forget.' He smiled. 'You know Mama, you forgets things here lately. Nothing to be ashamed of—it happens to the best of us.' Can you believe that old man had the nerve to say *that* to me?"

I smiled. "Mama—" but my words just stayed with me. What was there to say? She never intended for it to be mailed. And my daddy was just...being proud.

"I know we were wrong, Johnnie Mae. But when your story got selected, he was so excited. And to be honest, I was proud myself. I knew you had talent in that area. I know you say it's not your desire to be a writer, but you do have a way with words—whether written or spoken. Talent like that should not go to waste. Especially, when you inspire such fire in people. Great-Grandma Nam-o tried her hand at writing. You know, most of her writings are still in that trunk I sent to your house. Maybe one day, you'll look at them—see what you might do with them. I know she would have liked knowing that."

"Sure Mama," I said holding her up with a hug. I didn't even bother to tell her how I had found that article already and all I had gone through about it.

"I hate he and I didn't get to see you open it though. That's why we had held on to it so long...wanting to see the expression on your face when you saw what we'd done. And of course you found the contract and the check inside too? I did have to get you to sign the contract, but you signed the darn thing before I could tell you what it was. That's when I decided to just let it all be a surprise."

"Mama...I'm going in to talk with Daddy now," I said as I continued to hold her up while we walked back to the waiting area. I kissed her on the cheek. "Everything's going to be all right...I just know it is." I smiled.

"Oh, I know that too. Now you go on in and visit with him a spell. You know...he always did listen to you."

I tip-toed over to where he lay. It's funny when you think about it...I wanted more than anything for him to awaken and should have stomped and slammed doors just to get him to do so. But instead, I tip-toed...like he was asleep and I didn't want to disturb him. Like I would when I was a little girl.

"Daddy," I began. "It's me—Johnnie Mae. Johnnie Mae, Daddy. You know, the name you thought was just right for me. The one I seem to have hated most of my life." I pulled up a chair and sat beside him, touching his hand as I looked at the tubes that ran in and around him. "I've got a few things to say...more than a few actually. Now I know you hear me—you've always heard me. Anyway, when I finish...I'm hoping you'll open your eyes then you can tell me some things. You know, about planting and stuff; I'm sure there are a few more lessons you think I need to know.

"All right Daddy, so I'll start first. Let's see, where to begin. Should I start with the good or the bad news...or the news that should have been good but turns out to hold some bad news?" I looked over at him and smiled.

"Why don't I get the bad news out of the way first. That way we can linger more on some happy thoughts than sad. Solomon's over to his mother's. He hasn't actually *left* me, but he's a tad upset. Okay...more than a tad. And if Mama knew, she'd be upset with me too. But you, you just always let me be me. I know you thought I've made a few really bad decisions, but you've never said so." I took a breath.

"Okay, so now I suppose you want to know why Solomon's gone? Fair enough question. You see, I'm pregnant. I guess you could classify that in the good news section, except, I didn't think I wanted to be pregnant...not yet anyway. Look at me, as smart as you thought I was and I seem to be wrecking my whole life all by myself. You know Solomon...and Mama too as far as that goes, wants me to have a baby. I've known for over two weeks now that I'm pregnant but guess how many people knew it before yesterday?

"You give up? Three. My doctor, the nurse, and this guy named Landris. Oh, you'd like Landris I think. He reminds me a lot of you. He'll tell me just what I need to know and keep right on trucking. He was the one who explained why you guys probably named me Johnnie—too strong to be named anything prissy. I had to have a name to live up to what I'm here on this earth to do. Can you believe that Daddy—Johnnie Mae's not a bad name after all! And I'm doing wonders with it. Don't you think?

"Come on Daddy, it's hard to hold a conversation by yourself. Don't you even want to know the deal with me and Landris? I call him Landris but his first name's George. Okay, so I'll move on to something else then. I got this job offer, but of course you and Mama caught that much when you came over the other day. It's a vice president's position. If I take it; I'd have to relocate to Atlanta. Solomon won't move to Atlanta—I know that. He won't much less visit, let alone live. So that was my dilemma. I was trying to decide if this job was important enough for me to even chance losing Solomon. On the other hand, if I turn it down I may or may not get some of that same revenue flowing into my own company. Mr. Bijur was so nice about everything. He appears sincere about wanting me for that position...even came back and offered me more money. He's giving me a little extra time to decide.

"Now, what else. Being pregnant is kind of weighing in on me though. Before when I got promotions, I just made sure I didn't come up pregnant. This time, it's a little late for hindsight.

"I know I could have an abortion...now I'm not saying that's what I'm going to do, but it *is* a possibility afforded me. But I think if I were going to do that, I would have done it by now. Daddy, I really *do* want this baby. I just need you to get better so you can teach my baby some of the things you taught me when I was growing up. You remember Daddy? How I believed you were everything. And then that one day you and I were downtown minding our own business. You were going to buy me a treat if I was good...and I *was* good Daddy, wasn't I?

"Then those two white guys came along...young enough to be your own children. They came up and said all those things to you. Words that clung to the air like icicles from a roof. One of those words still stops warm air cold. How can one word have so much power? A word used to down rate, to heap an inferiority complex on those it's hurled upon by another who feels superior. From those who felt they had a right, were obliged even, to use it—that nasty, hateful, degrading word.

"And now in a different time, the word isn't so much spoken as implied. Jokes about fried chicken, collards and watermelon after one supposedly inferior ends up beating the reportedly superior in a one on one matchup.

"No. I choose not to even think of the word. I don't want to hear it...not even a variance of itself. I don't want to read it in required school or college literature. I don't care if they do claim the books to be American classics. I don't want to feel it as it cuts me to my bones...leaving its foul stench in air I am forced to breathe. And no amount of cleansing can truly rid its bitter nasty smell or taste.

"You told me, 'To act as though the word *never* existed is to ignore a part of history...even if it is the *ignorant* part.' You said people needed to remember so that *this* history would never repeat itself. You wonder why my generation, who never had to endure it the way your generation did, can be so militant about it? Why it fills *our* jaws with wind, our eyes with blood, cause our breathings to become irregular, our hearts to beat fast like Conga drums, our hearing to become intense, our hands to shake in rage? Why, when it was more our ancestors' burden to carry without any viable recourse?

"How, I asked *you,* could you smile when they degraded you, talked about you, called you a *'boy'* when you knew you *were* and *are* a man? How could you smile and say 'yessur' and 'nawsir' to those who had never shown respect to *you?*

"I remember what you said to me that day when I didn't understand how you could shame me so. Why you picked up that paper, when you were the man and they were the *boys?* You said, 'There's more than one way to win a war. I put it on...I take it off when *I* please. Can be as simple as putting on and taking off...an old coat.' That's what you said. You told me you used what was necessary to protect your family. 'When you're out in the bad weather, you do what's required to keep the wind and the rain out. But when you're inside, you can pull off that old coat with all its dirt, grime, and bird's mess and simply leave it outside.'

"You said there was coming a day when you'd be able to burn that old ratty thing—watch it as it goes up in flames. 'Remember this,' you told me, *'that every shut eye ain't sleep, and every good-bye ain't necessarily gone.'* " I stood up to stretch a minute.

"Daddy, I didn't understand back then. And I vowed to *never* be like you. Never allow anyone to disrespect me the way you did. I was determined I would make something of myself. But Daddy, I see how wrong I was about you. You're smarter than I gave you credit for. You knew how to wear that coat, yet take it off. I don't know how to put it on or take it off Daddy. I'm afraid if I do the wrong thing, everyone will find out who the real me is, and they won't believe it is truly *me.*

"Does that make sense? I'm so confused now, I don't think even *I* know what I mean. Daddy...please wake up. I need you to tell me a story; one that makes sense for strawberry plants. Daddy...it's my fault you're even in here. I cursed the person who stole that section from my journal...but I had no idea. If I had known, it would have been all right. Why did you have to go and be so proud of me?!"

I patted his hand and wiped the tears from my eyes. "Come on Daddy. Don't do this to me! And you know what I'm talking about too. I couldn't live with myself. Don't put me in that position. You hear me Daddy?! I forgive you for what happened on the street that day. I understand; I was wrong to have turned away from you like I did all these years. Please give me another chance. I had no right to judge you or your actions. I see just how strong you really were—because it would have been easier to have jumped on or fought so many times. But it takes a strong man to restrain himself.

"And you did, didn't you? You did it all for your family. 'Who...' you said, 'would be there to take care of my wife and children right...if something were to happen to me?' No...you weren't being a coward. You are my hero—the bravest man I know. And Daddy...I am so honored to be known as...a rose of Jericho. A man named for a wall that stood and protected, fulfilling its purpose, then came down. That's what it's most famous for—the fact that it did *come* tumbling down.

"And now look at me. Because of what you did—because *you* decided to *calm*—tumbling down—look where I am today. People say *yes ma'am* and *no ma'am* to me...they call my name with respect. So, yes...I do thank you Daddy.

"I remember your friend, Evangelist T. L. Moore asking the question once: 'In the right path, moving in the right direction. Am I alone?' Do you remember that Daddy? Remember what you told him? That no, you were not alone. And you're not alone now, either Daddy.

"Do you hear me? Please hear me, Daddy. Please."

The Rose of Jericho

But I would not have you ignorant, brethren, concerning them which are asleep, that ye sorrow not, even as others which have no hope. For if we believe that Jesus died and rose again, even so them also which sleep in Jesus will God bring with him.   I Thessalonians 4:13-14

Countess W. Gates' Journal

Mr. Gates regained consciousness, the day after Johnnie Mae had sat and talked to him for what seemed like eternity. I don't know what all she said, but he woke up mumbling something about a rose and some wall coming down.

"Man, you been sleep for days, and you wake up worrying about some old roses?" I said as I nearly cried all over him.

"Coun-tess, what a lovely sight for these two old eyes to see first thing."

"Oh, you old sweet talker you."

"Have I asked you to marry me yet?" he said and I frowned because I knew something wasn't quite right.

"Now Jericho, we been married going on forty-two years."

He smiled and looked straight up at me. "Oh I know that woman, I'm old...not lost my mind. I was just gonna ask you to marry me again...today, 'cause you look just like my bride on my wedding day."

I waved at him. "Oh you old thing! What I'm gonna do *with* you?" But what I had been thinking every day since he arrived here was...what would I do *without* him.

He asked to talk to all the kids. The doctor and nurses said he didn't need to tire himself out, but he wasn't hearing it. And he had something to say to them all.

Solomon stopped by the hospital; that's when I found out he had left home. When he told me what had happened, I talked to him just like he was one of my own.

"You're wrong!" I said.

"But what about Johnnie Mae," he said.

"She's wrong too; yet two wrongs don't make a right. Both of you are too old to be acting this way. And I'm not going to have *my* grandchild—not this grandchild I prayed down from heaven—growing up in no mess like this. So you two had better talk it, fight it, then love it out if you have to. Unless there's something else I need to know here?"

He took his hand and rubbed his head. "No," he said.

"You love her?"

"Yes I love her."

"Then what kind of love is that? Leaving your wife and child at the most inopportune time. I expect more from you than this Solomon! Unless I've been wrong about you all this time?"

He kissed me on my cheek. "No ma'am. You are right. I don't know what I was thinking."

"You weren't! That's the problem with young folks. You don't think. You merely react. When you get a little more seasoned like me and Mr. Gates, you begin to think first—then you react more appropriately. Not always right...but, nonetheless, much better." He started walking away. "So where are you going?" I said.

"To call Johnnie Mae—"

"No need. Mr. Gates is woke! Asking for everybody including you. She'll be here shortly. You can make it right then."

Mr. Gates is conscious. Johnnie Mae's going to have a baby! Thank you Jesus for hearing your child's cry!

 J. M. Taylor's Journal

Daddy's woke! I knew he would. After I all I had told him, he wouldn't dare let me have the last word. Solomon was at the hospital...he had already seen Daddy, but seems Mama got a hold of him. Just like she did with me when I stepped foot in the hospital. Told me off so bad—shoot, I thought she was going to make me go outside and break my own switch.

Solomon apologized as did I. I had already planned to call him after coming from Dr. Richardson's office, but there was a message on my machine saying Daddy was asking for us. I told Solomon what Dr. Richardson said...that me and the baby were doing just fine. Then I whipped out a picture of a sonogram and you would have thought I had already delivered the baby! He was going around showing the picture to everybody!

"Look, here at my baby! See, how beautiful! Looks just like its mama."

How he saw any similarity between me and that black and white photo, is beyond me. But I laughed like everyone else.

"Lord, what you gonna do once that precious angel gets here?" Mama teased.

After Donald came out, there was no one left but me. I thought it was too much on Daddy—talking to so many at one time. The nurses weren't going to allow it at first. But I think Daddy said something about being grown...nobody telling him he can't talk to his family...he'd just go home and talk to them if they didn't let him talk here. Needless to say, they gave in—allowing only five minute visits though.

When I walked in, his face looked almost like it was glowing.

"Baby Girl...Johnnie Mae...come on in. I have a lot to say. These militant nurses wanting to treat me like I'm a child. Seventy-years-old, and they're treating me like I'm two."

"Daddy, don't you think you should do what they tell you so you can get well?"

"Have you taken a look at this old house lately?" He patted his chest. "It's falling down...in...and leaning all around me. There's only so much fixing up one can do before it's just time to move out and find yourself another place."

"Oh Daddy, you know you're going to live forever—"

"I know. Just not in *this* building. I'm not fooling myself and I don't want you doing it either. Now the rest of them, they don't want to accept how serious I am. I know it; I don't need nobody acting otherwise for my benefit. But there are some things I got to be sure about first. You remember the papers I signed—that living will?"

"Why don't we talk about this another time?"

"When another time? I got to say what I got now...now's all the time I'm sure of." He started coughing so I decided it best not to upset him—to just listen.

"Okay Daddy. You talk; I'll listen. But you know they're due to kick me out in a little less than five minutes."

"I don't want to be left hooked up to no machines, you hear? When it's time for the seed to die and fall back into the ground, nobody ought to mess with that process. I don't want to be left on no machines you understand me. It just drains deep pockets dry for no reason. Eventually, we all gonna leave *here.*"

"But you might—"

"I'm tired, Baby Girl. Tired. Done been through a heap in my day. There are a few things I want to say to you; but first, promise me you're going to make sure they don't leave me hooked up to any machine—if it comes to that."

"Daddy, I can't promise you that because you...or I don't know—"

"Promise me, Baby Girl. I know I can count on you—if you promise me."

"I don't think I should have to make a decision like that. Daddy, what if it's the wrong thing to do?"

"What's wrong? To leave a person to die in dignity? If I were home, I'd just sleep on in my Jesus. That's what I want when it's my time. I don't want to meet St. Peter with tubes hanging all out of me," he laughed a little. "I sure would love to smoke my pipe right about now." He looked at me. "Do you think they'll have nice pipes in heaven?"

"I don't think so Daddy."

"Promise me Baby Girl?" Daddy said grabbing hold of my hand tight. "Promise me."

"I promise. I'll do what needs to be done...*if* I have need to. I just don't think this will be a question because you're going to get better and be back home in no time. But *now* you need to rest and do what the doctors tell you—"

"You were once *so* upset with me," he said. "That time when you thought I had no pride—I was *Stepin' Fetchit*. When those two young white boys came along and seemed to have blocked your sight of me. But my pride, Baby Girl, was in knowing you and the others were gonna have a chance. Where do you think you might be right now had I said, *No, I won't let you treat me that way?*

"If they'd have killed me right then and there or had me jailed on trumped up charges, who then would have taken care of my family for me? Oh but I did fight now. In my own way, I fought! I fought smart too. I brought forth offspring and taught them things...because I knew one day, the tide would turn.

"When I was bowing my head, picking up...seeming to be put down I was saying, '*Yessur.*' On the inside I was saying, '*Yessur!* but I've done outsmarted you in more ways than you'll ever know.' '*Yessur,* I planted seeds on this earth and no matter what kind of weather, they're going to survive.' '*Nawsir,* even if you try and trick these plants I planted with a blast of warm weather, then turn cold after they've decided to bloom, the strongest ones gonna still bear fruit. And of course, the result of that, is they gonna end up bigger and better in the end because there's less competition for nutrients.'

"That's how I fought. I knew it was not the time, but our ancestors gave us one thing—a will to survive regardless. Everybody don't fight the same way. But the race is not given to the swift nor to the strong, but to him that endureth.

"Johnnie Mae...you asked why we named you that? What else do you name such a determined girl who came here crying in the wilderness? And you did have a set of lungs on you! Lord, we had picked out Angel for you, but one look and listen to you, and we said, 'No, she more like a John.' I said, 'But we can't name no girl John.' So we thought on it a while and decided on Johnnie Mae.

"That's why you carry that name. Though I'm doubly sorry you dislike it so. Still, a name is just that—a name. You make something out of the name; the name don't make something out of you. That's what I've always believed. Take that *Orpah* woman what come on TV. Did you know the name *Orpah* come out of the bible—"

"Daddy...it's *Oprah.*"

"Say what?"

"Her name's Op-rah...not Or-pah. I think they got two of the letters switched when they wrote it on her birth record so it's *Op-rah.*"

"Yeah?" he said almost laughing. "Well see now, that even proves my point the more. They didn't even spell the dear child's name right—still, look what she's done with it!"

I smiled and looked at the nurse who was signaling me it was time to go.

"Daddy, I've got to leave now. But I'll be back...tomorrow. We can talk some more then. Daddy...I love you. Now you get some rest, okay?"

"Tomorrow. Okay, then. Tomorrow." Then he closed his eyes. "Baby Girl, have I ever told you why peaches, plums, apples and fruit like that are so sweet and tempting? Why nuts have such good meat inside those hard shells?"

"No Daddy. But you can tell me tomorrow, okay? I've *really* got to go and let you rest." I pointed at my watch and at

Daddy so the nurse would know I was leaving but that he was finishing up something.

"It's because they want the animals and people to be attracted to them. The trees bear so much fruit that if something don't carry them away from right underneath them, there would be too many trees in one spot. Eventually, there would not be enough room or nutrients and they would all die. You see, the most important thing to the tree is its seeds. It's all about the seeds. The fruit is actually a byproduct of survival.

"The fruit's just a ploy to entice animals and people to help spread their seeds to other places. So see, the tree survives by way of its seeds. Still—the gimmick is the fleshy part. People mistakenly think that's what a tree is all about. The flesh. But in reality, it's all about spreading its seeds across the land.

"Yes I have bent when I've needed to; fought when it called for it. I've stood through all kinds of weather. Been hot many days...cold others. But in the end, all people see is the fruit. Yet it's the seeds—that's what it's *really* all about."

He opened his eyes and looked up at me. "And Baby Girl...I know about Donald. How he took some of our money with all his scheming, wheeling, and dealing. I've spoken with him about it; told him myself I expect him to act more like a real man from here on out. He should do better. But if he doesn't, I need you to watch out for Mama for me."

Quietly, he closed his eyes again. I kissed him. He smiled, then nodded gently. And nothing but peace, filled the room.

* * *

"Green green the crab apple tree...where the green grass grows tall. Miss Johnnie, Miss Johnnie your true love is dead. And he brought you that letter to turn back your head."

That young woman visited my dreams that night. Only this time, she sang alone. She bowed her head, seemed to wink first, then smiled at me. And just as quickly—she was gone.

Countess W. Gates' Journal

After Jericho talked to all the children, Johnnie Mae being the last to see him, he asked for me. Told me how much he loved me, and how that love was eternal. I patted his hand and told him he could tell me all this when we got home to our own bed. He smiled and said he was tired...wanted to rest now.

I knew he had tired himself out, what with trying to impart lessons to five children, their spouses, and a few older grands. So I kissed him and oh, how that man kissed me. I told him he didn't kiss like no old man...an old man in a hospital bed at that. He took my hand and squeezed it tight. Then I left him...to rest.

He had insisted I go home to get some rest myself. "What good you gonna be if you end up in here too?" he said. I told him I would be back first thing in the morning. He nodded and said that would be good.

They called me early from the hospital. Said the aneurysm had burst...in his brain. They had him all hooked up on even more machines. I had gotten there as fast as I could...driving— Lord forgive me—eighty miles per hour.

He never did open his eyes. For one week, that machine breathed life for him and his body as we waited on him to tell us another story...teach us another lesson...tell us words of love and encouragement. But he refused to open his eyes just one more time. Let me look into his soul...just one more time.

Johnnie Mae had power of his living will. That's one of the things he reminded her of when she talked with him last...I know he did. He always said he didn't want to be hooked up to a machine to live. When he was ready to go, he wanted to ride that chariot in style. Didn't want them having to sit there and wait for us to let him go. So he had signed (some years back) for Johnnie Mae to take care of something like that—just in case I found I couldn't. And of course, he was right. He knew me better than anyone on this earth. The doctors said he was all but gone, but I said he would not leave me, so leave him be.

"Give him just a few more days; I'm sure he'll come around and show all you how wrong you were. He's gonna be just like he was...piddling in the yard, maybe not as much now as in the past. No, I won't allow him to piddle as much when he comes home. And we were planning to go on a cruise together—"

"Mama, whatever you want," Johnnie Mae kept saying.

She kept saying it until days became a week. The doctors said he was all but gone. No brain activity. All that kept him here now...were machines. But I couldn't do it. I couldn't tell them to go ahead and take him off. Johnnie Mae had to do it. She had to be the strong one of the whole family. None of the others could have done it; that's why he told Johnnie Mae. He knew she would not let him down.

So she authorized them to take him off the machines. It was the right thing to do. If he was to live, he would do it. If he was ready to go on to glory, we shouldn't artificially try and hold him here. So she signed to take him off the machines. And it wasn't no time before he stepped up in that fine chariot...drawn by a team of God's finest horses...beautiful black and white shining horses. I know; I saw them when they swooped away with him. He was sitting up there, looking just as handsome as ever...waving and throwing me good-bye kisses. No, not good-bye...more like *See you later.*

"Every shut eye ain't sleep; every good-bye ain't gone," I whispered his favorite phrase. "Later," I said throwing him one more kiss back. "I'll see you later my dear."

Then all my children...except Johnnie Mae, grabbed and hugged me. And we cried. Johnnie Mae stood alone over the empty shell that now lay on the bed and tears rolled down her face. Sol had to come take her away to get her to leave his side. I don't know what she was thinking at that moment, but I hope she knows how much I and her father appreciated her and what she had to do. Nobody else would have been strong enough to let him go.

But she alone...thank God...was.

 J. M. Taylor's Journal

Tomorrow for Daddy, never came. A week on the machine, and I had to do as I had promised him I would. I signed for them to take him off. Within an hour, they pronounced him dead. By my authority, they had taken him off the machine. Because of me... What if tomorrow he was to have opened his eyes again? He couldn't now...because of me. And I don't care what any of them say, think, or believe...the truth is my father is gone—because of me.

 Countess W. Gates' Journal

He died June fourth; his funeral...a celebration of life. I like the way Pastor tied the walls of Jericho falling, the rose of Jesus, to how our Jericho would also rise again. I only hate Mr. Gates would never see Johnnie Mae's child. But then, he's probably in heaven now watching over her little one. If he had gotten there before, he likely would have bounced that baby on his old bony knees—sang it a song or two...or three. Yeah, he's watching...I know he is.

Weren't many plums on the tree this year. First the unseasonably early warm weather, then that sudden cold snap all but destroyed only the strongest blossoms. Yet...those few that did survive were stronger, bigger, healthier—yes, sweeter... though Lord only knows...why.

 J. M. Taylor's Journal

So it's the fourth of July as I sit here—me and my best friend, my journal—reflecting on the happenings of this past year. Surprise! I am now an aspiring author. It's funny how things work out. That short story, *Moroccan Rose,* attracted so much attention, Mitchell had to call and ask if it was okay to give out my number to the many editors and agents who had bombarded him. He was so pleasant, it's hard to believe this was the same guy I talked with back in May.

I signed with a publishing company to write a novel based on *Moroccan Rose.* I'm not sure what the title of the book will be. Maybe *The Rose of Jericho*—that would be a good one. Everybody thought I really had lost my mind when I told them my news over the feast I cooked myself—thank you very much.

"You're going to do what?" Donald had said. He was there, but just him and his daughter from his first marriage (he and Jessica are getting a divorce to Mama's vehement objection I'd like to say. Well, I would *like* to say that. But to all of our surprise, Mama seems just fine with it. Go figure.).

"I'm writing a novel," I said again. "And I'm directing all my attention to penning the best one I can possibly produce."

"I think that's wonderful, Baby! If that's what you really want to do now," Mama said as she came and hugged me.

"Well, it's not like I didn't have some help arriving at this place and time," I said smiling as I winked.

"Your father would be *so* proud." She looked down at her hand where her silver wedding band still circled her finger tight. "Fact...I'm sure he is."

I smiled too.

"I'm happy for you," Pearl said. "You're going to be great at this, I just know you will."

"Thanks...Sister. I'm happy for you too. What with that short story you ended up getting published, and now another one—" I said.

"Yeah. and I want to thank you for not being too upset with me about my first story. I had no idea it would actually win or get published."

"Don't worry about it. But how on earth did you *ever* come up with such a strong protagonist. I love your character, although I admit, I don't think I know of *anyone* even remotely similar to her. A rich young snob with everything already in the world, suddenly finding herself starting from scratch? Come on—it'd have to be pure fiction. Who knows of *anyone* like *her* in real life?" I said teasing her.

"Hey, wait a second. Did you just call me...Sister?"

I smiled and touched her on the hand. "I need to get more ice," I said as I left her there and walked to the kitchen.

"J. M.?" Rosalyn said, holding the kitchen door so it would close gently. "I just wanted to thank you for inviting me, here with your family, friends, and all."

I glanced at her hair—her afro now exchanged for a tame, unnatural, ripple of glossy waves.

"Let's just let bygones—be gone," I said. "I liken it to what the one strawberry said to the other: *'If we hadn't gone to bed together, we wouldn't be in this jam today.'* Look, I'm willing to move forward, if you are Honey."

"Honey?"

"Yes...Honey. That *is* what you say you would prefer being called. Right?" I said smiling.

"Why yes. Of course, J. M."

"Johnnie Mae," I said. "It's okay if you want to call me Johnnie Mae. In fact, I've grown rather fond of it here of late."

"Johnnie Mae? Well now I don't know about that. Old habits are hard to break. You've been J. M., since we first met."

Just then somebody put on my new CD with, *Love Me in a Special Way* by DeBarge. I smiled, experiencing every word.

I rinsed out my glass and poured myself some orange juice. "Well, whichever, is fine with me." I raised my glass as to say *cheers,* then downed it.

"J. M.—someone's at the door to see you," Solomon said, glancing briefly at Honey.

"Who?"

"George Landris. I told him to come on in, but he just asked if I would let you know he was outside."

"Thanks, Solomon." I looked at Honey and she smiled and nodded.

Landris stood at the door looking as fine as ever. "Landris, why wouldn't you come in?"

"I'm sorry Johnnie Mylove, I didn't realize you had a house full of guest. I was heading out—for Atlanta—and wanted to stop by and see if you might not have changed your mind."

I smiled, stepped outside and closed the door softly behind me. "Landris, I want to thank you for everything. I mean it. You were...are...and always will be—it seems—just what I need at the moment."

"Then your answer is still *no* I take it?"

I laughed. "*Give up* is not in your vocabulary I see."

He took my hand. "Not when it comes to you. And you realize I *will* be calling and checking up on you from time to time...see how things are going."

"I would expect no less...from you."

"And if you ever need anything...anything at all, I'm only digits away. Don't you *ever* hesitate, not even for a second, to call me. I'll be there."

"Oh, you'll no doubt be so busy, you won't even remem—"

"When I told you I was willing to wait, I meant just that. But I always have to prove myself to you...so, we'll see when the time comes." He leaned down, kissed me on my forehead, my right cheek, then my left, and lastly gently brushed twice across my lips. He looked into my eyes. "Sweet Lady, if I don't leave now, I know I'll never leave you. Are you positive this is what you want? I shaved my head you know." He laughed.

I nodded. "Yes. I know. I'm sure. And...you'd better go."

"Yeah," he said shaking his head. "I'll let you know when I'm settled. Maybe you'll come visit me sometimes?"

I smiled without saying a word.

He shook his head and surveyed my body from top to bottom. "I hope you know...you look *good!*"

"Landris—stop," I whispered and smiled.

"I'm for real. You tell Mr. Solomon, he'd better take *damn* good care of you. He's a fortunate man. What I wouldn't give to be in his place, Alaiyo."

"Alaiyo?" I said. He forever spoke other languages to me.

"Alaiyo is a Yoruba word. It means *One for whom bread... food...is not enough.*" He took my hand. "Mee saloby you, langa alla mee hatty, so langa mee leeby. And *that* is Surinam to say *I will love you with all my heart, so long as I live.*"

Landris transferred to Atlanta. He had put in his request back when I was first offered the job there. Oh well...that's what happens when you ask for something. Most times you get it (even if later you *do* change your mind).

Having a shaved head made him look much younger. Even *if* he never intended to shave those gorgeous locks. Seems one of Honey's kids "accidentally" got a gob of green slimy, sticky stuff all in his hair the first time he met them. There was no other way to get it out, he was told, other than to shave his head and start anew. I tried not to laugh when he told me, but it was just...so funny. Of course, his company loves his new look, although he is planning to eventually grow it all back. That is...when and if it will grow back.

There is much I could write or could have written about Landris and I; but one thing I have learned—there are some things that should only be journaled in the heart.

A Yoruba proverb declares: *Nobody knows the mysteries which lie at the bottom of the ocean.*

Still, the deeper one is willing to dive, the greater the treasures await to be un-, re-, or dis- covered.

 J. M. Taylor's Journal

I had just finished the last of the novel and was getting it ready to send for review when I doubled over in pain. I called Solomon, and he was about as excited as a new father comes. It was not the easiest of deliveries, but Dr. Richardson and Solomon hung in there with me. I salute those who have more than one child. I might have decided to never have another baby again, had I not seen and held the fruit I had just bore...gathered so precious...inside my arm.

Solomon beamed, strutting around with the baby like a peacock strutting his own beautiful feathers. He got to take the baby to the nursery for their part of the process.

"Can you believe it?" Solomon asked upon returning. "I still feel like I'm dreaming. Your mama saw the baby; she's waiting to see *you* now." He kissed me and dashed for the door. "I'm calling Mudear. What name should I tell her?"

I smiled and didn't even hesitate one second. We had talked about a lot of different names, Jarrod was one if it was a boy, Patrice or Angelica if a girl. But having considered the little face I had gazed into earlier, I knew this precious being's name with certainty now. Solomon smiled, then nodded after I spoke it.

Mama came in beaming from ear to ear. "My Christmas present," she said. "I just saw my Christmas present! Finally, *exactly* what I always wanted."

I laughed. "A *little* early for Christmas though."

"Only by a week."

"Still early." Then I thought about Landris and could actually hear him say, *Early...like you,* and I laughed.

"My grandchild...living...breathing, with all ten fingers and all ten toes."

"You didn't?" I said, "Mama, you didn't go in there counting the baby's toes, did you?"

"That's what we did back in my day. Habits are hard to break," she said giving me a kiss on the forehead.

"Knock, knock," the nurse said peeping in. "Look what just came for you!"

"Oh look at these!" Mama said as she rushed to take them from her. "There must be two dozen roses here!"

"Three," the nurse said. "We counted them at the front desk; five different colors too."

Mama looked at me and raised an eyebrow. She sat the flowers down, searching diligently for the card. "Well...let's see who *these* lovelies are from."

"No Mama let me—" but it was too late. Her eyes were already skipping across the small card. I held my breath, fearing words she might be finding. She laughed. "Lord—good help sure is hard to find these days!" she said.

"What does it say?" I said, still holding my breath.

She handed the card to me as she spoke. "Punctuation marks all in the wrong place. Words running into one another. Some words looking like chicken scratch. I *guess* you can make some sense out of what it's supposed to say."

I read the card and smiled: *Congratulations—Forever. Mee saloby you, langa alla mee hatty, so langa mee leeby, Johnnie Mylove. Mr. Landris.* I pulled the card up near my breast and breathed, smiling as I stared at the five hues of roses. I could hear Landris...speaking with clarity to each of the colors with his special admiration, "Red means...Pink is...Yellow...White... and Brown..."

"So," Mama said, "what did you and Sol decide to name *my* grandchild?"

I looked up at her and smiled. "Princess," I said. "Princess Rose Taylor."

Mama smiled and with reverence said, "Princess Rose." She then looked up at heaven. "The Rose of Jericho," she said then mumbled something about, "Pink for a girl; purple for royalty." She smiled and fumbled for her purse. "I stopped by your house...to make sure everything's ready for you and the baby when you leave here tomorrow—Solomon told me where the spare key was—and I saw your manuscript scattered all over the floor. Since I was picking it up, I couldn't help but read the first page—I hope you don't mind?—and I made a copy of it."

"No, it's fine. But why'd you want a copy of the first page?"

"I thought it was just wonderful! I wanted you to read it for me...let me imagine...get a feel for how it'll be when you record the audio book."

"Mama, they may not even publish this. We just have to see what they say—"

"Oh, they're going to. If they don't, I don't know what *their* problem is." She handed me the freshly folded paper. "Read it...if you feel up to it, that is."

I held it, smiling at words now having life of their own and read each word aloud.

"It was a mild, more spring than winter, weather all across the South including Alabama that seduced quadrillions of dainty color blooms to burst forth early...opening wide like the mouths of a brood of hungry baby birds. So the week before the official marching in of spring—the year two Friday the thirteenths did a tango back to back—when an unrelenting breeze pranced just above the softened soil in its attempt to convince a hard freeze to at least 'entertain' the idea of shacking with it—the year my father died—their just-as-abrupt separation would leave only the strongest blossoms to survive. However, a herd of nutrients waited patiently to stampede, then flourish, those who did dare endure. Healthier? Oh yes! Though what was responsible for their sweetness...I'm certain...I'll never *truly* understand."

The End